CONTENTS

INTRODUCTION	v
SNOWFALL James A. Moore	1
HAUNTED HARBOR Amanda DeWees	9
THE HEADLESS HORROR Charles R. Rutledge	33
NOT MORE LOVELY THAN FULL OF GLEE Leanna Renee Hieber	49
WHO WOULDN'T GO Cliff Biggers	57
THE FORTINGALL YEW William Meikle	73
HOLD YOUR BREATH Jeff Strand	85
THE CAMPO Josh Reynolds	93
I USED TO LIVE HERE Kealan Patrick Burke	109
BY CHANCE OR PROVIDENCE James R. Tuck	121
THE HERON IN WINTER John Linwood Grant	141
THE WRECK OF THE CHARLIE SOL Jim Beard	163
THE DOLLMAKER James A. Moore and Charles R. Rutledge	185
CONTRIBUTORS	231

A Winter's Tale

Horror Stories for the Yuletide

Edited by
Cliff Biggers, Charles R. Rutledge
and James R. Tuck

A Winter's Tale: Horror Stories for the Yuletide
Edited by Cliff Biggers, Charles R. Rutledge, and James R. Tuck

© 2020 by Pavane Press and Individual Authors
All rights reserved.

Cover art © 2020 by Lynne Hansen
LynneHansenArt.com

This book is a work of fiction. Names, characters, business, events and incidents are the products of the authors' imaginations. Any resemblance to actual persons living or dead, or actual events is purely coincidental.
No part of this book may be reprinted, stored in a retrieval system, or transmitted by any form or any means, electronic, mechanical, photocopying, recording or otherwise without the prior written permission of the author, Except as provided by USA copyright law.

ISBN: 9798578070228

INTRODUCTION

Today, we think of the end of December as a time of joy, of holiday celebration, of contentment and tranquility.

But for a much longer time, people viewed the coming of the winter solstice as a time of apprehension, concern, and more than a little fear. It was a time of darkness, where communities would gather en masse for festivals where they would dance and sacrifice and perform magic to encourage the sun to return from its distant retreat, to restore light and warmth to the world. What better time than the period of cold darkness and barren fields and orchards to reflect on the fears that never wholly leave us? To contemplate the end of this world's journey and if there may, or may not, be one after.

Even the Yule log finds some roots in fear—a burning log to replace a bit of the warmth and light that had retreated with each passing day until the arrival of the solstice. It is the fire that must burn for twelve days to keep the worst of the winter away until the sun began its return.

Humans have always felt our mortality in the cold and the dark, we huddle together around the fire, knowing that without it there are things in the night that once hunted us, that still would save for our meager flame.

Any wonder, then, that the bleakness of winter should become a time for tales of ghosts and spirits and specters?

The tradition of wintry ghosts stretches back for centuries, but the Victorians turned it into an art form all their own. One of our most beloved Christmas tales, Charles Dickens' *A Christmas Carol*, may be sentimental to the point of being spiritually inspiring, but it also has moments as disturbing as any existential horror tale. That was far from Dickens' only foray into the realm of the Christmas ghost story. Instead, he was a master of bringing gothic elements into the holiday season, and devoted the Christmas issue of his magazines *Household Words* and *All the Year Round* to ghostly tales.

Later, the sentimentality of those early Victorian ghost stories would take a harsher, more distressing turn: by the time of Henry James' *The Turn of the Screw*, the aim wasn't to inspire sentimental reflection, but to disturb and frighten. The same was true of stories by writers like M.R. James, E.F. Benson and Amelia B. Edwards.

Whether their intent was to inspire or to frighten, the Victorians had one thing right: there is an inexorable connection between joy and fear, and they celebrated the season of joy with ghost stories that both frightened their audiences and relieved them with the knowledge that their own existences were less terrifying.

We're many generations removed from the Victorians, but we're not as different from them as one might think. That's the philosophy behind *A Winter's Tale*: to bring a touch of winter's chill to your spirit as well as your body with an assortment of tales of the eerie, the ghostly, and the disturbing.

In these tales, you'll find monstrous creatures, haunted forests, menacing apparitions, ghostly voices, eerie inns, and more. Some are Victorian in tone and substance, others less so—but each sets out to remind us that some "auld acquaintances" simply refuse to be forgot...no matter how we might hope, and wish, that they would.

SNOWFALL

JAMES A. MOORE

The night was very nearly silent. Outside the snow was falling, veils of spectral white that drifted lazily from the heavens, and inside the chill was kept at bay by the fire that Stephens, the butler, had started before the gathering commenced.

Dinner was finished, and the ladies had retreated from the dining hall to the red room, where they spoke of the sort of things women chatted about when they gathered together, free of their husbands.

It was Christmas Eve, and the men had gathered in the trophy room where Hawkes did his business while at home, and where he and his fellows joined together for brandy and a few cigars. Edmond Hawkes drew a match to his pipe and gently sucked the fire into the bowl of freshly packed tobacco, puffing away calmly until the sweet, aromatic smoke plumed up into the air.

Not ten feet away, Louis Humphries pulled at his cigar and then set it in the glass ashtray to his left. "Where is Langstrom hiding himself tonight? I thought he'd be joining us for certain."

"He was supposed to be here." Hawkes spoke with the same

calm he always seemed to muster, regardless of the circumstances he faced. It was his nature to be calm. "He responded to the invitation with eagerness, as I recall. He was supposed to be here with his new fiancee, if all went well. A young lady he met on his trip to Paris last year. Had a devil of a time convincing her to come here, apparently, but she finally agreed."

Harper responded, his words coming from the great mutton chop mustache he'd developed some time after their last meeting in the summer months. "From Paris to Sutton? Must have been a devil of a time, indeed."

"There's much to be said for living in the country," said Hawkes. "I might have to travel to London from time to time, but the nights are quiet, and there's little by way of crime out here."

Harper chuckled, and waved a hand. "I'd hardly be the one to argue that fact with you, my good man. I could easily find myself joining you out here, but for the fact my job demands more time in the city than yours. But I imagine that Sutton might be too quiet for a Parisian to endure. No shows, few restaurants, and far too much silence on a winter's eve." The man moved to the closest window as he spoke, and looked outside at the snow that whirled in the air and danced in ghostly waltzes. It was a night that promised great drifts of freshly fallen snow by morning.

Hawkes looked out the window again, seemingly fascinated by the snowfall.

Humphries picked his cigar from the ashtray and studied the burning ember at its end. "I remember courting Rebecca when I was a younger man. Now here's Langstrom, as old as any of us, and he's found himself a third woman to be his bride. He must have a great deal more energy than me."

"I dare say Langstrom was never meant to be alone." Hawkes spoke softly, and stared out the window past Harper. "Some men might be fine on their own, but not our Langstrom. If ever a man was meant to have a bride, he's the one. Lost on his own. He always has been."

"Worst sort of luck he's had then." Harper sighed and continued watching the snow. "Two times married and twice widowed."

"Olivia, wasn't it, his first wife?" It was Dennings that asked. He was relatively new to the group and had only met Langstrom in passing. "Was with him in India when she died?"

Hawkes nodded. And worried the tip of his pipe for a moment before answering. "Olivia Marie Evans Langstrom, She was a beautiful bride, and doted on her husband."

"What happened to her? How did she pass?"

Hawkes replied, "Drowning. They were in Calcutta, as I recall. Langstrom was working for the British East India Company, and he was looking over the latest contracts with several firms when the monsoons came upon them. Olivia had the misfortune of being in the path of a flood that swept their entire home into the sea." Hawkes cleared his throat and again looked out into the snow that whipped and writhed outside. "Horrible bit of luck, that. Such a lovely young lady and lost to the world."

Harper nodded. "He was devastated, of course. I've never seen a man so at a loss as poor Langstrom was when he found out. That was the last of India for him. He came home on the next available ship, though he couldn't bring Olivia back with him, of course. She was lost at sea and never found."

Hawkes nodded and sighed. "I didn't think he'd ever recover, but then he found Elizabeth, and he was a young man all over again. Well, not that he was old by any means. Still at an age when travel was easy, as I recall."

"Elizabeth!" Harper nodded his head. "I'd forgotten her name, though I daresay I'll never quite forget the look of her."

Dennings looked toward the other man with one raised eyebrow.

Harper responded as if the man had asked a question. "Oh, Olivia was a beauty, but Langstrom's second wife, Elizabeth, was very much the stuff of dreams."

Hawkes nodded and sucked at his pipe.

Harper continued. "I remember seeing her for the first time and being smitten. She was as graceful as she was lovely, and as charming as any woman I ever met. And like Olivia before her, she doted on Langstrom."

"Well, most women do. He has his own charm about him, doesn't he? I don't think I've met a woman yet who didn't find him pleasing. Been grateful more than once that he isn't the sort to dabble with married women, or I might very well have lost Anna to him." It could be said that Hawkes was joking, but instead of laughing the gathered men nodded their agreement.

"Poor Elizabeth," Humphries took out his kerchief and wiped at his brow. "So young when she died."

Hawkes did not speak, but he once more nodded his agreement.

Dennings sighed. "Dare I ask?"

"Another drowning," Harper said. "A tragedy, to be sure."

Hawkes cleared his throat and pointed to the window with his chin. "It happened out here, only a few miles away. Poor Elizabeth fell through the ice, while she and Langstrom were skating. He could not get to her before the waters pulled her deeper. I was there with Anna. There was nothing to be done for it. She fought hard to break through, or even to return to the very spot where she fell through the ice, but it wasn't meant to be."

Humphries nodded and wiped his brow again. He sat close to the fire and liked it there, but could not quite escape the heat.

All of them grew silent when Stephens entered the room to refresh their brandies. The man was quick and efficient, sweeping in like a gust of air and leaving with the same speed.

Humphries spoke again after Stephens had left. "Langstrom was ruined. of course. He had no extra weight to him, but lost easily a stone in weight. He wouldn't eat, couldn't sleep, and likely would have lost himself to spirits if he'd been left alone. Times like that let you know who your friends are."

Harper nodded. "I think we all took a turn at staying with him."

"Well, he's always been a good friend, hasn't he?" Humphries coughed into his hand and then looked around at each man in the room, as if daring them to disagree.

"One of the best, to be sure." Hawkes set his pipe down for a moment and again stared out the window and into the snowy night. "Marked by tragedies. What a pity."

"Well, hopefully he's found a new lady to be his bride." Harper did his best to sound cheerful. "He deserves a bit of happiness, I daresay."

For a time no one spoke, each man lost in thoughts. It was a comfortable silence but the lack of words held a fine edge to it.

Finally, Humphries spoke. "Do you suppose she said yes?"

Hawkes picked up his pipe again. "He's a handsome enough man, and successful. Certainly he can be charming. I would hope so, for his sake."

"I wonder what kept him from joining us." Dennings looked out the window at the growing snow. "I expect the weather might have something to do with it. I can see being caught out there easily enough." The thick, white snow continued to fall, and the swirls of snow continued their silent waltz as the winds caught that snow and hurled it into dervishes that mimicked the ballroom escapades of youth.

Hawkes nodded again and tapped the bowl of his pipe over the ashtray closest to his seat, knocking loose the embers. "You're all staying here, of course. I'll hear nothing of anyone trying to get home in this."

"And grateful we are for the invitation, old boy." Harper spoke for them all. Trying to head anywhere in the current weather would have been madness.

"It's always possible that his new paramour said no, isn't it?" Humphries spoke softly, but clearly. "I'm afraid he has a history of losing wives early on."

"Deucedly bad luck. Still, one can hardly blame him for accidents that happened." Hawkes shook his head and once more looked out the window, frowning.

"If he's told his intended about his history, that might be enough to scare almost anyone away, especially if she's young and easily frightened."

"Come now, Dennings. He's hardly the first man to seek a younger bride." Harper's voice was calm enough, but there was that edge of warning when he spoke.

"I'm not judging him, Harper. My own wife is ten years younger than I am. I'm merely saying that priorities might be different if she's younger. She might seek a younger man, or someone more physically capable of keeping her safe than Langstrom. He's not as young as he once was. I daresay none of us are."

"If that's the case, he's better off without her, I'd say."

"He's still not a man who fares well on his own, our Langstrom. If his man, Watkins, wasn't so capable I expect he'd never be dressed on time." Harper shook his head. "I know how harsh that sounds, but he's never been good without a woman at his side."

"To be sure, Watkins is a treasure, but Langstrom's hardly incompetent."

"No, not at all," said Hawkes. "Still, he tends to focus better when there's a woman in his life. This new woman, I can't say as I even know her name, but he's better for her, I think. More focused and quicker to action. Without that focus, that woman to make him focus, that is, I daresay our Langstrom is at a loss."

Harper nodded. "Then let's hope the lady in question said yes, if he's built the nerve to ask her already."

"Well, the plan was to ask her this last week, while they were in London." Hawkes looked at his pipe bowl and then reached for his pouch of tobacco. "I expect, one way or the other, that he already knows her answer." He frowned as he spoke and his voice drifted slowly into silence.

"Do you suppose a negative answer would be enough to make him stay away?"

"Not hardly." Dennings shook his head. "I've never known anything to keep him from a celebration."

"Oh, he's not without a heart, Dennings." It was Harper who responded with a chiding tone. Whatever was between him and Dennings, he seemed determined to scold the other man at every opportunity.

"That's not at all what I'm saying, and you know it. No, I merely mean that he has a love of life. He's not the sort to brood."

Harper acquiesced with a rueful expression.

"I agree, however. I think he'd have shown up just the same. I'm actually a bit worried about him." Hawkes struck a match and lit his pipe before going any further. "Heartsick or not, it's not like Langstrom to simply not show up after accepting an invitation."

"Should we go out after him?" Humphries frowned to himself.

"I've half a mind to send Stephens." He stared out the window, frowning as he studied the flows and eddies of the falling snow. "And half a mind to hold off. It looks devilish out there."

"Perhaps we should go ourselves." Humphries looked out the window as he spoke.

"The whole lot of us have had too much to drink, old boy. We'd likely get ourselves lost in the drifts." Hawkes spoke directly, and none of them could honestly disagree. Wine with each course, and brandy afterward. Without waiting for an answer from any of the men, Hawkes rang the bell near his right arm.

Stephens approached before the bell had stopped its light ringing.

Hawkes leaned in close and whispered to his man. A moment later Stephens was gone from sight.

"The matter is handled." Hawkes nodded to himself and around the room his guests nodded along.

"Well, that's good then. Stephens will be careful?" Harper frowned as he spoke, ever the worrier.

"Stephens won't go himself. He'll send one of the coachmen, possibly both of them."

"Well, that's for the best then."

They were silent for a time before Hawkes spoke again, softly and solemnly. "I fear they won't find a happy answer for us."

"Why do you say that, Edmond?"

"I'd like to think it's the wine and the brandy. I would, but I'm not so deeply inebriated to have lost my senses."

"Whatever do you mean, old sport?"

"I've been watching the snowfall, you see. Sometimes it falls straight to the ground. Other times it whips in the wind and looks for all the world like a dance. And if I'm being honest with you, in the time we've been sitting here I could very nearly swear I've seen Langstrom dancing just out there in the darkness, moving sometimes in a box step and others in a proper waltz, but always dancing with a different woman. I've seen him dancing with Olivia, and with Elizabeth, but also with another lady I do not recognize."

"Well, why didn't you say something?"

"You misunderstand me. I have not seen our Langstrom. I've seen the snow falling and making spectres. It's the snowfall, Harper. It moves and dances and looks like Langstrom." Hawkes pointed with his pipe's tip, his hand moving just so, mimicking the movements of a dancing drifting along to the music, and Harper's eyes moved out to see where he was pointing.

"It's rather close, I daresay. Surely it's your imagination, but I can see where you might feel that way." He spoke firmly, but the words lacked conviction.

Nearly three hours passed before Stephens came to let his employer know that Langstrom's coach had been found. Sometime during the storm the driver had missed a curve on the road, and the coach and horses had driven into the waters of the river.

The horses found their way back to the land but the coach did not. The bodies of the driver and his charges had been found.

There were no survivors.

Edmond Hawkes nodded and looked out to the continuously falling snow outside. Dawn was coming soon and it was Christmas day.

Langstrom had always loved to dance.

HAUNTED HARBOR

AMANDA DEWEES

I blame Roderick for tempting the fates.

After so much merriment during the holiday season, we had decided to spend the rest of January by the sea. He wanted peace and seclusion to work on a new commission, and as soon as he had selected a destination I had decided to join him. As unlikely as it seemed to all who knew me, I had grown just a trifle weary of London life.

Roderick, of course, knew me better than any living soul—indeed, better than any soul living or dead. He regarded me thoughtfully, his deep-set hazel eyes searching my face.

"Are you sure that's how you wish to pass the next fortnight? Away from all society, with no diversions except collecting sea shells?" he asked.

"Some peace and quiet will be welcome after such unrelenting festivity. Besides, I have a stack of plays to read," I said, not adding that I hoped to begin writing one. That was a secret I was not ready to share even with him—not until I knew whether my attempt would succeed.

He was still unconvinced. "At this time of year there will be no neighbors, no company at all—except of course for the sailors you lure with your siren song."

"I shall have you for company," I said, "and you are all I desire."

It was a beautiful prospect, just the two of us on our own. I imagined the exhilaration of taking long walks on an empty shore, then coming home to warm ourselves by a driftwood fire. Indeed, just the image of him striding along a bleak, wintry coast in a carrick coat with the sea wind whipping at the cape collars and tousling his curly black hair was enough to convince me that we needed this holiday together. I decided that moment to purchase a carrick coat for him before we left London. As an actress, I cannot resist the lure of the dramatic, even in menswear.

It was then that he spoke the fatal words.

"Won't you be bored?" he asked.

As a spirit medium who can often sense supernatural forces, I ought to have felt a foreboding pang. Glimpsed a shadow looming over us, or heard an ominous crack of thunder. Instead, all unaware, I said, "A little boredom would be welcome after so much activity. Two weeks alone with you and away from everything else sounds like heaven!"

Now that I think about it, perhaps we were equally to blame. But at the time neither of us had any notion of what lay ahead.

Since he was committed to one more performance before he could leave London, I decided to travel down a day ahead and prepare the cottage with the help of the servant we had hired. I am not very domestic, but I knew how Roderick liked things, and I enjoyed spoiling him.

From the moment I stepped off the train, I knew I was near the sea. The air was redolent of fish, a fragrance that was not wholly pleasing but at least carried the reassurance that I was indeed far from the center of the city. I was met by Mrs. Marsh, the housekeeper, and during the drive from the train station I learned all about her and her former master.

"I used to keep house for Captain Turner," she explained as the coach jounced over a rutted lane scattered with broken shells. "That was toward the end of his life. He had no one else; he'd lost his wife many years before I knew him."

"Has the house stood empty since his death?" I asked, and received a shake of the head. She was only a few years my senior, with a sturdily corseted figure and a benign face softened further by a double chin. She kept darting little perplexed looks at me as though trying to determine whether she had seen my face before. No doubt she had seen an engraved likeness of me in the newspapers. During the heyday of my acting career I had frequently appeared in print.

"It was ten years ago that the captain died," she said. "The house was rented right away to a young man and his spinster sister. I don't know much about them, as the sister did all the housekeeping except for a maid. They left just weeks ago, so this will be the first time I've set foot inside for a good long while." She sat up straighter in the cart as we left the track for a narrower path. "I confess I am curious as to how well the old place has been kept up."

The way she said "the old place" revealed an affection that was not evident from the words alone. And the moment our conveyance crested a rise and revealed the house overlooking the shore, I understood her emotion. The house was surely less than a half century old and most pleasing in proportion. I was glad to see a bay window as well as a balcony from which Roderick and I would have a magnificent view of the ocean. The front garden was covered with frost now, but in warm weather it must have been beautiful. The only discordant note was an ugly monkey puzzle tree that obscured one side of the facade.

"Why, it's lovely," I said, and the surprise in my voice made us both smile—in my case sheepishly. "Pardon me," I added, "but I had no idea what to expect from a house built by a sea captain. For all I knew it might have been a converted sailing ship."

She raised her voice to be heard over the sound of the ocean crashing against the shore. The beach was of loose rock and pebbles close to the track but sandy where it met the foaming waves. "The captain was newly wedded when he had the house built. He wanted his bride to be happy there while he was at sea."

"Was she very young when she died?"

Mrs. Marsh nodded sadly, jiggling her chins. "That was well before my time. All I knew of her was what little clues he dropped from time to time, not realizing. He was still mourning her up to the day he died."

Fortunately the coach drew up by the gate then, putting an end to this sad topic, and our driver hopped down to carry in the trunks and the large hamper of food and other necessities. Mrs. Marsh handed me the key, and I unlocked the front door and pushed it open. She was hard on my heels as I stepped over the threshold.

The shutters were still closed, so the interior was steeped in gloom. As my eyes adjusted I began to make out the shapes of sheeted furniture, and then, without warning, a woman's face appeared out of the darkness, staring at me from across the room. *My* face, hanging disembodied in the air.

I gasped before I could help myself. With every moment my eyes adjusted more, however, and I started across the room for a closer look. It was a painting, and the eerie effect of a disembodied head floating in the air had been created by the dark hues of the rest of the portrait. As for the woman herself—

"Why, she looks like you, Miss Ingram!" Mrs. Marsh exclaimed.

There was a superficial resemblance, at least. The woman was young, with a great deal of curling fair hair, and the general shape of her face and features bore some similarity to mine. Her nose was a bit more classical, her chin more rounded, and her forehead higher, but from across the room these differences were less obvious.

"Is that the captain's late wife?" I asked.

"Yes, ma'am. I must have dusted that painting a thousand times. He was firm about keeping it spotless." She cocked her head to one side and looked from me to the portrait. "That must be why I thought I recognized you, ma'am. You could be sisters."

That was a bit of an exaggeration, and I decided it was time we set about making the house livable. As Mrs. Marsh went from window to window opening the shutters and letting light into the room, I began to pull the cloth covers from the furniture. The last inhabitants had left so recently that scarcely any dust had gathered, and the furnishings that emerged were welcoming—fat armchairs, a plump divan, handsome cabinets that I later learned had once been used to store nautical charts, and a piano.

As soon as there was sufficient light, I couldn't resist exploring. The captain's house—Harbor Home, I learned he had called it—was charming, with high ceilings and unexpected windows everywhere. The upstairs room with the balcony proved to be the largest and finest of the bedrooms, no doubt where the captain himself had slept. Perhaps when he was unable to sleep he had stepped out onto the balcony to look out over the sea and think about all the adventures he had had there before leaving it behind for life ashore.

"Roderick and I will take this room," I told Mrs. Marsh, who produced a set of bed linens that we hung outdoors to air for a few hours before making the bed. I set about unpacking Roderick's trunk and putting his things away. Mrs. Marsh prepared a cutlet for my supper, and long before my usual bedtime I was yawning and ready to retire.

"That'll be the sea air," she informed me. "You'll sleep hearty tonight, Miss Sybil."

I bade her good night and took a candle to light my way upstairs. It sent friendly little shadows over the walls as I changed into my nightdress—my coziest red flannel one. Roderick was wont to poke fun at it, but I had no intention of catching a chill from an ocean gale.

Now that night had fallen, the room felt less pleasant and welcoming. The wind shrilled around the edges of the French doors, and even with them closed I could hear the ocean. It was a lonely sound, I thought, though during the day I had found it invigorating. What was that poem about the "eternal note of sadness" in the ocean's roar?

My trouble was that I missed Roderick, I decided as I climbed into bed. This lonely feeling would vanish once he arrived. And thinking of him, I fell asleep.

I'm not certain how long I slept, but some time in the night I woke briefly. Someone was in the room. I felt the mattress sink under his weight as he lay down beside me.

"Roderick?" I murmured, so sleepy I could not even open my eyes. "How did you get here so early?"

There was no answer. Still drowsy, I reached out to touch him, but no resistance met my hand. My groping fingers came to rest on the counterpane. No one was in bed with me.

That opened my eyes fully. Lighting the candle, I looked closely about the room. All seemed just as it had been when I went to bed, except that now I was wide awake and alert. Just to be certain, I got up and peeped in the wardrobe and under the bed, feeling foolish. Still, it was a relief to know for certain there was no intruder here. That left only one likely explanation: a ghost.

"Who is it?" I asked. "Is it Captain Turner?"

Though I listened hard, I heard no reply. I caught the faintest whiff of a presence besides mine, but not enough to tell whether it meant good or ill...or was simply reenacting scenes from its life with no awareness of me at all.

Well, if the specter hoped that I would let him be my bedfellow, he was doomed to disappointment. Removing a pillow from the bed, I make an improvised bed of an armchair, where I curled up and tried to go back to sleep.

And sleep I finally did, only to discover when I woke that someone—or something—had taken the counterpane from the bed and draped it over me, tucking it around my shoulders for all the world as though it had been concerned I might take a chill in the night.

"You didn't tell me the cottage was haunted," I said to Mrs. Marsh at breakfast.

She nearly dropped the cream pitcher she held. "Why, I never heard such foolishness," she said, looking at me with a pained expression, as though I had disappointed her. "There's no ghost here, Miss Sybil."

"I am quite certain there is."

She was shaking her head stubbornly. "I never saw hide nor hair of any ghost while I served Captain Turner, and if anything had troubled the next tenants, we'd have heard, ma'am. In the village. Mr. Bayliss's sister who did all the housekeeping was always in and out of the shops same as me, and she never so much as hinted such a thing."

"Perhaps she was afraid of being disbelieved," I said, pointedly.

The housekeeper folded her hands before her and took on an air of wounded dignity. "Ma'am, I will have you know that I am a member of the Little Whiteside Spiritualism Association. I fully believe that restless spirits move among us. Did my mother not see the ghost of her great-great-grandfather Jedediah standing at the foot of her bed when she was no more than a slip of a girl?"

"Mrs. Marsh—" I began.

But she was in full flow. "This cottage is no more haunted than a balloon. Miss Bayliss and her brother were perfectly happy here until he was posted overseas. Now, who's been putting these silly fancies in your head?"

"They are not silly fancies," I said. "Someone got into bed with me and then later covered me with the counterpane. I don't think it was you, Miss Marsh, and that leaves but one explanation."

"I expect you were dreaming," she said with a sniff. "Missing your husband, and all. If there were a ghost at Harbor Home, I would know."

"Never mind," I said shortly. It was true that Roderick had been in my thoughts when I went to bed, but that did not alter my conclusion. Once Mrs. Marsh experienced a ghostly presence cuddling up to her, she would be singing a different tune. And Roderick would believe me when he arrived.

As it happened, Mrs. Marsh was the one to welcome him, not I. I was upstairs reading in the captain's room—which had resumed its pleasant atmosphere in the light of a sunny day—and only realized he had arrived when I heard his voice downstairs. Immediately I ran downstairs to find Mrs. Marsh helping him off with his coat, fortuitously freeing his arms just in time for him to put them around me.

"There's my Sybil," he exclaimed. "As much of a minx as ever."

"Why do you say that?" I asked, then decided that I would rather kiss him than hear his answer. So it was a minute or two before he was physically able to respond.

"Having your portrait shipped here," he said, his hazel eyes warm as he gazed down at me. "That is quite a feat to carry out without my knowing, I must say. Did you plan for it to be a companion for me before you decided to join me in person? Or were you worried that I would forget what you look like?"

I swatted him on the shoulder, but not hard. "The painting was as much a surprise to me as it is to you. Besides, it's only a passing resemblance."

That made him grin. "Meaning that you find yourself more beautiful than the portrait's subject? I shall have to make a close study before passing judgment."

"Rogue," I said, and drew him into the dining room. Perhaps some luncheon would temper his mischievous remarks.

But this was not exactly the way things fell out. Roderick held my chair for me, like the gentleman he can be when he chooses, but when he went to take a seat opposite me the chair abruptly shot back several feet, dumping him on the floor.

The suddenness was as startling as the sight of my husband in such an ignominious position. "Are you all right?" I exclaimed. "That looked painful."

Roderick got to his feet, glancing all around for the cause of the chair's strange behavior. No one was in the room but the two of us.

"How did that happen?" he exclaimed. "Is the floor built on an angle?"

"I couldn't say. Surely that alone wouldn't account for it." I raised my voice and called, "Mrs. Marsh, did you wax the floor yesterday?"

The housekeeper entered from the kitchen and looked perplexed when we explained what had happened. Roderick and I regarded at each other in puzzlement.

"Neither of you has had this happen?" he asked, and I shook my head.

The chair stood against the wall. It had not moved since it slid out from under Roderick.

"I must have somehow knocked it away," he said, though he sounded unconvinced. When it remained motionless as he put one hand on it, he drew it close to the table and gave it a hard look before seating himself.

Or, rather, being unseated, for again the chair slid out from under him in less time than it takes to pen the words. Mrs. Marsh exclaimed and fell back. This time Roderick managed to grab the table and keep from dropping to the floor, but it was an undignified pose, and as he straightened I saw little patches of red on his cheekbones. He did not like being made a fool of, any more than I would.

Out of curiosity, I pushed away from the table and rose, then seated myself once more. The chair made no sudden moves or, indeed, any moves that were not of my doing.

Roderick and I regarded each other with concern. "This isn't a propitious beginning," he said dryly.

"Could it be an earthquake?" the housekeeper ventured.

"I don't see how," I said. "It would have affected other objects in the room."

Roderick said, "Maybe the house doesn't like men. Or Americans."

I suspected I knew what was going on, but it needed one more experiment. "Roderick, come kiss me," I said. "Mrs. Marsh, you may avert your eyes if you wish."

She chose to do so as Roderick came around the table to me. "What is in that clever mind of yours?" he asked.

I feigned surprise as I rose to my feet. "Must I give my husband a reason to kiss me?"

That made him laugh and take me in his arms. "I've no objections," he was saying when over his shoulder I saw a heavy porcelain urn rise up from the table and hover in the air.

"Be careful!" I cried, and Roderick ducked as the urn came flying through the air. He was just in time. The porcelain grazed his dark hair before smashing into the wall and shattering to fragments.

I sighed in vexation. Usually I enjoyed being right, but this time I was not pleased at all.

"Dearest," I said, "I'm afraid you can't stay here. It appears that there is a jealous ghost in residence—and it does not like you one bit."

NATURALLY RODERICK DID NOT TAKE KINDLY to the idea of lodging elsewhere. For a start, the nearest neighboring house along the shore was so distant it was barely in view—and was shut up for the season to boot. The village of Little Whiteside had rooms to rent, but it was miles away. The prospect of being separated in this way was frustrating to both of us.

Still, seeing the fragments of the vase scattered on the floor convinced Roderick that he was actually in danger while he was in the house. So he grumbled only a little—enough to soothe my vanity—before he accepted his fate.

"Unless there is a shed or an outbuilding where I could sleep," he began, but I shook my head.

"You would freeze," I said.

"But I could look," he said, starting for the front door. He paused only to don his coat and take up his violin case, and Mrs. Marsh followed close behind with her ring of keys. They were already well down the front path as I approached the door. Before I reached the threshold, the door slammed with a force that seemed to shake the house.

When I tried the handle, it didn't budge. "Roderick?" I called.

I could hear his steps approaching. "Sybil, are you coming?" he replied. I could hear him rattling the handle. "What in the blazes—"

I sighed. "Evidently something is quite determined to part us." Though I realized now that it was futile, I put all my strength into jiggling the handle.

"Are you certain you haven't locked it, ma'am?" came Mrs. Marsh's voice, and it was a good thing she was unable to see my face at that moment.

"Quite sure," I snapped. It wasn't the sort of thing one could do by accident and without knowing, but it sounded as though she blamed me for this predicament. "Stay there a moment, both of you, if you please," I directed them. With a show of nonchalance in case I was being watched by unseen eyes I strolled back to the kitchen and tried the door there, only to find that it, too, might as well have been set in cement.

"Blast!" I muttered and returned to the front of the house. I could see Roderick and the housekeeper peering in the front windows. Roderick was wrestling with the sash of one.

"No luck?" he called through the window, and I shook my head.

"We'd best try the windows, then. Is the catch of this one fastened?"

I nodded, and for a moment I felt a little tentative hope that this means of egress might have escaped the ghost's notice. But the catch refused to turn, and when I moved on to the next, my heart sank as it, too, refused to budge.

"It won't turn," I said, trying to keep calm. "None of them will."

At that, Roderick removed his coat and rolled up his sleeves. The look of determination on his face would have made the stoutest enemy quail. After some shouted discussion through the closed window, he and I made our way around the cottage, me on the inside and him on the outside, trying all the windows and re-trying the doors until my hands were red and swollen. No matter what we attempted, there was no way for him to reenter or me to exit. I could hear the rising tension in his voice, matching the increasing alarm I felt.

He even picked up an anchor that was doing duty as a garden ornament and, with a warning to me to stand well back, hurled it at a window with force enough to fell a giant. But it glanced off the glass without so much as cracking it. He and I stared at each other bleakly through the unblemished glass pane.

Roderick was safe, but I was a prisoner—and alone with the ghost.

THE THREE OF us spent a great deal of the afternoon conversing loudly through closed windows. Finally I was able to persuade Roderick and Mrs. Marsh to return to the village to spend the night. Roderick agreed with glowering displeasure, but I knew his ill humor was caused by worry and frustration.

"Until tomorrow, dearest," I said, and placed one palm flat against the window. With a long look at me, he did the same on the other side.

"I'll be thinking of you every minute," he said, standing very close to the window.

It was as near as we could come to a farewell embrace. And we were not even allowed to enjoy it, as one of the branches of the monkey puzzle tree chose that moment to take a vicious swipe at his head. Perhaps Roderick was not as safe as I had supposed and the haunt could show his displeasure outside the house.

"You'd best go," I said. But when he and Mrs. Marsh finally turned and walked away, I felt a terrible sense of loss.

"This nonsense must end," I announced to the air. "No one gets to make a fool of my husband!" Except perhaps myself, but I did not add that.

There was no response, but I felt a kind of smug pleasure wrap around me, as though the house itself were congratulating itself on having ousted its rival. Was old Captain Turner infatuated me because of the similarity I bore his wife?

Then I took myself in hand. First I must take stock. How long could I endure this imprisonment, considering my provisions? I must find out how much food Mrs. Marsh had brought and how much coal and firewood was inside the house.

I then made a list of experiments to try. Could I send or receive letters slid beneath the doors? Crawl up the chimney? (Doubtful.) Could I make a way out where none presently existed? Though Roderick had had no luck with the anchor, I tried hurling various heavy objects against the windows. None of them damaged the glass in any way that I could see, and while at first I derived some childish pleasure from giving free rein to my frustration, the fact that I was having no effect on my prison eventually made me more cross than ever.

"What I want to know is *why*," I snapped as I put on a kettle for tea, which I hoped would aid my thought processes or at least my temper. "You and your wife are both dead, if you'll pardon my being blunt. Why haven't you been reunited? Why are you still pining for her, or rather me?"

Despite my wide experience as a medium, there was still a great deal I didn't know about spirits who had passed beyond the veil.

And, to my frustration, it seemed that most genuine mediums were in the same predicament; only the sham ones claimed to understand all the workings of the ghostly realm.

For all I knew it could be possible that the captain and his wife had been unable to find each other. She had died young, after all; perhaps all the years that passed between her death and his had created some sort of obstacle. Especially if the captain's mental faculties had begun to erode, as seemed entirely possible, he might actually be confusing me with his wife.

Perhaps, I mused as I poured my tea, I was attempting to communicate with the wrong person.

Thus it was that as soon as twilight deepened into dusk, I took a seat on the divan opposite the portrait of Luella Turner, calmed my mind, and reached out for Luella's spirit.

But I knew almost at once that it was futile. I could capture no sense of her here. The only trace of her presence was the portrait, and though I concentrated for an hour or more, I could not call her up.

I was weary after this day full of shocks and surprises, so again I retired early. Tonight, however, when I set foot over the threshold of the captain's room I felt such jubilant adoration that it almost knocked me backward.

"So you plan to sneak into bed with me again?" I muttered. "I think not." Snatching up the counterpane and a pillow, I returned downstairs to sleep on the sofa. Nor did I undress, in case ghostly eyes were watching. Instead I pulled the blanket over my head and unbuttoned my bodice by feel. In the same manner I unhooked my corset and the waistband of my skirt. At least I could sleep in relative comfort—and I felt a certain satisfaction in having stymied any potential supernatural ogling.

I WOKE EARLY, having forgotten to draw the curtains to block out the dawn, and the first thing my eyes happened upon was a vase of fresh daffodils set upon the hearth. I regarded them uneasily. The idea of my ghostly admirer having conjured them up out of nothing was unsettling. Did that mean he was growing stronger?

Nevertheless, my mood was hopeful. Determined to contact Luella Turner's spirit, as soon as I had had my morning tea and some bread spread with currant jam I set about a thorough search of the cottage.

I started with the captain's own room. It was tempting to be deliberately messy as a morsel of revenge, but I surmised that it would be wise to keep the old fantod in a good humor. After all, he had proven he was willing to hurl heavy pottery about with no consideration for life and limb. Thus, as I pulled drawers out of the bureau and felt all along the hems of the drapes in my search for secret hiding places, I made sure to leave everything tidy in my wake.

It was vexing, after exercising such consideration, to unearth no findings. I moved on to search downstairs, but my efforts were thwarted there as well.

By this time the morning was sufficiently advanced that I could expect Roderick to arrive soon. I had hoped to have made some progress to share with him.

Flushed and irritated, I sat back on my heels. What other hiding place could there possibly be? Or was I doomed never to find any of Luella's belongings? Her portrait seemed to be smiling at me in a patronizing way, as if it knew something I did not.

Of course! The portrait. Springing to my feet, I went to regard it more closely. When I took hold of the frame and made a tentative effort to lift the painting from its hook, I realized how heavy it was. Better to leave it in place, then. I held the bottom of the frame away from the wall and felt along the back. Almost at once my fingers touched folded paper, and I drew it out eagerly. It was a letter.

Once I began reading, I realized why it had not been secreted where the captain could easily lay hands upon it. He must not have wanted to see it again.

My dear Alfred,

I think you will not be entirely surprised by this letter. You know how lonely I am when you are away at sea; I have made no secret of that. Yet you have said it is impossible for you to take up a trade on land that would allow us to be together. This would be too terrible a sacrifice for you to bear, and it would be cruel of me to demand it of you.

So I have gone away with Adolphus, the farrier. We shall live as husband and wife in a town far from here where we are not known. I wish you no ill, Alfie, and I hope you will be able to forgive me.

Regretfully,
Luella

He must never have stopped loving her, or else my welcome at the cottage would have been very different indeed. It was possible that the poor confused spirit really thought his wife had returned.

Settling this matter was going to be more complicated than most of my previous attempts to lay spirits to rest. I would most certainly need the aid of all of Roderick's and my friends, and doubtless many others. I took up a post in the bay window to keep watch for him so that we might start effecting this ghostly reunion as soon as possible.

Although the time felt long for me, it must not have been more than a quarter of an hour later that I saw their figures in the lane. As soon as they came close enough to see me I began hammering at the window panes to gain their attention and beckoning the to come faster.

Roderick's eyes brightened at the sight of me awaiting them, and when I held the letter up against the window, he and Mrs. Marsh quickened their pace. I was relieved to see that Roderick remembered to be wary of the tossing branches of the monkey puzzle tree as he strode up the walk with the housekeeper.

I had been right about the carrick coat. It looked splendid on Roderick with its cape collars snapping in the breeze. But I must not let admiration of my husband's physical presence distract me from the urgent matter at hand.

"She is alive," I shouted through the window before they could greet me.

"What? Who?"

"Luella! Alive! At least, there is a good chance she is. Mrs. Marsh, have you ever heard talk in the village of a farrier named Adolphus? He would have been before your time."

She screwed up her face in thought. "I can't say's I have, Miss Sybil."

"Will you ask, then, please? Especially among the older residents. We simply must find where he and Luella Turner settled."

"Do you really think she's still alive?" Roderick's eyes were bright with the excitement of a challenge.

"She was significantly younger than the captain, after all, and she certainly does not seem to be with him in the ghostly sphere. We must find out—and bring her here if she can be persuaded." It was a good thing that I was trained in projecting my voice in theaters, or else I would have been quite out of breath by this time from shouting through the closed window.

Roderick stepped even closer to the glass and lowered his voice slightly. "Are you well, Sybil? Was it an unpleasant night?"

His solicitude made me smile. Dear boy, how much I missed him already. "It was fine aside from being separated from you. Please, dearest, let's give this crotchety spirit what he wants as quickly as possible so we can be together again."

His smile was a touch bittersweet. "Let it be noted," he said, "that no man ever had better motivation for such a quest."

EACH DAY RODERICK came to report on his activities and progress. I wasn't certain how much the captain's ghost understood, for he continued to act sulky with Roderick. If the spirit had but realized it, Roderick was working on behalf of the captain's interests as much as ours. Like many a jealous man, however, he did not let rational thinking overrule emotion.

Roderick told me of all the telegrams he had sent, revealing that he had also managed to recruit our friend Detective Inspector Strack to set his men to work searching. Roderick drew me a figurative picture of a huge network of people combing the continent for the captain's erstwhile bride. It was almost overwhelming.

"How kind everyone is," I marveled, then had to repeat it more loudly so Roderick could hear me through the window. What a nuisance this Pyramus-and-Thisbe nonsense was.

"Some are kind indeed," Roderick said. "Many more become agreeable when I scatter money their way. And Strack, of course, would exert himself in every possible way to look good in your eyes."

It was true. This was not the first time Roderick and I had benefitted from my having a police detective as an admirer. "He is most obliging," I reflected. "I must make a point of being particularly flirtatious with him upon our next meeting to show my gratitude."

"I cannot think of any reward he would like better." He grinned. "Perhaps I shall even contrive to look jealous to add an extra flourish."

I was touched. "That is so considerate of you, dearest," I exclaimed. "We must invite him to pay us a call once I'm released from my enchanted tower."

"Ah, yes. The enchanted tower." The merriment left his eyes, and he glared upward at the captain's balcony. "If this captain were only flesh and blood, I would make him regret coming between me and my wife."

My husband looked quite fierce, and ferocity is a devilishly attractive mood on him. I took a deep breath and tried to quash visions of all the marital delights he and I were being denied during this separation. It was enough to make me quite cross, and the captain's ghost must have found me an irritable companion for some time after Roderick had reluctantly taken his leave.

As for how I endured my captivity: I forced myself to be practical. If I was truly a prisoner, I must find ways to occupy myself lest I run mad. In addition, with the house surrounded by fog for so many hours of the day, it would have been all too easy to fall prey to lonely fancies that I was cut off from the rest of the world, that I truly was held captive by a magician's spell.

So I did my best to keep busy. I read the stack of playscripts I had brought with me. I tried to begin writing my own play, but after a few false starts it was clear I was too distracted by my circumstances—and that I would find the process much easier had Roderick been there to offer aid and advice. That train of thought led dangerously close to panic, however, as I could not help but wonder if we would ever be reunited without a wall between us, so I betook myself to other tasks.

I tried again and again to make contact with the captain's spirit, but he persisted in his wordless wooing. As my diet of bread and jam grew wearisome I considered trying my hand at learning to cook, but the likelihood of my burning the cottage down with myself inside dissuaded me.

Most important, I refused to let myself consider how long my imprisonment might last. I could not look ahead without panic, so I did not look beyond the next day or two.

After what felt like a month at least but was really just three days, the huge web of searchers that Roderick had summoned up bore fruit. Adolphus was not a common name, after all, and being coupled with a particular profession made the man and his *soi-disant* wife easier to trace.

Thus, on the fourth day of my enforced tenancy, when my husband arrived in a dogcart he was accompanied by a strange woman in a shawl and bonnet. Once they descended and drew close to the house I could recognize her as the woman from the portrait, but considerably older. I was fascinated.

Roderick performed introductions—through the closed window, of course—and a look of vexation crossed our guest's face at this impediment to conversation. She stepped back to look up at the captain's room and said in a carrying voice, "It's Luella, Alfred. You may as well open the door. After the trouble to which you've put this young couple to find me, why don't you let me in so that we may talk?"

There was a moment during which I actually held my breath, and everything around us seemed to do the same. The wind died, and there was complete silence even from the gulls—and then the front door slowly creaked open.

Luella stepped inside, but the door slammed behind her before Roderick or I could reach it. Thus thwarted, I turned my attention to my visitor. It was strange to look into her face, almost as though I were looking into my own future. Her fair hair was threaded with white, but since the two blended so imperceptibly, it created the sense that time had dealt kindly with her. Despite her crows' feet, her eyes were still vividly blue. Her figure was still handsome, if not quite as slender as in the portrait. What was more important, she looked confident and capable, a woman who was not easily frightened.

"How wonderful of you to come," I exclaimed, taking her hand. "I cannot thank you enough."

She smiled and patted my hand. "Alfred always was an obstinate man," she said in a low, pleasant voice. "That is something I have not missed." Then her eyes drifted toward the staircase. "He could be sweet on occasion, though," she mused. For a few moments she lingered, lost in thought, as her eyes took everything in. "So little is changed since I left," she said, almost to herself. "The portrait...the furnishings...even the piano."

She fell silent, and I wondered if she was recalling happy times before she had decided to leave. Then she gave herself a little shake and straightened her shoulders.

"I'd best get on with it and see what sort of humor he is in," she said lightly.

"Good luck," I said, and she acknowledged this with a little bob of the head before starting up the staircase.

Her footsteps proceeded all the way up to the room. Then I could hear her speaking in a mild tone, which was followed by what sounded like wind bursting through the windows and sweeping around the room, knocking its contents about. There was a great crash, then silence.

"All is well," she called before I could shout up to her.

Despite her assurance, I was nervous. I heard Luella's voice grew stern, and the noise died down. There came one dismal clatter, as of a sulky little boy kicking a can. Then Luella laughed, and her voice dropped to a tone that I could no longer hear.

Roderick demanded through the window, "What is happening? Is she bringing the old boy to heel?"

"Shh," I cautioned, since I did not feel we were safe yet should the ghost choose to make another display of temper.

The creak of floorboards announced Luella's descent. Her hair was coming loose in front, as if blown by an angry wind, and she looked tired yet exultant. "He'll behave himself now," she said. "There should be no more trouble."

As if to prove her words, the cottage door gently swung open. I gave a cry of joy and raced through it, and Roderick caught me in his arms and swung me in the air before setting me on the ground once more. It wasn't until I felt his arms tight around me that I fully realized how frightened I had been that I would never feel his embrace again, and as if sensing this, Roderick held me close for a very long time indeed. He and I had a great many things to say to each other, but most of them could be said silently.

Eventually it dawned upon us that Luella had joined us, and we came to our senses, remembering it was impolite to ignore our rescuer and, moreover, to subject her to an unbridled display of marital delight.

"We cannot thank you enough," Roderick said, still hugging me tightly.

But she smiled. "I owe you thanks as well," she said. "My Adolphus passed away just over a year ago, and I've been lonely." Giving the monkey-puzzle tree an affectionate pat on the trunk, she said, "I think I'll take over the lease on Harbor Home. I believe I understand Alfred a bit more now than I did when I was a young lass, and he and I may rub along together quite comfortably now."

This seemed like a dangerous gamble to me. "And if you don't?" I asked.

"If we don't," she reflected, "at least he seems like a companion who will add some interest to my life."

That was so true of Roderick and me that we shared a secret smile. Long before we realized we were in love, each of us had found the other a stimulating presence. If Luella and her ghostly husband got along even half that well, Roderick and I could rest easy.

AFTER RODERICK and I returned to the village, we took a snug room in a public house for the night. There we had the privacy to pursue one of a married couple's favorite pastimes: deciding who was to blame.

"Clearly the fault is yours," Roderick said, "for being so irresistible."

I scoffed, though I was pleased. "That is just your own bias as a husband," I said. "You are the one who engaged the haunted cottage."

"No, you are clearly the cause of all the trouble," he said placidly, lying back in bed with his arms behind his head and watching me take my hair down. "This entire episode just goes to show that you are so adorable that even dead men fall in love with you."

"Do you know," I said reflectively, "because I am so happy to be reunited I think I am going to let you win this discussion." I nestled down next to him, and he kissed the tip of my nose. He showed an inclination to kiss me in more places, but first I had something to tell him. I placed a finger against his lips.

"When we were separated," I said, "and I wasn't certain we'd ever be together again—"

His brows drew together. "You needn't remind me, Sybil. I'll never forget how damned powerless I felt."

"Hush, now. You were magnificent. But I realized that I hadn't told you about something, and I know now that I wouldn't want us to be parted with anything unsaid."

"Such as?"

Now that I had committed myself, I hesitated. "Well, I do feel a bit shy about discussing it. Perhaps after all I shouldn't say anything more until I'm certain it will happen."

By now he had sat straight up in bed and was staring at me. "Sybil...are you trying to tell me you're going to have a child?"

I burst into laughter. "Of course not, you ridiculous man! No. I only meant that I'm thinking of writing a play."

All the breath went out of him in a whoosh, and he collapsed back on the bed. "Oh, thank heaven. A play! If that's all it is, you've nothing to worry about. You'll be brilliant."

"Do you think so?"

"I know so." He drew me close once more. "Have you decided what you'll write about? Maybe a beautiful vixen who draws men to their doom with her seductive wiles?"

"When I do decide, you shall be the first to know." I stroked his curly dark hair back from his forehead. "I intend to stick close by your side for a good while to make up for the time we were parted."

"Good," he said huskily, and kissed me. "We are always better together than apart."

As Shakespeare might have said, there needed no ghostly sea captain come from the grave to tell us this. But since all had ended well, I could forgive old Captain Turner for his drastic measures.

I wondered if Luella was even now curled up asleep at Harbor Home with the coverlet tucked around her by her ghostly captain. And safe in my husband's arms, which were warmer and more secure than any coverlet, I fell asleep.

THE HEADLESS HORROR

CHARLES R. RUTLEDGE

Port Erroll, Scotland. 1895

A south-east wind had brought heavy banks of sea-fog to the coast of Aberdeenshire, and more specifically to the fishing village of Port Erroll. Abraham "Bram" Stoker strode along the mist-shrouded, crescent shaped beach which stretched away on the other side of the sand dunes from his hotel. Bram's wife and son were still blissfully asleep in their rooms, but it was Bram's habit to take long walks while thinking about the novel he was currently writing. The rather macabre surroundings were admirably suited to Bram's latest narrative.

Bram squinted as the wind blew a fine spray of mist and sand into his face. He was near an area known locally as the Sand Craig, where large rocks were revealed at low tide, and where he often sat for hours, musing on the events of his imagined worlds. The weather wouldn't allow for a long period of contemplation this morning, however. He would finish his walk and head back for breakfast.

Just as he began to turn, a flurry of movement near a group of boulders caught his attention. Moving closer, Bram saw there were several bluish crabs scurrying amidst the rocks. Then he saw a pair of boots and caught a whiff of a ripe, sour smell that not even the insistent wind could completely dispel.

Bram stepped to where he could look behind one of the larger stones. The boots belonged to the body of a man who lay in the shadows of the boulder. The man's head was missing. Bram stepped back, clamping his teeth hard to keep from crying out at the sight.

The crabs were feasting on the torn flesh of the man's neck and tearing at his fingers. A solitary seabird sat upon the lifeless chest, taking its own share of the grisly repast. It glared at Bram with beady black eyes.

Repulsed, Bram rushed forward, brandishing his walking stick. The bird flew away with a screech of reproach. Bram kicked sand at the crabs and shouted. The crabs scuttled away, but they didn't go far. They could wait.

Bram made himself look down at the corpse. He felt bile in the back of his throat. What could possibly have happened to this man? Where was his head? Bram looked all around, suddenly aware of how isolated he was. He could see little more than ten feet in any direction in the dense fog. Anyone could be hidden by the mists.

The thing to do now was to find someone in authority. He knew there was a coast guard shack on the hills above, but in the fog he would be as invisible to it as it currently was to him. Port Erroll had two police constables. He would seek them out. He hefted his walking stick and started back in the direction he had come, glad of the path left by his footsteps in the sand. He didn't look back to see the crabs return to their meal.

He had hoped the rising of the sun might help dissipate the fog, but if anything the light had grown more dim as heavy clouds moved in. The barometer had been falling for days. There would likely be a storm later. At least the wind was at his back now, and not blowing in his face.

Bram heard something crunching on the sand off to his right.

He stopped, listening intently. When the sound wasn't repeated he resumed walking. The noise came again, and this time it sounded like footfalls somewhere behind him. He glanced over his shoulder but could see nothing. He picked up his pace, stabbing at the sand with the tip of his stick as he went.

The footfalls seemed to come more quickly too, and he had the distinct feeling something was moving up fast behind him. Like the traveler in Coleridge's poem, he didn't look back again, though he was sorely tempted.

Despite his growing alarm, Bram was suddenly forced to halt in his flight when a shadow appeared ahead of him. Something was coming toward him out of the fog. He gripped the handle of his heavy walking stick in both hands, ready to strike.

Then a voice said, "Why, it's Mr. Stoker!"

Bram let out an intense sigh of relief. He could see now the specter of the mist was a man known as Lang Jim, one of the constables he was on his way to find. He was a tall man, thus the nickname "Lang," taller even than Bram, who had often been called a giant because of his stature.

"Ah, constable. You don't know how glad I am to see you."

"Lord, sir," Lang Jim said. "You're as white as can be. Are you ill?"

Bram shook his head. "No, just near frightened out of my wits. I found a body on the shore. I was on my way to find you."

"A body? Did you recognize him, sir? I'm looking for Neil MacDonald. His wife said he never came home last night. I believe you know him."

Bram said, "I do know Neil, but I can't tell you if it was him. The man's head was missing from his body."

"Good God. You'd better show me, if you can stand to look at it again."

Bram had no desire to ever see the headless man again, but he said, "I'll lead you to him. He's near the Sand Craig."

ALL IN ALL, it was almost two hours before Bram was able to return to the Kilmarnock Arms hotel. His spirits lifted a little when he spotted the stonework facade appearing out of the fog. The owner, James Cruickshank, was waiting for Bram when he entered. During his various visits to Port Erroll, he and Cruickshank had become great friends. Bram was glad to see the familiar long, jovial face, given what his morning had been like.

"There you are, Bram," Cruickshank said. "Mrs. Bram asked me to tell you that she and young Noel have gone to Ellon to do some shopping and to view Ellon Castle. Mr. Shepherd was going that way and offered to drive them in his gig."

"Thank you, Cruikshank," Bram said. He found it charming that the villagers referred to his wife as Mrs. Bram. "Did Florence say when they would return?"

"She said they would be back late in the afternoon, but before dinner."

That sounded about right. The ride to Ellon, which was where the train from Aberdeen made it's final stop, would take about three hours usually. It was just as well they were away from Port Erroll for the day. Perhaps the matter would be cleared up before their return.

Bram said, "I suppose I've missed breakfast."

Despite what he had seen, Bram found that he was ravenous. Lang Jim and his fellow constable Lang John (apparently all Scottish policemen were tall) had asked Bram to say nothing of what he had witnessed. They had taken a small boat across the bay to pick up the headless body, rather than carry it along the beach where everyone could see them. Bram had thought both men were acting a little strangely, but then he'd never seen them faced with something like this, and it was, indeed, a macabre situation.

"You're in luck," Cruickshank said, "We've one guest who's still eating, and I've never seen a man put away so much food, so the cook is still at work, and complaining that she needs to be getting to luncheon preparations."

"I owe the man a debt then. I'll go to my usual table."

"And I'll have a pot of tea sent over first thing. You look like you could use it, Bram."

"I could indeed. Thank you."

Bram turned and went into the dining room. Though it was ostensibly summer, a fire burned in the grate on one side to ward off the morning chill. Only one table was occupied, and that by the largest man Bram had ever seen. The man was seated, but Bram estimated that he would tower several inches over his own six foot, two inch frame. The table utensils looked like those from a child's tea set in his enormous hands. The man noticed Bram's appraisal and gave him a not unfriendly nod.

"You're welcome to join me, Mr. Stoker," the man said in a deep, rumbling voice.

"Are we acquainted, sir?" Bram asked.

The big man shook his head. "I've seen you at the Lyceum, where you're the manager, I think. My name is Kharrn."

Looking at the man, Bram wouldn't have thought him the theater going sort. And he wondered that he didn't recall seeing him there. He was certainly memorable. Perhaps he'd used a private box. Bram crossed the room and pulled out the chair opposite Kharrn. "Thank you for the invitation, Mr. Kharrn. I will join you. I'm not much in the mood to eat alone just now."

"Just Kharrn will do."

"As you say. And please call me Bram."

One of the maids brought Bram's tea and poured him a cup. He received it gratefully. He asked for several items from the kitchen, assuring the maid that he would settle for anything the cook had left.

Kharrn said, "Is something troubling you?"

Bram looked at his new companion. His skin was deeply tanned and up close he could see an old, white scar ran down one side of Kharrn's face. His eyes were a very clear shade of blue.

"Nothing I can talk about at the moment, but thank you for your interest. I had a very harrowing experience this morning. Later today I'll probably be at liberty to discuss it. In the meantime, perhaps you'd care to tell me what brings you to Port Erroll. It is a bit out of the way. I only discovered it by accident, myself."

Kharrn said, "I'm looking into a mysterious death."

Bram felt his heartbeat quicken. "A death. Are you a detective of some sort?"

"Nothing official. A man was killed three days ago between here and Boddam. A friend contacted me in London."

The village of Boddam lay north of Port Erroll, past Slains Castle.

"Did you know the man who was killed?"

"No, but there was something strange about the killing, and I've long been a student of the outre. My friend thought I might be able to offer some insight."

Bram didn't want to ask the next question but he did. "What was strange about the death, can you tell me?"

Kharrn seemed to consider it for a moment. "The police appear to be keeping it quiet, but the corpse was missing its head."

"My God," Bram said.

Bram tried to keep his expression neutral. For a moment, he considered telling Kharrn about what he had seen on the beach, but he had promised his silence to the constables until they could identify the dead man and inform the family. Surely something would be announced later in the day.

"I don't think God had much to do with it. At least not the one you mean. Something more sinister, I think."

Bram's food arrived and he fell to. He didn't think it wise to excessively interested. Kharrn seemed a shrewd sort.

The big man finished his breakfast and rose from the table. He was even taller than Bram had thought. Perhaps seven feet. "I enjoyed talking with you, Bram. I hope we can speak again later."

"I would welcome that, my friend. Perhaps you might join me for dinner and meet my wife and son."

"I would be honored." Kharrn said, 'Though this evening I have a previous engagement." Before he left, he reached behind the table and lifted a flat, leather case. It looked as though it might contain something heavy, though the big man hefted it easily enough. He gave Bram a final nod and left the dining room.

WELL PAST LUNCHEON, Bram was still waiting for word from Lang Jim. Perhaps the constables were having trouble identifying the dead man. That would certainly be understandable.

Despite the events of the morning, he wanted to get back to work on his book. He preferred to work outside, but the damp, windy day wouldn't be conducive to that, so he sat down at a small desk in his room and consulted his notes. He was calling his latest work *The Un-Dead*, as it dealt with the subject of vampires. Bram had long been interested in sensationalist literature, and he had originally thought this novel would be as quickly written as some of this other works.

It had grown in the telling, however, and it looked to become his most ambitious novel yet. He had spent considerable time in the London library, consulting reference volumes, and making copious notes from books like *Roumania: Past and Present, The Book of Were-Wolves,* and *Round About the Carpathians.*

Bram became so lost in his work, that when he next looked up, two hours had passed while he was wandering in the land beyond the forest, as his setting Transylvania was known. He stood from the desk and stretched. Consulting his watch, he saw the time was nearing four in the afternoon. Florence and Noel should be returning from Ellon soon. He decided to take a short walk to clear his thoughts, and perhaps he could learn how the constables' investigation had progressed.

Bram stepped out of the hotel to find the day was even more overcast. He hoped that his wife and son wouldn't be caught out in a storm on their way back. He decided to walk northwards this time. Best to stay away from the beach for now.

He started up The Terrace, a narrow lane with only a few red granite cottages scattered along the way. Port Erroll was in some ways, a village divided by its inhabitants. The "upper village," the area where the hotel sat, was where the tradesmen lived, and the "lower village," closest to the harbor, was where the fishermen and their families made their homes.

As Bram walked, he became aware of a prickling at the nape of his neck, that familiar feeling of being watched. He turned suddenly and found that someone was indeed staring at him. A gaunt old woman stood about ten feet away, and her glare was so intense that her eyes almost seemed to glow.

"Good afternoon, madame," Bram said. "Is there something I can help you with?"

The woman said, "Na, laddie. But there may be something I can do for you."

"I'm afraid I don't understand."

"You don't understand, and that's the peril of it."

Bram considered just walking on, but something in the woman's baleful gaze held him. "Perhaps you can explain it to me then."

"You've been close to something today, laddie. Close to something few men have seen and lived. You were lucky this morning in the fog, but you will encounter it again, and soon."

Bram said, "You'd have me believe you're a fortune teller of some sort?"

"Yes, I'm a seer. Believe of don't. My name is Gormala, and I am known here."

Bram heard thunder rumble in the distance. The day seemed colder somehow. "And you've seen something about me?"

"You and yours. Listen well, Abraham. There is a Bochdan plaguing the countryside."

Bram had heard the term before. Bochdan was a general name for apparitions, hobgoblins and evil spirits.

"This fiend has no head and he seeks the heads of others," Gormala continued. He took Neil MacDonald's head in the blackness just before dawn and he almost took yours. He will stalk again tonight."

How had this woman known about the man with the missing head? As far as he knew the constables still hadn't released any information. Perhaps she did have some sort of second sight. He suddenly wished his friend Hall Caine were there. Hall had great knowledge of the supernatural.

Gormala grinned. "Yes, laddie, I know what you saw in the fog. Most of the village knows by now but they won't speak of it. They never do. Lang Jim and Lang John will tell Neil MacDonald's wife he met with an accident and that will be that. All here know 'tis best not to speak of the headless one."

"I'm sorry, madame," Bram said, "I'm having a difficult time believing..."

But Gormala cut him off. "I told you. Believe or don't. But the headless one will stalk again soon, between here and Ellon. Look to your own, laddie. Look to your own."

At that moment a tremendous flash of lightning rent the clouds and thunder seemed to shake the ground. Bram looked around him as he felt a few drops of rain. When he looked back toward Gormala, he found her gone. There was nowhere she could have gone to so quickly. No near building or copse of trees that could hide her. And yet, gone she was.

Bram decided it was time to get back to the hotel and started back the way he had come. Florence and Noel might have returned by now.

Bram halted in his tracks.

Florence and Noel. They were his family. His own. And they

had gone to Ellon. The old woman had said the Bochdan would walk again, and in the direction where his wife and son had gone. What if the old woman wasn't mad? He started off again at a faster pace.

When he got back to the Kilmarnock Arms he went immediately to the front desk. Cruickshank wasn't there but Elizabeth Masson, was standing behind the counter. Bram didn't know Beth that well, but she and Florence often passed the time of day together.

"Ah, Beth," Bram said. "Have you seen Florence and Noel this afternoon?"

"They haven't returned from their day trip as far as I know, Bram. The storm is coming this way from the direction of Ellon so they might have been delayed."

So they were still out there. Probably on their way back by now. There was a good chance they wouldn't make it before dark. Bram gritted his teeth. The old woman's warning had disturbed him more than he realized. A headless creature. It seemed impossible. And yet he had seen Neil's body and he had been sure something had been following him the in the fog.

"Beth," Bram said. "I need to find a horse or a dogcart."

Beth's eyes widened. "Do you think something has happened?"

"Let's just say I'm becoming concerned. With any luck, I'll simply meet them on the road on their way back."

"Well of course, Bram. Mr. Banes, who drove you from the station, can probably help you, though he may not want to go out in the storm."

"I'll help him," a rumbling voice said. "I have a horse and cart in your stable."

Bram turned to find Kharrn standing behind him. "It isn't necessary, Kharrn, though I'm grateful for your offer of aid. I can go talk to Banes."

"I'm going, so you might as well come with me. Come on."

With that Kharrn turned and started out of the hotel. Bram made a hasty goodbye to Beth, and followed.

"Kharrn," Bram called after the man's broad back. "This is probably a fool's errand."

Kharrn stopped and faced Bram. "You're afraid the headless one is out there. So am I."

"You know about it?"

"That's why I'm here. I told you about what happened at Boddam. I was planning on hunting the creature tonight. By all accounts, it likes to find travelers in lonely spots."

"You believe it's real, then?"

"I believe something killed those men and took their heads away. Be it man or demon from hell, I intend to stop it."

Kharrn's blue eyes glittered with an intensity that was almost frightening. Bram had to resist a sudden impulse to take a step back. The big man turned and continued stalking toward the stables.

Within a quarter of an hour, the horse and cart were ready to go. Kharrn and Bram climbed onto the driver's bench and Kharrn took the reins. The rain was still light as they headed toward the bridge leading out of Port Erroll, but the clouds hung low and dark, and thunder rumbled along the horizon. Kharrn turned the dogcart toward the west.

The rain began in earnest about sundown, making visibility poor, so Kharrn had to drive the cart slowly. They lit a lantern, and that allowed Kharrn to keep the road in sight, but did little else to dispel the gloom.

It was strange and unreal night journey. They traveled in their own small globe of light, and all around them the rain fell. Bram could hear nothing but the susurration of the waves of rain and the low rumbling of thunder. Occasionally lightning would reveal the landscape beyond the twisting road.

They were perhaps an hour out of Port Errol when Bram heard a different sound. The sound of human voices screaming.

"Good God, Kharrn. I pray we are not too late."

"There's a light ahead of us," the giant man said. "Looks like a lantern."

As he spoke, Kharrn reined in the horse. He reached behind him and retrieved the flat, leather case from where he had stored it. He threw open several clasps that held the case closed. The lantern's feeble light glittered on something metallic.

From within the case Kharrn withdrew a big, twin-bladed ax, like the kind Bram had seen in illustrations of Vikings. The thing had to weigh upwards of thirty pounds, but the giant man held it in one hand as he vaulted from the driver's bench and landed in the mud. He was off in an instant, running full out toward the wavering lamplight and the screaming voices.

Bram leaped into the mud as well and hurried after Kharrn. He took only a moment to wonder about the ax. His wife and son were in danger, perhaps already dead or injured. He would worry about the giant man's choice in weapons later.

As he got closer to the light, Bram could see that it was, indeed, thrown from a lantern, which hung on the side of Mr. Shepherd's wagon. Shepherd lay in the mud beside his dead horse. Or at least Bram assumed it was Shepherd's body. He had no head.

A second later, Bram saw Shepherd's head. It was gripped by the hair in one fist of a gigantic creature who towered over Kharrn, although the thing had no head of its own. To Bram's disgust and horror, he saw that half a dozen human heads in varying stages of decomposition were attached to a belt around the apparition's waist.

For a moment, Bram hesitated, shocked by what he was seeing there in the rain. Then he heard Florence scream. She and Noel were pinned against the side of Shepherd's wagon. The headless one was stalking toward them. Now Bram could see that it held a sort of cleaver in its free hand. It was long and heavy, and covered in rust and dried blood, but the blade looked keen enough. Bram scrambled toward his family.

"You! Creature!" Bram heard Kharrn yell.

The headless one stopped moving forward. Slowly, ponderously, it turned toward Kharrn. It couldn't actually "face" him, or anyone else, but it seemed to know he was there. Somehow it "saw" him. It started toward the big man, brandishing the cleaver and waving Shepherd's severed head.

Bram hurried to Florence's side. He put one arm around his wife's shoulders and the other around his son.

"Bram," Florence said. "Thank God you're here. That...thing just appeared out of the rain and attacked us. It killed Mr. Shepherd."

Bram said, "Listen to me, dearest. I want you to take Noel and run. Perhaps Kharrn and I can delay the thing. Just get away."

Bram looked back over his shoulder just in time to see the headless creature close with Kharrn. It hurled Shepherd's head straight at the big man. Kharrn dodged nimbly to the side, but as he did so, the headless one swung the cleaver in a murderous arc.

Kharrn brought up the big ax and met the monster's stroke. Sparks flew as the cleaver bounced off the ax blade. Kharrn continued the motion, sweeping the cleaver aside and leaped inside the headless one's reach. He brought the ax down in the center of the thing's chest, sinking it deep.

The creature ignored the ax and swung its free hand out, catching Kharrn across the face and knocking him away. Then the thing reached up, and grabbing the ax, pulled it from its chest. Bram saw brackish blood oozing from the gash in the creature's breast.

Kharrn was on his feet, but the ax was out of his reach and the headless one was lumbering toward him, swinging the cleaver in great sweeps. Lightning chose that moment to flash and the combatants were thrown into stark relief. Bram saw the tip of the cleaver strike Kharrn's chest, ripping through his shirt and waistcoat, and tearing into his flesh.

The big man roared, more in anger than pain, Bram thought.

Still, Bram ran toward the headless one, yelling and waving his arms, hoping to distract it from its assault on Kharrn.

It was just enough. The creature seemed to hesitate, and Kharrn ducked under the next swing of the cleaver and slammed one massive shoulder into the headless one, causing the thing to stagger backwards.

Kharrn rushed past the creature and snatched his ax from where it lay in the mud. The headless one was right behind him, but he spun and buried the ax in the thing's knee. The knee gave out and the thing toppled. Kharrn whipped the weapon free and struck a quick blow to the hand that held the cleaver, causing the creature to lose the weapon.

The headless one tried to grab Kharrn with its other hand but the giant man drove the edge of one of the blades downward between the second and third fingers, splitting the monster's hand to the wrist.

Bram had never seen anything so savage. The giant man, who had seemed so polite in the dining room of the hotel, was now acting like a berserk beast, hacking away at the monster. He continued chopping long after the headless one had ceased to struggle.

At last Kharrn's fury seemed to be spent and he backed away from the fallen monster. Now Bram saw something else. The creature seemed to be disintegrating as the rain washed over it. Robbed of whatever unholy power had animated the headless body, it seemed to be falling apart.

Bram made his way to Kharrn. "Are you all right, Kharrn? Are you injured? I saw that blade strike you."

"I'll be fine. Let's get your wife and son back to shelter."

"Yes, I quite agree. Is that devil gone for good, do you think?"

"It's destroyed, if anything like that can ever truly be destroyed. It won't be back in your lifetime."

Bram thought Kharrn used that last phrase oddly, as if Bram's lifetime would be vastly different from his own. Oh well. Another question for later. Now he just wanted to get Florence and Noel, and himself for that matter, out of the elements.

DAWN CAME clear and bright the next morning. The storm had pushed through, carrying away the sea fog. Bram stood with Kharrn in front of the Kilmarnock as the big man loaded his luggage into the dogcart.

"I wish you would stay and truly meet Florence," Bram said.

Kharrn grinned. "I think your wife has seen all of me she wants to see, Bram."

"You may be right. She and Noel were both exhausted and are sleeping still, but I'm sure she would like to thank you properly for saving both their lives."

"You've thanked me enough for the both of them."

Bram said, "I don't know that I can ever thank you enough for that, my friend. Kharrn, you came here looking for that headless creature, and I sense that you know of other things beyond the knowledge of most men. There are so many questions I'd like to ask, not the least of which is the origins of that strange ax of yours."

"That is something to discuss another day. Right now, I have to be on my way. As you said, there are other things out there that people don't know about. It is my fate to find them. Perhaps we'll meet again."

"I truly hope so."

The two men shook hands and Kharrn climbed onto the dogcart. With a final nod at Bram, the giant man set the horse in motion and the vehicle rattled away. As it did so, James Cruickshank came out of the hotel.

"Good morning, Bram," Cruickshank said. "Beth told me you and Mrs. Bram were caught out in the storm last night. Care to tell me about it over breakfast?"

Bram smiled. "Perhaps I shall, Cruickhank. But I've a question for you too. What can you tell me about the woman called Gormala?"

"Gormala?"

"Yes, an old woman who claims to be a seer of some sort. I owe her a debt of gratitude."

Cruickshank looked puzzled for a moment, then he said, "The only Gormala I know of was said to be a witch."

"Yes, that's the one."

Cruickshank shook his head, "That couldn't be, Bram. My grandmother told me stories of the witch woman, but Gormala died long before I was born."

Bram stood for a moment, listening to the waves and the sound of the gulls. There in the bright morning sunlight he recalled how the old woman had seemingly vanished and for a moment he felt as if a shadow had passed over him. "Let's go inside, Cruickshank. I think I could use some tea just now."

AUTHOR'S NOTE:

I couldn't have written this story without the help of Mike Shepherd, the author of When Brave Men Shudder, *a book about Bram Stoker's love for the fishing village of Port Erroll, now known as Cruden Bay, and the time he spent there writing Dracula. Not only was Mike's book of material assistance, as Sherlock Holmes would say, but he was kind enough to answer my many questions about the village and its inhabitants, and to fact check the finished story. Anything I got wrong is my fault. Thanks again, Mike!*

NOT MORE LOVELY THAN FULL OF GLEE

LEANNA RENEE HIEBER

It was said that the artist had abandoned the fine house in the mountains; that richly appointed chateau with the turret where countless rooms stood silent, adorned with art and colored glass. Rumor had it that the cellar was an open pit and the upstairs floorboards creaked and thumped.

It was said that he'd left the village haunted after the untimely death of his young bride. But then again, the peasants below were full of superstition. It wasn't that anyone had seen her, but the disappearance of her lovely glee was a haunt in reverse. The absence of a once beautiful treasure was the living's own ghost to bear.

She was talked about. Her memory had life and in it, she was again not more lovely than full of glee as the very mention of her made the elders smile. Then they'd cluck their tongues and ask the rhetorical question of what happened to her. They knew in their hearts; out, out, brief candle. She'd been snuffed.

It was Christmastime—Christmas Eve to be specific—when the artist made his way back to the sorrowful site, in hopes that the season of peace and forgiveness could create an alchemical change in his heart and his fortunes. What better time to reckon with the past and turn a new page, a heart made pure as the mountainside under a fresh blanket of undriven snow?

When the artist's driver reached the end of the lane, the old man hesitated.

"Go on, sir," the artist assured. "I'll walk from here. Turn around, get that shivering mare into a warm stable. I'll be all right." He unleashed his leather case from the back of the carriage. "I'm home again. And I have to make my peace with that."

The hunched driver crossed himself and turned his hack sharply, murmuring a benediction for the artist's soul and something about "*her*" that became lost in a gust of wind.

The chateau loomed ahead at the end of the tree-lined lane, its form like a skull on the edge of a cliff. The last of the day's light glinted off eye-like windows, and the land below was ushered swiftly away in a sheer drop.

With a crunching tread through deepening drifts, the artist made his way forward. He glanced up at a noisy blackbird grumbling in a treetop, noting that the branches arching above him had begun to gnarl and knot; claws in a tangle.

A warning from the morning halted him at the property's wrought-iron gate which yawned open at the latch. He recalled the woman in the train bench in front of him; when he handed his ticket over to the conductor and said what town he'd be stopping in, she turned around, mourning veil nearly obscuring her wrinkled face.

"Take care, there, my son. Yuletide or no. It is a place of curious endings."

These words had chilled him enough to make him reconsider his return. He had opted not to go through the town and up the rugged pass, but instead continue on the rail north and take the higher road, privately, back. He was sure if he'd paraded through the central pass there would be whispers and cruelties spoken not enough out of earshot. His sorrow was heavy enough without gossip weighing it further.

Stepping up the overgrown flagstones to the hefty, carved oak front door, the artist noted the glass on either side was broken, the lock forced. He shouldn't have been surprised that brigands took evident shelter here, assuming the place was abandoned. They hadn't been wrong. After the funeral, the once romantic nest had become as silent as the lily-marked grave down below. The artist didn't dare look down the side of the mountain at that valley churchyard. The only comfort he could muster was what he hoped still lay ahead, hung on the walls inside: his art.

Once inside the foyer, he struck a match to light the front braziers and then struggled with the resistant wick of an oil lantern. Lamp finally lit, by jaundiced light, he began his tour of plaster walls lined with paintings and dark wooden roof-beams decked with spiderwebs. The colored glass lining the windows was as dark as the night sky. But his art remained safe within. He sighed in relief.

In the main hall were his vast landscapes. Ruins. Abbeys. Castles.

Up the curving stairs were the faces. Patrons. Scholars. Nobles.

They were works of great renown; each a captured flash of fervor and obsession. Now, here, they were his witnesses.

He hadn't stopped painting during his time away; he did have to eat, to survive, and there were no other skills to which he was suited. But looking at these pieces here, remembering them again, feeling them in his fingers as if he were still sculpting the paint into just the right texture, nothing he'd painted of late had the life of these earlier works.

And nothing, of course, had the life of *her*.

Perhaps that's why all the art had been left alone. Deemed haunted.

There were footprints tracked in the dust ahead of him as he climbed the curving stone stair, the lamplight illuminating a limited arc ahead of him, two pairs of feet then just one as the furthest chamber was reached. He paused at the open door. The prints of the boots were hardly fresh so it had been some time since the trespass, and as the steps were few, the place must have been denounced as eerie enough to ward off subsequent intruders.

At the end of the hallway stood the turret room that had held his most precious treasures. His best work. The place where he captured her adoring look. Forever. To the last.

The night was a dark one and very little light came through the lancet windows ahead.

If the artist wasn't mistaken, even the lamplight hesitated at the threshold, as if it didn't dare disrupt the deep shadows within.

Trembling, he took a deep breath and stepped into the chamber. The bedcurtains across the room were open and the bound book that had chronicled all the artistic works within the house lay open to a final page atop the rumpled bedclothes.

His mind swam. Had a friend, the week she died, offered to add in one final entry? The artist didn't remember and was too unnerved to look. Instead he bent to set the lantern upon the floor, cast the book aside and lay down upon the dusty bed, folding in upon himself to weep.

It wasn't that he hadn't mourned then, it was that he'd gone into a detached state and felt like he was only now waking up, jarred to the truth of the empty place. Her vacancy. He had been so obsessed with the look of her and how to translate it he hadn't considered the reality of her.

"It is a place of curious endings."

She had ended. Here. And yet. What was art but a chance at eternal life?

He tried to bring the image of her to mind, of her beautiful face, even as she was laid out in her winding sheets. But all he could see was the flurry of brushstrokes in his mind's eye. All he could seem to recall was the drag of horsehair on the palette and the angle of the dim light. He had tried so desperately to capture what was always said of her: glee above loveliness. The final result was, of course, stunning, unearthly, but it had been cast aside when the health of his model- his *wife*- vanished.

"Forgive me..." he whispered to the empty room.

Bare trees scraped against the narrow windows like the scratch of fingernails.

The portrait was there on the wall, behind a curtain. After the funeral the artist had placed it in the deepest of shadows. All he had to do was lift the lamp, draw the shade, and confront his fated masterpiece. Face down on his coat sleeve, he steeled himself and wiped his streaming eyes on his cuff. That's when he heard a footstep.

A light footstep. From the corner of the room. A slow, pervasive paralysis crept over him.

Another step. The creak of a floorboard. He did not dare lift his head now. Another step at the head of the bed. Shifting his face, unable to help himself, he peered between his fingers. The curtain over his wife's oval portrait was drawn aside.

The frame was empty!

A sound left his throat, something strangled and shocked. The shadows to the side of him, mere feet from him, moved. In a scramble, he reached for his lantern, lifting it up with a choking "Who's there?"

There she stood.

Shaking, the artist lowered the lantern, but its arc was wide enough to capture her whole form at the head of the bed, dressed in the dark gown she'd been painted in. "My God..."

There was a glow about her like a phantasm, and yet her small, slippered feet were planted upon the ground—as much solid as shade. Her face looked just as he'd painted her. But the curve of her smile was terrifying.

Then the figure spoke. Her voice was soft. Musical. Glancing off the artist's ear as if from across the hall, not right before him.

"Hello, husband." She smiled an obedient, sharp-toothed smile. "How do I look?"

He gaped at her. She took another light step forward, coming around the bed towards his cowering form. Her feet sounded on the boards and yet no dust was disturbed in her wake.

"Am I not more lovely than full of glee?" she asked. "Is that not what always was said? It is important to remember what has been *said*."

He fell to his knees, crossing himself. "A...miracle...Though...how can it be that you are here now? I buried you, my sweetheart."

She drew close. Cold hands that abrased like dry canvas shot out to cup his cheeks. "You did, my husband..." She murmured hungrily. Her dark eyes flickered to the wall. "But my life was here all along. You saw to that. Down to the last spark of my body's vitality that you gave to the glint in my painted eye. Did you not think there may be more than one way to take and give a life?"

Still in her unsettling hold, he tilted his head to the side, not understanding her question. She did the same in an eerie mirror.

"The storytelling," she explained. "The tales told of me. I suppose you wouldn't have thought of it. Your art was in paint, your mind in lines and strokes. I understand. But you're here now to see the power of the word. It giveth and taketh away."

His wild fervor was held by her sharp fingernails. Her smile broadened, gleeful indeed, as she bent to kiss him. He shuddered in her grasp. His color leapt from his cheek to hers.

A spark leapt up; that ineffable, glittering light, that unfathomable mystery. She caught the luminous wisp in a deep breath, rolled it on her parched tongue and swallowed it whole.

The artist slid to the floor, motionless.

The book that chronicled the entire gallery of the chateau, indeed works of great renown, stood open to the very page that told of her demise. Her sacrifice. That the book was open proved it had been read. Someone had come to bear witness to her tale. But it was as yet unfinished. She plucked a pen from the prone artist's pocket and added to the narrative which had ended, abruptly, with her death. She continued the tale:

"Yes, dead she may have been, but what has the finest wit of our age said? 'Life imitates Art far more than Art imitates Life.' Perhaps, but it must then also be said: Death imitates Art far more than Art imitates Death. If art captures life then I was never wholly dead and words have resurrected me. I have stepped out of the frame to begin anew."

Church bells tolled the midnight mass to proclaim a special child was born to a peasant, urging the world to tell tales of sacrifice and eternal life.

She stepped out of the turret, strong footfalls treading the sonorous floorboards. She kept walking until she reached the town below where tales of her reached further still; not more cautionary than full of fear.

WHO WOULDN'T GO

CLIFF BIGGERS

Andrew missed Grandma Bess's voice. The Christmas songs had never been the same after he broke her three years ago.

It was an accident, of course. The delicate glass ornaments seemed to become more fragile with each passing year, and hers was one of the oldest. Metallized blue finish with a flocked white snowflake pattern stenciled on front and back. He remembered seeing it on his grandmother's tree when he was five years old. When she died and the family was laying claim to various belongings of hers, he spent an hour rummaging around idly, disinterested in the furnishings and silverware and jewelry that so fascinated the others. When he saw the box labeled "Christmas," he knew what his choice would be.

The next Christmas, he placed her ornament in a position of prominence. It helped him to remember Grandma Bess the way she had been before old age and dementia had taken her away little by little. By the end, she couldn't carry on a conversation. What she could do, though, was sing. Her memory of names and events may have been taken from her, but those songs were so anchored in her mind that every time she heard a song she liked, she would sing in her beautiful voice. And Christmas songs were her favorite.

Music had always been a part of Christmas for his family, so he played a few old familiars as he reflected on the ornament. Grandma Bess didn't sing right away—and when she did, her harmonious voice was so soft that he almost didn't hear her at all. "Adeste Fidelis" was the song that drew her back. As the song went on, he recognized her distinctive voice.

From then on, it became a nightly ritual. He would play the song every night, and she would sing along.

"Merry Christmas, Grandma Bess. I'm glad you're here."

Andrew never told the rest of his family about her. But every evening, he would creep downstairs once his wife and his son and his daughter had gone to bed. He would plug in the Christmas lights, and he would hum along while Bess supplied the vocals.

One night, caught up in the holiday spirit, he asked, "Grandma Bess, what was Christmas like when you were young?" No answer—just another song.

Andrew would sometimes fall asleep on the sofa next to the tree as he listened to her songs. "No one loves Christmas as much as your dad," his wife would tell Ryan and Katie. Andrew would smile and nod.

Christmas passed, and Grandma Bess's song was packed away in a nest of protective tissue.

The next year, the tree went up on Thanksgiving evening as always, heralding the beginning of the Christmas season. He was so eager to hear Grandma Bess's voice that he hung her ornament first. Once satisfied that it was in the proper place, he turned his attention to the tree skirt.

As he struggled to spread it into place, the quilted fabric caught on a lower tree limb, jostling the tree ever so slightly. But that was enough. The glass ornament rocked slightly as the wire hook slipped from the branch. It popped when it hit the oak floor, with a sound much like that of a breaking light bulb.

The tree was quiet after that.

COUNTRY ROADS STAND AS constant reminders that nature always wins. Almost as soon as the pungent asphalt mix cools, the cracks begin. Tiny cracks, not even visible for the first year or so.

But the edges don't crack They crumble. Without the protective confinement of a concrete curb and gutter, the edges of country roads yield to eroding rain and tenacious weeds and shifting red dirt. Little pieces separate. Larger chunks follow. Cracks radiate from the crumbled edges, presaging future breaks.

The crumbling edge must have been what did Ryan in. That's what the officer said. The road probably looked fine, but the front wheel must have hit that edge, which gave way and pulled the motorbike off the road and into the ravine below.

The same motorbike that Andrew and Ellie had given their son as a Christmas gift when he turned eighteen. The motorbike he had requested for three Christmases in a row until they finally gave in.

The spring overgrowth was so dense that it took the police three days to find him. The officer wouldn't let Andrew or Ellie to see the body. "This ain't the way you'd want to remember him," he said.

Andrew struggled with their son's death, but Ellie was devastated by an overpowering guilt. She had been the one who had given in to Ryan's persistent requests for the motorbike. "It's what he really wants, Andrew. What's the harm in it?" Those words haunted her.

With guilt came despair.

The various holidays passed uncelebrated. There were no fireworks or bunting or cookouts on the Fourth of July. They didn't even speak of Ryan's mid-September birthday. The lights remained off on Halloween to discourage any trick or treaters.

That year, they had decided not to put up the tree. Ellie

dreaded the approaching holiday. "What is there to celebrate?" she asked. Andrew didn't have an answer. So the boxes remained in the garage.

Thanksgiving dinner was done—not a turkey and dressing feast, but a modest meal of rotisserie chicken, mashed potatoes, and instant stuffing—and the dishes were washed. Andrew anticipated a dreary evening on the sofa.

But Katie had a different idea.

"Hey, dad, ready to get started?" She stood next to the artificial tree, which she had assembled while her parents were cleaning up. The tree skirt was already in place, the boxes of ornaments open. Katie knew that her parents needed Christmas...and so did she.

I guess we're doing this then, he thought as he half-smiled at his wife...who didn't smile back. *We're doing it for the children,* he started to say—but this year, there was only one child.

Even so, that one child deserved a Christmas. And thus the decorating ceremony began. But Katie was the only one whose heart was in it.

A FOREST green ornament with two irregular white stripes around its circumference and a dash of white at the stem, just below the hanger loop. Ryan had added the white paint when he was eight years old. "It looks sad when it's all one color," he told his parents when they asked why. "Now it looks happy, like Christmas."

It spoke to him the first time three nights after Thanksgiving. Andrew was dozing on the sofa. Rather than waking him up to tell him to go to bed, Ellie and Katie had left him. It was almost two in the morning when he woke up, more weary than he was before he had dozed off. He was just gathering the energy to go upstairs when he heard it.

Up on the housetop, reindeer pause...

The voice was distant, barely audible...It seemed to come from a faraway place, like those AM radio stations he used to tune in on sleepless Christmas Eve nights. So far away that he had to strain to understand it.

"Ryan? Can you hear me, son?"

Merry Christmas, Dad. I knew you'd be here.

Andrew rubbed his face with the heel of his right hand to wake himself up, just in case he was still asleep and dreaming. Then he heard his son's voice again, once again singing "Up on the Housetop." The same song Ryan had played over and over when he painted the ornament ten Christmases ago.

"I miss you, son."

I know, Dad. I know a lot now...

"Remember that Christmas when you were six?" Andrew interrupted. "That Star Wars play set that you wanted that I couldn't find anywhere?" He didn't want to hear about now. He wanted to hear about how things used to be.

"I remember. You hid it in the closet in your and Mom's bedroom, and I found it—

"That's right—you found it when you went in there for something else, and you were so afraid that we would take it back once you saw it..."

Yeah...Gifts were everything back then.

Andrew wasn't sure how to reply. How he wished he could give his son one more gift.

FOR ALMOST FOUR WEEKS, Andrew would sit downstairs after everyone had gone to sleep, eager to spend a few moments with his son. If Ellie noticed his absence, she never said anything about it.

The time with Ryan never lasted long enough. His son's voice would start off relatively clear, but as they talked it became more garbled, more difficult to understand, until it was finally gone.

The nature of the conversations disturbed him more than their duration, however. For the first week or so, Ryan had taken part in Andrew's talk of Christmases past. But as Christmas approached, the reminiscing gave way to a disturbed agitation. It came to a head on Christmas Eve night; it was almost midnight when Andrew paid his late-night visit.

Dad? Something's wrong...

"Nothing's wrong, son. You're back home. It's Christmas, and you're back home."

But it's not right, Dad. I can't see you. I can't see anything. I don't know where I am. I don't belong here. I'm scared, Dad...

"It's okay, Ryan. It's Christmas Eve. It's the best night of the year."

No. I don't want to be here, Dad. Help me—

The final word was clipped.

"Ryan?"

No reply.

Andrew looked at his watch. Just after midnight. It was Christmas.

BY MID-MORNING, the gifts had been opened. Katie was texting her friends, telling them everything that she had gotten. Ellie brought in a large black trash bag, eager to clean up the remnants of giftwrap and ribbon and bring this particular Christmas to an end. "Do you want to start taking the tree down?" she asked.

"No...No, I think I'm going to leave it up until New Years Day.'" Andrew couldn't tell her the reason for his reluctance.

"Do we have to? I hate looking at it."

"I really want to. It would mean a lot to me, okay?"

Ellie started to reply, but she wasn't ready for a Christmas morning argument.

The day passed slowly. Ellie was weary and more than a little irritable by the time dinner was over. Katie went up to her room, continuing to focus her attention on her iPhone and its endless stream of "What did you get for Christmas?" texts from her friends.

Andrew knew it would be easiest to wait Ellie out. He idly watched television (or pretended to) until she finally got up from the sofa without a word and went to bed. Once he was sure that she had closed the bedroom door, he leaned in the direction of the tree.

"Ryan?"

No response.

"Ryan? Can you hear me? It's Christmas, son."

Nothing.

He took the green ornament off the tree, holding it gently. He leaned forward until his lips were just an inch from the ornament and whispered "Merry Christmas, Ryan."

No words came to him from the ornament...but for a second, he thought that he heard a sound.

A frightened, barely voiced whimper.

The morning of December 26th, Andrew took the tree down and packed the ornaments away.

ANDREW SHOULD HAVE SEEN the signs. Ellie's despair grew even more intense after the holidays were over. "Give her a year," their friends said. "It takes that long to get over a death in the family."

A year passed, but Ellie's depression only deepened.

"Maybe you should see the doctor again, babe," he suggested.

"What for? No one can fix what's wrong, can they?"

"The prescription that Dr. Gantry gave you isn't working for you. Maybe there's something else they can suggest. Maybe they can help you to—"

"To what? To *not* give our son a motorbike. To *not* let him die? To bring him back?" Her voice became more strident. That was all too common now.

"It's okay..." he said as he tried to console her with a hug.

"Its *not* okay!" she screamed. "It will *never* be okay!" She stormed out of the room, not quite managing to stifle her sobs until she reached the bedroom doorway.

Those would be her final words to him. Turned out that Ellie found a way to make that prescription work for her after all.

"It's the best thing for Katie, Andrew. You...well, you haven't been yourself since we lost Ellie, and her mother and I really need the time to reconnect with our granddaughter anyway. I'm glad that you understand. It'll only be for a few days—we just thought that spending Thanksgiving with us would be better than just the two of you here all alone in this house." Concern and sympathy struggled for dominance on Ellie's father's face.

"I I appreciate it, Chet. You're right—Katie deserves a good Thanksgiving."

"You know, we'd be glad to have you join us. You're always welcome, Andrew. Margaret makes so much food that a dozen extra people could show up and we'd still have a week's worth of leftovers."

"I appreciate it, but I don't think I'm ready for a big holiday quite yet. I'm just going to stay here and use the time to clear my head. Besides, we have a holiday tradition of our own that I want to keep going."

"The Christmas tree?"

"Yeah. Figured I could set it up while Katie was gone. Surprise her when she comes back. It'll do me some good to keep a happy tradition going. Do me a favor, though—bring me some of that chocolate pecan pie when you drop Katie off, okay?"

"Sure. I'll bring some dressing, too. If I don't get rid of it somewhere, Margaret will have me eating it until the Fourth of July."

ANDREW HAD turkey and dressing for dinner, just like always. Difference was, this year, it came out of a Hungry Man frozen dinner box. He gave the meal very little attention, though—it was just a necessary ritual before he could begin the decorating ritual.

The tree was assembled and festooned with garland in less than thirty minutes. Then it was time for the decorations. The first ornament he placed was the forest-green one with irregular white stripes. Then he placed another thoughtfully chosen ornament right next to it. The second ornament was too red to be fuchsia, but not scarlet enough to be a true Christmas red. It had never struck him as a Christmas color, but as soon as she had seen it at the small artisan craft shop, Ellie had immediately claimed it as her ornament.

Satisfied that the two ornaments were positioned properly, he sat on the edge of the chair, leaning towards the tree. The two ornaments were at eye level. He turned on the twinkling lights, watching their reflections on the ornamental glass. Next, Andrew chose his Christmas playlist to set the mood before pulling a chair close to the tree.

"Ellie? Ryan? Merry Christmas."

No response. Andrew waited for what seemed like too long. He was beginning to lose hope.

Andrew?

Was that an undertone of sadness?.

"I've missed you. I'm so glad you're here."

I'm not sure where here is.

"Well, we're together now—you, me, and Ryan. Right, son?"

Dad? Ryan's voice was unsteady. *Is it Christmas again?*

"Of course! And we're together, just like always. I wish you could see the tree. I did the garland just the way you liked it, Ellie. And I put up all those Santa ornaments you liked, Ryan. It looks great."

I wish I could see it, Ellie said. *I can't see anything. It's so dark...But I can hear the music.*

"My special playlist—all of our favorites."

It's not right, Dad.

"Sure it is, son. I've got that silly 'Grandma and the Reindeer' song that you always loved, and the Mannheim Steamroller 'Silent Night' that made your mother's eyes get all misty, and—"

Not the music, Dad. None of this feels right.

"You'll get in the mood, Ryan. Ellie, remember when Ryan was three and we had that dancing Santa figure next to the tree? Scared him to death. He wouldn't come near the tree for a week without starting to cry. We finally had to take it back. Remember that?"

Yes...I remember.

"Do you the song that we all sang to get him to come back?"

"Up on the Housetop."

"Yes! That was the one! We'd sing it, and Ryan, you'd come in and yell out the 'Ho Ho Ho' part and the 'Click Click Click' part, then you'd just laugh. Why don't we sing it now? Siri, play 'Up on the Housetop.'"

The sound of Gene Autry drifted through the room

Andrew began singing along, but after a few seconds he realized that his was the only voice accompanying the recording. "What's wrong? Let's sing together, okay?"

I don't want to sing, Dad. I don't want to be here. I know that there's some place else I'm supposed to go, but I can't. It's not supposed to be dark like this, is it?

Andrew, he's right. Concern filled Ellie's voice. *I'm not sure why either of us is here. We don't belong here.*

"But it's Christmas season. The tree's here, and your ornaments are here, and you're here, just like you're supposed to be. We're a family."

Where's Katie? Is she there, too?

"No, she's with your parents. I wanted this to be our time. She'll be back next week."

Gene Autry sounded particularly cheery.

But Katie's your family. She needs you now, more than ever. I never should have done what I did, Andrew. I was just so lost after...I didn't know how to deal with it. I just hurt so much and I couldn't see how I'd ever be happy again. So I..."

"I know, babe. I remember. But I don't want to talk about that. We can be happy now. Let's be happy. It's Christmas. Let's sing along like we used to, okay? Alexa, repeat the song."

Over and over again, Andrew sang with a robustness that contrasted with his increasing concerns. If there were other accompanying voices, no one else would have ever heard them.

"I'm home, Dad! Are you—" Katie stopped in mid-sentence. She hadn't expected to see the Christmas tree—and she certainly hadn't expected to see it with lights, garland, and only two ornaments. Nor had she expected to see her father asleep in the chair next to the tree, still wearing the same clothes he was wearing the previous Wednesday.

"Dad?" No response at all. She wasn't sure if he was asleep, passed out, or dead. "Dad!"

Chet and Margaret heard Katie's startled exclamation halfway across the house, where they were bringing in her luggage and several plastic containers of Thanksgiving leftovers. They entered the room just as Andrew awakened.

"Hey, hon...Merry Christmas."

Katie started to reply, but couldn't find the words. She rushed out of the room. A moment later, the slam of a door resonated through the house.

Chet and Margaret exchanged a look, each hoping that the other would know what to say. Neither did. After the silence went beyond awkward and into the painful range, Chet struggled for words to break the tension.

"Andrew...Look, I know that...I was hoping..." Three false starts, and Chet still had no idea exactly what he should say.

"It's okay, Chet. I know this is a mess. I sort of let things get away from me."

"Yeah, you did. What happened? When we left, you said you were—"

"I was going to get the tree up and have things ready for Katie...yeah, I know. But I've been having trouble sleeping. I spent every night in here..."

"Doing what? Not decorating, obviously."

"No. Just talking. Singing songs. Remembering."

Chet put his hand on Alex's shoulder. "Son, it's obvious you're having problems. I don't think that Katie should—"

Andrew began picking up the clutter. "No. It'll be okay. It won't take me long to fix this."

Two hours later, the three of them had the house restored to a semblance of order. the tree was decorated, though somewhat haphazardly.

Chet and Margaret offered to stay overnight, but Andrew insisted it wasn't necessary.

"You get some rest, okay?" Chet wasn't the hugging kind, so he put his hand on Andrew's shoulder and squeezed firmly. That was the closest Chet ever came to showing affection.

"Yeah, I will. I'm pretty tired; I'll bet you that I'm in bed asleep before you guys are out of the driveway."

Neither statement was true. As soon as his in-laws were out the door, Andrew pulled his chair close to the tree once again, ready for another long evening with his wife and son.

KATIE OPENED THE DOOR SLOWLY, wincing at the resonant creak that seemed far louder than it actually was. Midnight. Dad should be in bed. She was hungry, and late night turkey and dressing was always the best.

She tiptoed down the hallway in her socks. Slow and easy. Stay to the right to avoid the loose floorboard in front of the bathroom.

She was about to creep into the kitchen when she heard her father's voice. He was still awake. Must be on the phone to someone. She didn't want to talk to him yet, but curiosity led her to peek around the corner.

He sat on the edge of his chair, just a foot or so from the tree. Rather than looking melancholy as she expected, he appeared quite happy. The tree lights enhanced the squint that always accompanied his smile.

"...and then you asked how in the world I could forget the batteries? Every present under the tree needed batteries!" His laugh was warm and honest, just like it used to be.

Talking to mom, Katie thought. She'd heard about people dealing with grief by speaking to the person they'd lost.

As she listened some more, though, this sounded different. Dad wasn't just talking to Mom—he was listening, as if she were replying to him. Sometimes he'd chuckle, sometimes he'd respond as if he were answering a question. It was like listening to one side of a phone call; she could almost discern what he thought he was hearing based on his response.

"No, we have to do the song." There was a tone of insistence in his voice. He fumbled with his iPhone for a moment, then she heard a tinny "Ho Ho Ho" emanate from the phone's speaker.

"Up on the housetop reindeer pause..." He stopped, then punched the stop button on his phone. "Come on, you have to sing along. Let's start again. Up on the housetop..."

Katie wasn't hungry any more. She tiptoed down the hallway to her room.

Once inside, she closed the door. But this time, she locked it.

BREAKFAST WAS BEREFT OF CONVERSATION. Both had things to say, but no idea exactly what.

Katie broke the silence. "Dad...Last night, I was in the hall, and I heard—"

Andrew grinned. "That's great, Katie! I wasn't sure how I was going to tell you. I knew it would sound weird. But now you know. That makes it so much easier."

"Know what, Dad? That you sit there all night long, talking and singing to an artificial Christmas tree?"

"Not to a tree—to your mom...to Ryan. We talk to each other."

"I talk to them, too. Every night, I tell them how much I miss them...that I love them..."

"It isn't like that. When I sit by the tree and talk to them, they talk back. We remember the good times. Christmases past. We sing Christmas carols."

"Don't say that, Dad. It scares me when you talk like that."

"Nothing to be scared of. It's wonderful! We're still a family."

Tears began to well up in Katie's eyes. "*I'm* your family, Daddy. You and me. We're all that we've got now!"

"You're wrong. Tonight you'll see what I mean."

ANDREW SPENT most of the afternoon dozing restlessly. Katie spent most of the day in her room.

The house was dark by six. Katie turned on the overhead light as she stepped into the family room to see what her dad was doing.

"Turn that light off," Andrew snapped. He pressed the remote button, and the multicolored lights sparkled. "The Christmas tree lights are all we need."

Katie was disinclined to argue. She sat on the sofa, across the room from her father.

He looked at her with the same sort of eagerness that parents often see on a child's face on Christmas morning. "This is great—everybody's together."

Andrew turned away from Katie and faced the tree.

"Ellie? Ryan? I'm here. You know who else is here? Katie, that's who! I told her about you, and she's here too. Say something to her."

The silence was so stark that it was as if the entire world had paused. Katie was surprised when she realized that she was actually straining to hear voices that weren't there.

"Honey? Say something to Katie, okay? Let her know that you're here." But a quiver of uncertainty was evident behind Andrew's smile.

Still nothing. Katie wasn't sure how she was supposed to feel. She had almost hoped that her dad would be right, even though she knew it was impossible.

The previous uncertainty rapidly gave way to agitation. Andrew shifted his gaze from the tree to Katie and back. Tears formed at the corners of her eyes as she watched him.

"Wait," he said in a broad, almost theatrical manner. "They want to do the song first." With that, he hurriedly removed the phone from his pocket, almost dropping it as he fumbled to open the music app. "You'll remember this, Katie!"

Even before he hit play, she knew what the song would be. The baritone "Ho Ho Ho" confirmed it. Her father began singing along with the Gene Autry vocals that had been a part of every Christmas as far back as she could recall.

She listened to her father's voice. His holiday joy was tempered by nervousness.

But there was something else. She had heard that song hundreds of times. But tonight, it sounded different.

What were those sounds in the background? Not voices—more like moans.

Her eyes opened wide.

Her father sang along, but it wasn't his voice that both

distressed her. It was those mournful sounds in the background—sounds full of anguish and misery.

She arose from the chair and walked slowly towards the Christmas tree. As she did, the nervousness on her father's face was replaced by joy. "Sing along with us, Katie!"

Andrew resumed singing with the same excessively theatrical vibrato that had made her giggle when she was young.

She lifted her arm, and her father reached out, assuming that she wanted to hold hands while they sang. Rather than taking his hand, though, she reached right past him to grasp a sturdy middle limb of the tree, pulling it to one side. Ornaments fell to the floor in a clatter.

The tinny sound of "Up on the Housetop" continued, but there were no other sounds—not her father's voice, and not those mournful noises. Anguish washed over her father's face. At his feet the floor sparkled as the fallen tree's twinkling lights were reflected in the shards of broken ornaments strewn across the hardwood.

Andrew gazed at the fragments of forest green and reddish fuchsia at his feet, then looked at his daughter. After a moment, he turned his head away, and Katie knew why. She had never caused her father to cry before.

The song continued, its light-hearted tone mocking them. Katie didn't want to hear any more. She picked up her father's iPhone and pressed stop.

In years to come, she would tell herself that the room was silent after that. But it wasn't true. She knew what she had heard—and she knew who spoke those words.

Thank you.

THE FORTINGALL YEW

WILLIAM MEIKLE

I was late in arriving in Fortingall, having missed a connection in Perth, so it was near midnight by the time the coachman dropped me at the doorstep of the kirk. Then there was only time to reacquaint myself with my old friend John, partake of several large glasses of his fine Scotch, and wend a weary way to bed.

So it was that my first sight of the old tree came in the flush of morning with a mist on the ground and a stiff breeze in my face. John had told me about the yew in his letters, of course, but there had been nothing that could have prepared me for the sense of history that the sight of it brought. It is an aged thing indeed, its original core having been long since hollowed out by time and weather, leaving a myriad of secondary branches gathered around the remains of a gnarled old trunk that looks more like stone than wood. John joined me for a pre-breakfast smoke as I circled the trunk below the canopy, feeling my way around the thing.

"I knew you would like it," he said. "I have it on good authority from a professor of Botany at the University that it predates Christ himself. Just think of what memories of Christmas past it could show us if we could only unfold them."

"I thought they placed yews in churchyards, not the other way around," I said, laughing.

"For all we know this old tree here is where they got the idea," John replied and I almost laughed again before I saw that he was being serious.

I did not get a chance to follow up on it for just then his housekeeper called us in for breakfast and I was treated to a mound of eggs, ham and toast that took three pots of strong tea to wash down and all I was fit for during the rest of the morning was sitting in an armchair in John's study while we caught up with our friendship.

It had been several years since our last meeting. They had been quiet ones for him here in his wee kirk in rural Perthshire, rather less quiet for me in the Transvaal with the regiment. Now here I was home: furloughed, lamed, and looking at the prospect of a bleak retirement in the face. That tale of the change in my circumstances is too long and far too dull to relate here. Suffice to say my friend John listened as a friend should, and his reply was not to scold or berate me for my depression but to fetch out the smokes.

Once I was feeling more like myself again, I turned conversation from my personal woes around to the business of the yew tree. It quickly became clear that John had been putting his quiet time to good use, for he had a treasury of knowledge of the tree's history at his command. He treated me to what he had learned and also much of what he suspected. It was fascinating stuff indeed, but little of it is germane to my story here except for what he said at the last.

"You know, there's even a story that Pontius Pilate himself sat under this very tree as a boy when his father governed this part of the country for Rome."

I had to laugh at that.

"It's Christmas, old boy, not Easter."

He didn't rise to the bait and I saw that he had something on his mind.

"Okay, out with it," I said. "You didn't ask me up here for the weather. What's up?"

Before he answered he took two sheets of crumpled paper from his pocket and smoothed them out on the table.

"I have indeed got a story.. But first, what do you make of that?"

I got up, rather reluctantly, and examined the paper. Both pieces had obviously been taken as rubbings, not from brass or stone but from wood. They showed what appeared to be a series of stick figures, most of whom were missing some part of their anatomy—no legs, or one leg but no head, that kind of thing. The figures covered the pages, twenty five lines to each, eight to a line, four hundred little men marching for a reason I could not even begin to fathom.

"It's Sherlock Holmes you need, not me old man," I said. "It's some kind of code, isn't it?"

"I think so. Although it is a peculiar one that has defeated me for a year to the very day. Are you ready for a snifter? I know it's not even noon, but it is Christmas after all."

I wasn't about to argue. Minutes later we were settled by the fire again with fresh smokes lit and glasses filled as he sat with the papers in his lap.

"As I said, it was a year ago today," he started. "I went out to watch the sunset and by pure chance happened to be lined up with the tree between me and the last rays of the dying day. I saw, at the base of the oldest part of the trunk, what I took to be ridges hacked into the wood by a blade. At first I thought little of it, then I noted their regularity and how they were tightly concentrated in a small space; it was something that had been done with a purpose in mind. The light was going from the sky quickly and somehow I knew I might not get another chance, so I ran indoors, giving my housekeeper a bit of a fright in the process, and came back to make these rubbings.

"Many a night between then and now I have sat here trying to penetrate the secret. And many nights I have gone out to stand by the tree at sunset but—and you will have to believe me on this—I have never again been able to find the little soldiers. It is as if they were only there for that particular minute, existing only for that single spot in time."

He went quiet then, both of us supping at our drinks and puffing smoke until I broke the silence.

"It is a mystery, to be sure, I replied, "but hardly one to get yourself worked up over, old boy. The old world is full of such mysteries; stones lined up with the solstices, menhirs used as calendars, that sort of guff. Surely this is just more of the same? The marks on the tree are still there, of course they are. They must be. It's just that they need the right light for them to show up."

"My thoughts exactly, or they were, last winter. But as the nights, and the sunsets went on and the marks never again revealed themselves I took to running my fingers over the wood, attempting to trace them by feel. I assure you, they are not there. Maybe they never were. And if you do not believe me, go look for yourself. You'll only find obdurate old wood, as I have done these many months."

I saw, too late, that the poor chap had got himself quite worked up. He'd invited me here hoping for some understanding, perhaps a sympathetic ear, and here I was offering him skepticism instead of friendship. I felt quite ashamed of myself. There and then I undertook to do something about it.

He had taken quite the huff with me and did not look up from the fireside as I took my leave and went once more out onto the kirkyard. I took more time with the old thing this time, sitting on my haunches close to the base of the trunk and running my hands over and around the aged bark, trying in vain to find the gouges that had shown up in the rubbings. I had a moment when I thought bad thoughts of my old friend, wondering whether this whole thing might be some fine Christmas prank of his. Then I remembered how he'd taken such a huff and I redoubled my efforts.

I must have been at it for a good twenty minutes and was no closer to feeling anything but cold bark when the strangest sensation came over me. It started in my fingertips, a buzzing vibration passing from the old tree through to my hands, my wrists, up my arms and into my head where a distant drumbeat started up, a martial rhythm that reminded me of nothing less than facing down the Zulu in the veldt. It quite discombobulated me and sent me back inside, where I sought sanctuary in the warmth of both the fire and a new glass of scotch in my belly.

By the time the housekeeper called us to lunch, John had quite forgiven me my earlier transgression. Over a fine meal of salmon, potatoes and greens, washed down by strong Scottish ale, we reaffirmed the joy of our long friendship and I made a promise to him to stand beside him at the sunset. The vibration in my head had faded with the ale, but I was no longer quite so sure that there would be nothing to see come the evening.

We spent the afternoon by the fireside again, sipping scotch and trying to make head or tail of the blasted marching stick figures—but for the life of me, I could see no pattern to the thing no matter how much I squinted at it.

"I've looked at it every bloody way I can think of," John said on seeing my exasperation. "I even showed it to a mathematician—David McLeish, you'll remember him from Edinburgh back in the day—he had the pages for two weeks in the summer but I brought them home none the wiser on their return. If it is indeed a code, it's a damned devilish one."

"Have you had any thoughts at all as to why it might have been carved in the tree? Or when?"

"Thoughts, opinions, yes. But nothing in the way of hard facts. I can tell you that judging by the position of the carvings and the state of the bark that I believe the marks to have been made at least as far back as the Roman era."

"Don't give me that Pilate tale again," I pleaded. "My incredulity will only stretch so far."

That at least got me a laugh and another glimpse of the old friend I remembered. Our companionship sustained us through the afternoon in tales and anecdotes of our time as students in Auld Reekie and, after a few more scotches I found myself telling tales I had told no one else, of that last battle, of blood and thunder and Zulu songs and a leg wound that will pain me on damp nights for however long I have remaining. John had always had a sympathetic ear and today proved to be no different. I talked for hours while he kept our glasses filled and smokes coming. When it was done I felt hollowed out and empty but strangely more like myself than I had at any time since leaving Africa. When the housekeeper called us to the dining room for tea, I even began to feel a long forgotten boyhood excitement for the forthcoming Christmas.

After a most pleasant tea, John had us out in the kirkyard again in time for the sunset but any hope of a ray of light on the matter was dashed by one of those particularly Scottish shifting mists that obscured everything beyond ten paces from the doorstep.

We stood there until the light went out of the sky completely and I could see by the slump of his shoulders that the disappointment was hitting my friend hard. I attempted to bring back the Christmas spirit by offering an early present, a Meerschaum pipe I had brought out of Africa for this very purpose. It did indeed bring a small smile to John's face, but it wasn't long before he was back to sitting in front of the fire worrying at the two pieces of paper again.

"Look, John," I said. "It's Christmas. Don't you have any duties to your flock that you should be about?"

"The flock is widespread at the best of times," he said. "We used to have a midnight service on this night, but after old Mrs. McKenzie died that was the end of it, for I would only be speaking to an empty kirk. Now all I do is ring the bells to see in the day. If we stay sober long enough you can give me a hand with that later."

He was showing a distinct lack of enthusiasm, I must say. I

attempted to bring him some cheer with some old soldier's stories, of battles fought, of rollicking drinking binges in the fleshpots and of comrades found and all too soon lost. He listened—as I have said, he has always listened—but he still had the two sheaves of paper on his lap, and every so often his eyes would drop to peruse the marching figures that so vexed him.

Staying sober proved to be beyond me under the circumstances. I'm afraid to say that I took to his Scotch with rather too much gusto. By the time it came round to almost midnight my head spun like a top and getting out of the armchair was almost beyond me.

"Stay where you are, old chap," John said. "I'll ring the bells and come back for a last snifter before bed."

Duty to both my friend and my conscience in the morning forced me to stand and follow him through the manse and out to the belfry of the old kirk.

We had to pass the yew on the way and once again I felt the strangest vibration thrum through me, this time coming up out of the ground through the soles of my boots and upward via ankles, knees, thighs and hips into the barrel of my chest where it got my old heart beating in time.

John turned and held his oil lantern up to see my face.

"Are you all right? Are you sure you wouldn't be better back by the fire? Come, I'll see you back."

Even as he spoke the vibration faded, gone as quickly as it had come. I managed a smile I wasn't sure I had in me.

"Nonsense. Just a touch of the whisky vapors; it's not the first time you've seen me under their influence. Lay on, MacDuff, and don't spare the horses. Can't have Christmas without the bells, can we?"

When we arrived in the belfry, John seemed much more like himself, the act of preparing the ropes and setting them up appearing to ground him back in the little joys that help to build reality. As for myself, I was happy to stand back and let him get on with it; the whisky had me feeling delicate and it wouldn't do to have anything come back up that should be staying down. Besides, John had it all well in hand. He checked his watch and smiled.

"Merry Christmas, old friend," he said, and pulled on the first cord. The peal of the bell rang loud, echoing through the belfry. I felt it move my guts about then the second bell kicked in, the vibration rose and rose again to a pounding that set my heart to beating in time. A blaze of pure white noise blasted through me as if I'd stood too close to a cannon going off and for a while I knew nothing but darkness and the beat of the great drum.

I came out of it unsure as to where in the world I might be, for the drums still echoed in my head and the pain in my gammy leg was as bad as at any time since I'd taken the wound. Then I tasted whisky at my lips and opened my eyes to see John's concerned eyes looking into mine. I was back in the armchair by the fire, having no memory of getting there from the church. John was speaking, something about how I'd put on too much weight for him to be lunking me about in the dark, but I wasn't really listening. I was looking at the two sheaves of paper that sat on the seat of John's chair. And just like that it all came together in my head, old battles, drums and remembrance, all rolled up and laid down in the tree for the future to see.

"A devilish code, that's what you called it," I said. "But I don't think Auld Nick had anything to do with it. It's not a code, John. It's notation, music of a kind I think or, more likely, a drumbeat. Look."

I reached for the papers and traced the stick figures with a finger.

"Imagine each figure as a representation of beats to the bar. So a figure with all heads, body and limbs would be six beats. Lose a beat for each lost limb, and what we have here is a rhythm. The only thing I don't know—yet—is where to start the beat. The head is the obvious place, so let's start there. Fetch me a pen and paper. We need to get this down."

It had all come out of me in a breathless rush and John just stood there gaping at me as if I had taken a blue funk.

"Pen and paper, man," I said. "I know what I'm about, and if I seem a bit excited you only have yourself to blame; it was your bally bells that brought it on."

I shook the papers at him.

"It's drum beats, I'm sure of it."

He fetched writing materials from his desk drawer and I interpreted each figure as he wrote the number I called out. We soon had lines of beats, six to the bar, eight bars at a time all laid out in a neat series of rows. By the time we'd finished and paused for a smoke and more whisky it was almost one o' clock in the morning but neither of us had any thought of bed.

"Now what?" John said.

"An experiment, that's what," I replied.

I reached for the paper where he'd written down the beats, but he pulled it away from me.

"Oh no, you don't," he said. "You've had quite enough excitement for one night. My house, my rules."

He put the paper down on his table and began rapping out beats on the old wood with his knuckles; no legs, no left arm, no head, no arms, one left leg, one right leg, just a torso, no head.

I felt the vibration in my gut again and heard an answering beat, far off as if lost in a wind.

"Slower," I said softly. "This is a lament, not a call to battle."

I didn't know how I knew that, I just did, just as I'd known on awakening about the nature of the code. I was proven right when John rapped out, slower, the next eight bars.

No arms, head and left arm missing, no legs, no limbs, head and left arm missing, no legs, no legs, no legs.

A definite rhythm developed, one that echoed around the room and set the beat going on my chest and head again, but still distant, still lost in the wind. I happened to catch movement in the shadows beyond the window, branches bending and swaying in time to the beat, and again I knew what had to be done.

"The tree," I said. "This needs to be done at the tree."

To John's credit he did not question me for a second, merely took up the paper and headed outside, picking up his oil lantern from the side of the door as he went.

I joined him in the kirkyard just as the mist lifted away and a full moon bathed the old tree in dancing shards of silver and grey.

"Look," John said in a hoarse whisper. "There."

My gaze followed his stare. There, etched in black against the trunk, proud in the moonlight, were the lines of stick figures. I felt the vibration, the beat, thrum from the ground and up and through me until it filled me with rhythm.

"Quick now, John," I said. "While we still have the moon."

He took to rapping on the trunk with his knuckles while I held the oil lamp and paper so that he could read it. The beat grew stronger still but something still wasn't right.

I put the paper on the ground, the lamp on top of it and stepped forward to the tree. The beat told me what to do; I slapped the trunk with both hands.

No arms, head and left arm missing, no legs, no limbs, head and left arm missing, no legs, no legs, no legs.

Then there was nothing but rhythm and beats, the slap of flesh on the tree and the dance of the stick figures. I was aware of John's presence, of his knuckles rapping out the same time I was keeping. There was no need for our notes; we were the beat and the beat was us and we were all lost in the lament for the dead. A shadow play took place in front of my gaze as if projected against the last of the mist, a silent battle of dancers in the beat. Swords flashed, bodies fell.

No legs, no left arm, no head, no arms, one left leg, one right leg, just a torso, no head.

Drums pounded in my head like cannons going off, I slapped the old wood ever harder as voices rose to join the beat, a language

I did not know but whose words came to me anyway there in the dance.

They dance in the deep with the worms in the dark
They dream with the earth in the depths
They dance and they sing with the gods in their sleep
And the Dreaming Gods are singing where they lie.

Somewhere in the distance John's voice joined mine as we sang and pounded and stamped out the last few bars of the beat. The dancing shadows fell apart into dust and light and moonbeams seeping onto the tree like water into a sponge.

Where they lie, where they lie, where they lie, where they lie
The Dreaming Gods are singing where they lie.

The beat continued even after we stopped, fading slowly, draining away somewhere far below us beneath the tree.

"In the deep, in the dark," John whispered, and just like that all was quiet, the moon went behind a cloud and there was only the kirkyard and the night and we two friends staring at each other in wonderment.

"WHAT IN BLAZES was that all about?" John said five minutes later as we made determined inroads into the last of the scotch by his fireplace.

"You don't see it, do you?" I replied. "I suppose it's because I'm a soldier that I do. At some point in distant history your tree saw a battle; I'm guessing it was your Romans against the locals, and the locals did not come out well in the fight. Afterwards, they set down their record; these days we carve our memorials in stone but they did it on the oldest thing they knew. They set the record of their dead in the tree, for them to remember, for us to remember."

I polished off the last of the whisky. I felt better than I had felt since taking my wound in the battle in the veldt.

"You have your flock for your Christmas service, John. I suspect they'll be here every year, now that they have someone to remember for them. And you can add one more to that, for as long as I live I too will be joining you."

I intend to keep that promise. I owe it to all the old soldiers.

At the dying of the year I shall dance and sing and drum and dream with them, and on one day to come I may even join them and go gladly into the dance.

And the Dreaming Gods are singing where they lie.

HOLD YOUR BREATH

JEFF STRAND

The initiation was very simple. Open the gate (covered with rust but always unlocked), walk over to the house and up the steps to Mr. Cook's front porch. Then hold your breath to the count of twenty. After that, having proven your worth, you could flee the yard and would never be expected to return.

It seemed like a small task to gain the respect of the other children in the neighborhood. Everybody had done it, they said. Even six-year-olds. A ten-year-old like Penny should have no fear. It wouldn't even take a full minute. And not once had Mr. Cook ever opened his door to confront the children on his property.

Of course, you couldn't do it in the daylight. That didn't count.

Oh, it didn't have to be at the stroke of midnight. Nothing like that. This was a safe neighborhood and night fell early in the winter. It wasn't unusual for parents to let their children play outside in the dark, as long as they stayed in their own yard—or at least the yards of their friends.

And it also wasn't unusual for children to disobey their parents.

Penny stood in front of the gate. She couldn't even remember the names of three of the four children who were with her—just Anne, who had beautiful blonde hair that probably didn't hurt when her mother ran a brush through it. At her old home, Penny had spent almost all of her time indoors, reading. Mom and Dad had said they wanted her to make some friends. "This is so exciting!" Mom had said. "You get to reinvent yourself!" And so, apparently, Penny was reinventing herself as somebody who would walk up onto a stranger's porch after dark and hold her breath for twenty seconds, just to gain the approval of new friends.

It was as scary of a house as she'd ever seen, but it wasn't as if ghosts or vampires lived in there. The trees didn't have knotholes with glowing eyes within. It was just a regular house, poorly maintained, and if anything she was at more of a risk of stepping on a nail than meeting her doom at the hands of a supernatural creature.

"Do it," said Anne. "Don't be scared."

Of course, the whole point was to be scared. The other children were interested in her bravery or lack thereof, not her breath-holding capabilities.

Penny opened the metal gate. It didn't creak, which surprised her. This definitely seemed like the kind of rusty gate that would let out an eerie creak when it was opened.

She stepped into the yard alone.

Mr. Cook's yard was overgrown with weeds, but the path to the front porch was made of pebbles. Unless a rat came scurrying out, she'd be okay.

She slowly walked along the path, trying to move as if she wasn't frightened, like she was casually going up to the house to sell the owner some Girl Scout cookies. She wasn't in any danger. It wasn't even that scary, if you really thought about it. There was no full moon, or wolves howling in the distance, or bats flying around. Just a normal house. Everything was fine.

Everything was perfectly fine.

She made it to the steps without anything bad happening. See how easy this was?

Penny walked up the steps onto the porch. The wood *did* creak, but not loudly, not so much that she thought she might break through, or awaken something underneath.

There. She'd made it. This was the easiest initiation ever.

She took a deep breath and held it.

One...two...

Simple. Anybody could hold their breath to the count of twenty. That was nothing.

Three...four...five...

Twenty seconds wasn't a long time. The house wasn't scary. It wasn't even all that dark out. If this was all it took to impress the other children, Penny would be the most popular kid in the neighborhood by spring.

Six...seven...

The front door remained closed. The curtains didn't shift. Nobody was watching her except her new friends. Mr. Cook might not even be in there. For all she knew, the only living creature in the house was a fly or two. And Penny most definitely was not afraid of flies.

Eight...

What was that sound?

Nothing. There was no sound. She'd imagined it.

Nine...

Had the wood creaked again? It shouldn't have. She hadn't moved.

Ten...

That wasn't true. She'd shifted her weight a bit without realizing it. That's all. She needed to be careful to make sure that she really *didn't* break through the wood, but there was nothing truly spooky going on.

Eleven...twelve...

More than halfway done. Was she counting too slowly? She thought she might be counting too slowly. Holding her breath was becoming more difficult, and it really shouldn't be, not if she was only up to the count of twelve.

Thirteen...fourteen...

Her lungs were starting to burn. She suddenly wondered if she was going to make it.

Had the doorknob moved?

Of course it hadn't.

She imagined the door swinging wide open, revealing Mr. Cook, a wide grin on his face as flakes of his skin blew away in the light breeze. *"Well, hello there,"* he'd say. *"Why, I'd love to buy some cookies from you. Or maybe I'll just eat your fingers instead..."*

Fifteen...

Only five more seconds. Just five.

Sixteen...

She was starting to feel like she might pass out. She thought her eyes might be bugging out of her head, even though that was ridiculous. Her face wasn't turning blue. Her lungs weren't about to pop like balloons. She was making all of that up.

Seventeen...

Penny was going to die.

Eighteen...

She couldn't do it anymore. She released the breath she'd been holding and then gasped for air.

Penny spun around. She wasn't going to run. There was no need to run. She could walk down the steps like absolutely nothing was wrong, and then proceed along the pebble path as if she didn't have a care in the world.

She ran.

She hurried down the steps then fled toward the gates, expecting the rotting hand of Mr. Cook to clamp down upon her shoulder. *"Now, now, where you are going, young Penny? You weren't done counting. Ten little fingers. Ten little toes. Twenty parts of you for me to eat!"*

She ran out of his yard and slammed the gate shut.

"You did it!" said Anne. "You're one of us now!"

Penny tried to smile. She hadn't made it to the count of twenty, but the other children didn't seem to have noticed anything wrong, so she probably had indeed been counting too slowly.

They walked away from the house.

"Why do we do that?" Penny asked.

"To prove that we're not scared," said Anne.

"I know, but why did I have to hold my breath?"

"That's because of Melissa, Mr. Cook's daughter," said one of the girls whose name Penny couldn't remember. She was the oldest of the group, maybe twelve years old. "A long time ago there used to be a pond near here. It's all drained now. One day Melissa, when she was a little younger than you are now, went swimming, and she went out too far because she didn't realize how deep it was. She thought it was shallow all the way across. It wasn't."

The girls all stopped walking to make it easier for her to achieve the proper atmosphere when telling the tale.

"She screamed and screamed for help. Lucky for her, Mr. Cook was watching his daughter. He swam out there, but she'd already gone under. Well, he searched and searched and searched, and just when he thought he'd lost her for good, he managed to grab her by the hand and pull her to the surface. He swam back with her, but when he got to the shore he realized that she wasn't breathing."

"Did she die?" Penny asked.

The older girl shook her head. "Mr. Cook knew mouth-to-mouth resuscitation. He held her nose and he breathed into her mouth. He did it twenty times. And on the twentieth breath, her eyes opened, and she was okay. He'd saved her life."

Wow. Penny hadn't expected it to be a happy story. "Does she still live there?"

"Oh, no. She's all grown up now. She moved away years ago." The older girl looked at her wristwatch. "Hey, we should all go home before we get in trouble."

Penny went home and told her parents that she'd had a very nice time and made some new friends. She didn't tell them about the initiation, since they wouldn't approve of her walking into a stranger's yard after dark. They didn't need to know *everything* she did. Some secrets were okay, as long as nobody got hurt.

At bedtime, she fell asleep right away.

She opened her eyes when she heard a noise in her room.

It was nothing. All houses made sounds, and she wasn't used to this one yet. Floors creaked. Pipes rattled. Strange dogs barked. It was nothing.

She closed her eyes and tried to go back to sleep.

Did she hear dripping?

The bathroom was across the hall from her bedroom. Maybe the faucet was leaking.

She opened her eyes again and sat up.

No, the dripping sound was definitely coming from her room.

Was somebody in here with her?

She reached for the lamp that was on her bedstand, but before she could turn it on, a cold wet hand clamped over her mouth.

"*Shhhh...*" somebody said.

Penny let out a muffled whimper.

"*You cheated.*" It sounded like a little girl.

Penny shook her head. She wanted to protest, but she couldn't speak with the clammy hand covering her mouth.

"*You only counted to eighteen! You stole my last two breaths!*"

Penny tried to explain, to tell the little girl that she thought she'd been counting too slowly, that she'd been scared the door would open, that it wasn't her fault.

"*I needed those breaths. You stole them from me. Right now I'm at home in bed and my husband thinks I'm suffocating. Do you want me to die? Do you want me to leave my children without a mother?*"

Penny bit down on the little girl's palm. She didn't want to hurt her—she just wanted the little girl to take her hand away so Penny could explain what had happened.

Her teeth broke through the girl's skin easily. Cold, foul-tasting water squirted into her mouth.

"There's only one way for me to stay with my family. You stole my last two breaths. Now I have to take ALL of yours."

The little girl opened her mouth wide—impossibly wide, inhumanly wide—and leaned forward, completely drowning out the sound of Penny's scream.

THE CAMPO

JOSH REYNOLDS

Venice in winter is a solemn sight.

The colors are muted, the canals dark. A sort of resigned solemnity hangs over the city. Tourists are thin on the ground and a pervasive silence shrouds the twisty streets. The city is a shadow of itself, and I said as much as my companion and I ambled along the empty, winding paths of the Cannaregio.

"I love this time of year," Moultrie drawled, in amiable disagreement. He was a few years older than me, though you wouldn't know it despite the silver in his hair. My hair hadn't gone gray yet, but I'd lost so much of it, it didn't matter. "One can breathe and see, without the threat of crowds of sweaty tourists and their gelato."

"I thought you liked gelato."

Moultrie chuckled. "I admit, I'm particularly fond of that place we went over near the Misericordia earlier." He patted his stomach and smiled contentedly. "Still, sometimes it's hard to see the city for the people, if you follow me."

"Is that why you invited me along, then? To see the city?" I pulled my coat tighter. The sky was still a smear of pink and orange overhead but night came swift to Venice, and brought a biting Adriatic chill with it. "Not that I'm against a vacation," I added.

Moultrie gave me a lazy look. "You didn't think twice about coming with me, Fowler. Not looking forward to spending the holidays alone?"

Being recently divorced, the jab hit home. I grunted and shook my head. "Sometimes I wonder why you and I are friends."

He opened his mouth to retort, but was interrupted by a sudden cry. It was thin and sharp—a child's yelp, abruptly truncated. We looked at one another, all thought of our burgeoning disagreement forgotten. "This way," Moultrie said, and took off. I followed with only a moment's hesitation.

The cry came again, closer this time—or so it seemed. Around us, the shadows lengthened as the sun shrank. The city was so small in the daylight. But as night came on, the streets unfurled and it became something vast and unknowable.

We followed the echoes across one of the little footbridges that connected the islands and down a narrow, unfamiliar street. I had no idea where we were, or whether we were even still in the same *sestiere*.

Finally, we slowed, listening. But the only sound we heard was that of our own footsteps on the damp stones. "Whatever it is seems to be over," Moultrie said, his tone doubtful. "It might have just been kids roughhousing. I think—wait, what's that?"

I spied the church even as he spoke. It nestled between several taller buildings at the end of the narrow alleyway, as if trying to remain inconspicuous. It was the smallest such structure I'd seen in Venice—barely more than a chapel with a square, gothic façade. "Odd place to find a church," he continued. "They're usually located on or near the *campi*."

Curious now, we drew closer. A pair of stone angels guarded the doors, slouched like weary sentries, their wings folded, heads bowed. I paused, struck by their expressions—there was weariness there, but also a fierce alertness.

Moultrie must have had similar thoughts. "Sentries on the walls of Paradise," he murmured, as he gave a cursory rattle of the doors. "Locked."

"Is that so surprising?" I realized that the church wasn't quite centred. Instead, it was angled slightly, so that the eyes of the angels were turned towards the all but hidden entrance to an unobtrusive side street.

"Curiouser and curiouser," Moultrie said, when I directed his attentions to it. "I wonder if that's where our crier in the night is. Or was." As he spoke, he patted absently at his coat and then sighed. He'd stopped smoking the year before on orders from his doctor, but hadn't shaken the habits of a lifetime. "Maybe we should check it out."

"It's getting dark," I said. "Let's head back to the flat. Or, better, go find dinner." My stomach gurgled as if in agreement. Moultrie gave me an amused smile.

"Just a quick look." He started down the side street. "Just in case."

I wanted to argue, but knew better. Moultrie had a passion for the outré, the stranger the better. Like me, he was a folklorist, though his interests were more wide-ranging than mine. He wrote on everything from ancient ballads to thoughtforms, and did the odd bit of consulting for friends in Hollywood.

I kept to more respectable paths, hoping to reach the end of the tenure-track before I was too old to appreciate it. But even so, I envied his freedom. Perhaps that was why I jumped at every opportunity to accompany him, my responsibilities permitting. Or why I followed him down dark alleys, when I damn well knew better.

A building blocked off the end of the street, but a thin, claustrophobic archway had been cut into the foundation. An iron gate hung ajar, its hinges rusted and a loose chain looped about it. I wanted to turn back, but Moultrie tapped his lips for silence. A moment later a thin, light sound trickled out of the passage.

I realized that it was muffled laughter, childish and shrill. I began to wonder if this were all some form of elaborate prank. "Let's leave them to it," I said. "Whatever this is."

"Aren't you the least bit curious? Come on," Moultrie said, as he made to squeeze through the gap. I considered abandoning him, but only for a moment. With a sigh, I followed him and we soon found ourselves in a smallish campo.

There was a disconcerting absence of the usual newsagents, cafes and the like. The few visible doorways were boarded over and the windows bricked up. Odder still, there were no other entrances. It was as if the campo had been utterly severed from the city by common agreement.

The only occupant of the square was a lonely wellhead sitting at its heart, equidistant from the surrounding buildings. Something about it put me on edge, though I couldn't say what. Perhaps it was the way the shadows cast by the setting sun danced across the nearby stones. Moultrie seemed equally discomfited. "The buildings look as if they're leaning away from it, don't they?" he murmured.

"This is Venice. Everything is leaning or sinking or both."

Moultrie shrugged. "Maybe. You never read de Castries, did you?"

"I'm not familiar with the name, no. Why?"

"No reason. Not your field, really. He theorized that the stones of cities held onto memories—bad ones especially. That they played them over and over again, refusing to let them fade. Sort of a precursor to the stone tape theory."

"I don't see anyone," I said, refusing to be drawn into another argument about residual hauntings. My words fell flat on the air. It was too quiet here. The only sound was the slap of water against the sides of the canals.

Moultrie looked around. "Maybe it was a cat." He was hunched slightly, hands thrust into his pockets, head bent, shoulders folded. I thought maybe it was just the cold. I felt it myself, seeping through the material of my coat. A piercing damp, and the taste of salt on the tip of my tongue. The chill I'd felt before hadn't gone away. If anything, it had only gotten worse. Feeling nervous, I cleared my throat. "Come on. Let's go get dinner."

Moultrie started across the square. "I want to take a closer look at that wellhead first."

"It's just a well. There are hundreds of them in the city."

Moultrie didn't reply. I hurried after him, and as I caught up to him, the thought struck me that the stillness of our surroundings was not simply silence, but somehow anticipatory. As if some unseen giant had inhaled suddenly at the sight of us. I tried to dismiss the thought as we neared the wellhead, but I couldn't shake my growing unease.

My grandmother had always maintained that she had a touch of the sight. Sometimes I wondered if I had it as well, for I was unduly sensitive to certain quirks of atmosphere and temperature. But I'd never seen a ghost, and had no wish to do so. I'd been inside one or two supposedly haunted houses in the course of my research, but never felt anything like what I was feeling now.

It was as if we were being watched—though by who or what, I couldn't say. There was nonetheless a definite air of observation about the campo. A watchfulness that I found increasingly oppressive. "It will still be here in the morning," I said, as we reached the wellhead. "We can come back. Unless you think it's Venice's answer to Brigadoon."

Moultrie laughed. "Hardly. I doubt either of us will find a new love here."

I felt a sharp pang at his words. I missed Ellen more than I cared to admit. Moultrie saw the look on my face and sighed. "It's no use moping, Fowler. Like they say, if you keep picking at it, it'll never heal."

"I'll keep that in mind," I said, sourly. "And I'm not moping."

Moultrie laughed again and crouched down in front of the wellhead. He pulled off a glove and gently traced a faded grotesquery carved onto the front of the wellhead, his expression intent.

For my part, I felt only revulsion as I studied the faint sheen of mold that clung to the whitewashed Istria stone. It was on the stones and walls of the nearby buildings as well. But it rose thickest around what I thought must be faint cracks in the foundation of the wellhead. An image of what it might look like inside rose up unbidden and my stomach gave a querulous twitch. I wasn't hungry anymore.

I spied several nearby drains that might once have collected rainwater. Upon a closer inspection, I realized that they had been filled with lead, effectively sealing them. "Moultrie—take a look at this."

He grunted, wholly focused on his study of the grotesquery. Shaking my head, I took in the curved metal lid and the smooth grooves around the rim where ropes had been used to haul up buckets. My eyes strayed to the trio of heavy padlocks that kept the lid sealed. It was usually done with bolts or melted lead. I wondered why this one was different.

I lifted one of the padlocks, and something—a loose sliver of metal, perhaps—stung my palm. I drew it back and saw that rust and mould stained my hand. Disgusted, I wiped it on my coat. "I'm ready to go," I said, palm still smarting.

Moultrie glanced up. "Not yet. Look at this."

"It's just a carving."

"Not the carving. Below it." I stooped and saw that letters had been carved into the stone beneath the grotesquery. "How's your Latin?" he asked.

"Worse than my Italian." I gave it a shot regardless. Even with the aid of the flashlight app on my phone, I couldn't make out the words.

Moultrie had better luck. "*Hic...jacet...*something," he sounded out, tracing the letters with his fingertips. "Last word is too faded to make out." He sat back on his heels, clearly frustrated.

"Here lies," I translated, after wracking my memories of high school Latin. I stood abruptly, suddenly aware of the cold and the shadows that surrounded us. The sun was almost gone now, and the last dregs of light drifted across us. Soon the campo would be shrouded in darkness. "Here lies whom?"

"That is the question, ain't it?" Moultrie pushed himself to his feet. "I'm going to take some pictures." He began to rummage for his phone.

"Let's go," I said. "We'll come back tomorrow. When the light's better."

"What's the hurry?" Moultrie said.

"I'm hungry," I lied. "Aren't you?"

Moultrie retrieved his phone. "Dinner can wait."

"So can this."

He paused and turned. "Something wrong, Fowler?"

"Low blood sugar," I said, letting a bit of sharpness creep in. My hand still hurt so it was easy enough. Moultrie got a familiar mulish look on his face and made as if to argue.

Salvation came in the form of a priest, or so I judged him to be from his vestments. An older man with flyaway white hair and lined features, he shouted something in Italian, so quickly I couldn't catch it. From his gestures he looked to be haranguing us. Indeed, he seemed desperate to get our attention.

Moultrie slid his phone back into his pocket and went to intercept the newcomer. His Italian was better than mine, and soon they were chatting away. Moultrie could be charming, when he put his mind to it.

As they talked, my attentions strayed to the edges of the campo, where the shadows were deepest. For an instant, I thought I glimpsed something—a flash of movement, or maybe a face—but it was over and gone before I could tell what it was.

I realized that it had gone quiet, and that the priest was looking at me. So was Moultrie. Both of them had queer looks on their faces, and I wondered if they'd seen it as well. "We're being asked to leave," Moultrie said.

"How unfortunate."

Moultrie smiled. "But he'll show us around the church tomorrow, if we like."

I sighed. "I assume we do."

Moultrie's smile widened, but he didn't reply. The evening shadows stretched across the campo as we headed back the way we'd come, led by the priest. It was as if they—or something—were following us. I imagined a stealthy, catlike padding in our wake, and unable to help myself, I looked back.

The campo was utterly dark, utterly still. A sudden metallic clang startled me. It sounded as if something heavy had fallen to the ground. I thought of the padlocks, though I could not say why. Maybe they weren't as solidly fastened as they'd appeared.

I wasn't the only one who heard it, for the priest whirled. His face was pale, his eyes wide. "*Lei si agita...*" he murmured, and hastily crossed himself. Moultrie glanced at me, eyebrow raised, but said nothing as the priest pushed past us and hurried back through the gate. He urged us on with frantic gestures and slammed the gate shut after we'd squeezed through it. He hauled the chain tight, and snapped a shiny new padlock in place.

"The old one broke," Moultrie explained, as we walked back to the church. "He was out getting a new one before the shops closed. That's why he wasn't around to tell us off earlier when we went in."

"Before we trespassed, you mean." I paused. "Did you tell him about the children?"

"Didn't seem relevant."

"They might still be in there."

Moultrie shrugged. "I doubt it."

It was only when we reached the little church that I felt able to relax. The sensation of pursuit faded as we passed beneath the stony gaze of the two guardian angels and I allowed myself a sigh of relief. The priest seemed equally relieved. He spoke to Moultrie again, and they shook hands. He didn't offer to do the same with me, for which I was peculiarly pleased.

"What was that he said as we were leaving?" I asked, as Moultrie finally joined me. "Something about someone getting angry?" I rubbed my hand as I spoke, trying to ease the growing ache. It felt as if a sliver of metal was stuck in my palm.

"Or waking up," Moultrie said. "My conversational Italian isn't much better than yours. Maybe we disturbed someone in one of the houses near the campo."

"Hard to believe. I didn't see any lights."

"Doesn't mean they weren't there."

I looked back towards the campo, half expecting to see a child's face pressed to the bars of the gate. But there was nothing there, save shadows.

After we left the church, we had a satisfying dinner at an establishment that Waugh had referred to as 'the English bar' in one of his novels. Or so Moultrie claimed. I'd never gotten on with Waugh, being more a Wodehouse man. Despite our differing opinions on literature, I tried the shrimp risotto on Moultrie's recommendation. I wasn't disappointed. Then, if there's one thing Venetians do well, it's sea food.

The meal was expensive, as were the drinks, but Moultrie was covering both, so I didn't give it much thought. The place was a tourist trap, but we were tourists, so it seemed fitting. We'd gotten seats near a window, and I had a good view of the waterfront.

As we ate, Moultrie expounded his theories about the iron hook set at the apex of one of the city's bridges—how you were supposed to tap it for luck, and if you refused, you invited disaster. I only half-listened, watching the last embers of the sun vanish into the wide, black sea. Idly, I thought of other sunsets and the wood frame mill house in West Columbia where Ellen and I had lived. Where I still lived.

We'd spent the better part of a decade turning the place into a home, but without her, it felt empty, hollow. As if she'd somehow taken all the joy with her when she'd left. Given how much I'd taken for granted during our marriage, a part of me thought it was only fair that she be allowed to keep the happy memories, few as they were. Fair or not, it hurt all the same. Perhaps Moultrie was right, and I'd gone with him to escape being alone.

I was still thinking of my broken marriage when I saw the woman. I almost mistook her for Ellen at first. She had the same dark hair, the same olive complexion. It was only when I took a second glance that I realized my mistake. Her eyes met mine for an instant and slid away. I felt there was something odd about her, but couldn't say what. My hand throbbed suddenly and I turned my attentions back to my food.

I pushed the thought aside and, feeling somewhat bolstered by our well-lit surroundings, said, "So what were you two chatting about? You and the priest."

"Hmm?" Moultrie said, as I interrupted his train of thought. "Oh, I asked him about the wellhead. I wanted to see if he knew what the inscription meant."

"And?"

"He does."

"And did he tell you?"

"He did not." He traced thin lines of condensation on the table as he spoke, as if drawing a map. "In fact, he seemed quite agitated by the question."

I recognized the look on his face immediately. "Is that why you want to go back?" I glanced out the window. The movement of the water made me think of the shadows in the campo. Suddenly no longer hungry, I pushed my plate aside.

"Part of the reason." Moultrie took a swallow of his beer before continuing. "The wellhead...the campo...it reminds me of something. A story, I think."

"What sort of story?" I heard a low laugh and turned. The woman again, talking to someone perhaps. She laughed again, and I felt the sound deep in my bones. She was attractive, but that wasn't it. Unnerved, I looked away.

Moultrie shook his head. "I'm not sure. I seem to recall it was about someone being immured, like Fortunato, but I might be confusing it with something else."

"For the love of God, Montresor," said, and finished my drink.

"Something like that. There was a crime committed—something nasty. Nastier than warranted a clean execution, I guess."

I shivered slightly at the thought. "Not a good way to go."

Moultrie laughed and signalled for the bill. "Is there such a thing?"

I was about to reply when I caught what I thought to be a hint of furtive movement at the window. At first, I took it to be a reflection, but there was no one behind me. It was as if someone were peering in at us. Then, between one moment and the next, it—she—was gone, and there was only the night pressing against the glass. The waitress came over then, and I forgot what I'd been about to say.

The walk back was quiet, save for a brief moment's disruption. A sharp sound echoed through the streets, and we stopped, startled. There had been a definite metallic quality to the noise, but I could not think what it might be. At the instant it had occurred, my hand had spasmed. There was no blood, no sign of a wound, but it still hurt nonetheless.

As the spasm faded, I thought I heard someone singing. Far away at first, but drawing closer. A gondolier perhaps, or a drunk. The song was in Italian—must have been in Italian. It seemed at once plaintive and demanding, and then it was fading away, fading north into the convolutions of the Cannaregio. Moultrie was talking about something inconsequential and didn't appear to have noticed. I said nothing. What was there to say?

By the time we got back to our little rented flat in the Cannaregio, the pain had faded to a dull ache. The alcohol had likely helped. I choked down a pair of aspirin and bade Moultrie a good evening. I was asleep so quickly, I barely had time to shed my shoes.

That night I dreamed of the wellhead.

Or, to be more accurate, I dreamed of Venice. Of narrow streets and lagoon mist, of deep shadows and muffled voices. I half-stirred, thinking Moultrie had fallen asleep with the television on again, but as I sank once more, I realized they were the voices of children. Laughing, singing, crying out. Running along the canals, and I was chasing them. I didn't recall leaving the flat, but I must have done.

I tried to catch them, but they slipped away from me just as I got close. Just as my hand—was it my hand?—snapped shut, shy of an arm. It felt as if they were all around me, pressing close and then whirling away, like leaves in a strong wind. I called out, but they only laughed all the louder. I thought they might have been calling out a name—but not mine.

Ellen and I had never discussed children. It was something other people did, having a child. But hearing their laughter, a pang cut through me. Made me wonder what if.

They led me on a riotous gallop through the streets until I was once more standing in the empty campo, with no idea how I'd gotten there or why they'd brought me. Before I could ask, I heard a clang and my tormentors went instantly silent.

I turned. The wellhead sat in the center of the square. Three padlocks lay rusted and forgotten on the ground. Somewhere, a child began to weep. Then another, and another, until the stones echoed with disconsolate wailing.

Someone began to sing. Softly at first, and then more loudly. As if they were drawing steadily nearer over some vast distance. As they did so, the wailing faded and soon was drowned out entirely by the unseen singer. I thought it might have been the same song I'd heard earlier.

It was coming from the wellhead. Out of the corner of my eye, I thought I saw something move, but ignored it. The wellhead was the whole of my world in that moment and I went to it, stumbling on numb feet.

I could hear only the singer now, and her voice—it was a her, I was certain—was unsettlingly familiar. Ellen, or maybe the woman from the restaurant. In my head, they became one and the same.

But what was she doing here? I called out to her, softly at first. The singer paused, and then started anew.

I reached out with my aching hand. The unlocked lid scraped against its rim, as if something were pressing insistently against it from below. Was she trapped down there? I don't know why the idea had occurred to me, but suddenly I couldn't shake it. I knew—I *knew*—she was down there.

She was down there and she needed me. Needed my help. She was calling out to me. But still, I hesitated. Something held me back. The whispers of children, the feel of small fingers plucking at my legs, my elbows. The singing became a raw, red rasp of sound. It didn't sound like a woman anymore. Instead, it reminded me of an animal's growl. It sawed at the air and my ears. Demanding. Greedy.

Something that panted in my ear, just over my shoulder. A low laugh, but not that of a woman. Eyes like twin lamps caught mine, and shaggy hair brushed against my cheek.

I smelled—God, that smell...

Then I heard the bells of the little church sounding as if from a great distance. And wings—pigeons, I thought, but so many and so loud it was like soft thunder. The rasp of sound rose to a shrill shriek and I was falling back—back...my head connected with something hard and the pain jolted me awake.

"Fowler. *Fowler!*"

I was on the ground. Moultrie crouched above me, shaking me. Nearby, the priest was watching, his lined features set in a solemn expression. It was morning, early enough that the sky was a blur of pink and purple. I was wet—cold. I tried to push myself up, and a jolt of pain pulsed through my hand. I gasped and pulled the injured limb to my chest. "Where—what...?" I croaked, utterly bewildered.

I was in the campo. But it had only been a dream—hadn't it? Moultrie leaned close, concern etched onto his face. "You were gone when I woke up. Thought you'd gone out for coffee, but you hadn't bothered to put on your shoes." He gestured to my feet, and

I realized they were bare and aching. As if I'd been running across cold stones all night.

"I don't understand. Was I sleepwalking?"

Moultrie hesitated and glanced at the priest. The old man looked away, his eyes straying to the wellhead. His expression was one of resignation. I wondered if it had been him ringing the bells I'd heard in my dreams.

"In a sense." Moultrie helped me to my feet. "We found the padlock on the ground. Broken just like the last one."

"It wasn't me," I protested. Again Moultrie looked at the priest, and I had the feeling that some understanding had passed between them.

"*Era lei,*" the priest muttered and made the sign of the cross in the direction of the wellhead. Moultrie nodded and looked at me.

"No, he knows."

"What was I doing? Why was I on the ground?"

"You fell—I think we startled you. As to what you were doing, no need to worry about it. You didn't manage it, whatever it was." As he spoke, the priest replaced the padlocks reverentially, his lips moving in what I took to be a silent prayer. When the last one was clicked shut, I felt a sense of relief that I could not explain.

"I don't understand." My head felt foggy. I looked at my hand. My palm was raw and bleeding, as if the flesh had scraped—or gnawed.

Moultrie was looking at my hand as well. "This has happened before, I think. Come on, let's get you out of here." He helped me back to the church, the priest following us. As the angels came into sight, I thought again of the sound of wingbeats. I could barely recall the dream now, though it had seemed so vivid while it was occurring.

"Someone was singing…a woman?" I said, hesitantly.

The priest spat on the ground. I realized somewhat belatedly that he must understand English. He shook his head. "*Non una donna,*" he said solemnly. "*E morto da tempo, inoltre.*"

I looked back at Moultrie. "The children...I heard them too. Just as we did earlier. I—I followed them, I think."

Moultrie did not meet my gaze as he helped me sit on the church steps. "No children come here, Fowler. Not for a long time. They know better, these days." He looked at the priest. "The only ones at risk are tourists."

"At risk from what?"

The priest smiled sadly. "*Il ricordo di una corsa malvagia.*"

"What does that mean?" I asked, as they helped me inside. Moultrie glanced back towards the passage, his expression solemn.

"Just a bad memory," he said, softly. "One that refuses to fade." He clapped me on the shoulder. "Let's see to that hand and go get a coffee." He forced a smile.

"I don't know about you, but I could use one."

I USED TO LIVE HERE

KEALAN PATRICK BURKE

Perhaps she let him in because it was Christmas and it was cold, or because my mother always had a big heart. I don't know. We didn't have much money ourselves back then, and yet-she never passed a homeless person without giving them whatever change she could scrounge from her purse. It's just the kind of person she was. This was 1981, and we were in a recession, so the sight of a middle-aged man in a threadbare coat looking glum was hardly uncommon. And this was how she found him, the man whose name she never learned because she didn't think to ask, standing outside the small gate to our little bungalow, looking up at it with something like envy.

If I close my eyes, I can see her there in our kitchen with its gaudy yellow and blue flocked wallpaper and tacky orange linoleum, going about her business, maybe shimmying a hip to Stevie Nicks (her favorite), while I, not even a year old at the time, napped in my crib in my parents' bedroom. (I wouldn't have a room of my own until we moved to a bigger house in 1989). For extra money, she sometimes babysat the Murphy kids from next door, but they were out of town for the holidays, so she would have been alone. Mom was brewing some tea on the stove and folding laundry when she glanced out the kitchen window and saw the man standing out there in the snow. Unlike nowadays, her inclination was not suspicion or fear, but worry. After studying the man for a few moments, perhaps waiting to see if he moved along, she went to the door.

"Hey there," she said. "Are you all right?"

So intent was he on the house, the thin man in the frayed dark coat took his time meeting her gaze. When at last he registered her, he nodded politely and tried on a smile. It was, like his clothes, loose and ill-fitting.

"Good morning, Miss," he said. "I hope I didn't disturb you."

"Oh, not in the least," she assured him. "Is anything wrong? You look a little lost."

"I suppose I am," he said. "Lost in memory."

When she looked quizzically at him, he went on.

"I used to live here. Back when I was a boy."

"You don't say. Well isn't that lovely."

He nodded, tried the smile again, and again it fell short, like a man ashamed of his teeth. "Circumstances brought me back this way again, and I thought I'd wander by, see if it was still here."

"And how does it look?"

He scanned the exterior of the bungalow with its peach colored walls and white painted shutters. "Familiar."

Had my mother entertained any hesitation about the man, they fled in that instant. She stepped away from the door and gestured into the hall. "Well, would you like to come in for a cup of tea and see if the inside is how you remember it?"

"I don't drink tea, but I would take a water."

Even back then, in those days of unlocked doors and neighborly warmth, not all people would have been so obliging. It wouldn't be long before my mother wished she'd been one of them.

With a nod of thanks, the thin man in the long black coat nodded his gratitude, unlatched the gate with a hand my mother later described as ladylike, but for the dirt caked beneath the cracked nails, and walked up the short path to our home.

SUMMONED by the whistle from the boiling kettle, my mother hurried to the stove, leaving the tall man in the hall. "Just water you said?"

"Yes."

After transferring the laundry to a basket on the floor, which she surreptitiously slid beneath the kitchen table, my mother brewed herself a cup of tea, and then poured the man a glass of water. She set both drinks at opposite ends of the table, and turned to address the man, only to find he hadn't moved from just inside the front door.

"Do come in," she said. "It's much warmer in here by the stove."

It was as if he hadn't heard. His attention was on the gallery of framed photographs hanging on the hallway wall. "You have a nice family," he said.

"Thank you. That's my parents there, and then John's parents next to them."

"John is your husband?"

"Yes, that's us in the picture at Niagara Falls. It's beautiful. Have you ever been?"

"No, I haven't. I haven't been much of anywhere to tell you the truth. Never had the chance."

"It's never too late."

He turned away from the pictures to look at her. Later she would tell my father that his eyes looked somehow artificial—though when pressed, all she would add is that they reminded her of the eyes of a department store mannequin, painted on to give the impression of being human.

"Sometimes it is," he said, and returned to his inspection of the pictures.

Abandoning her efforts to coax the strange man into the kitchen, and only mildly annoyed that he hadn't kicked the snow off his boots before entering the house, my mother sat down at the table to enjoy her tea. From that position, the doorframe bisected the man. She could only see half of him from the table.

"Ah, the child," the man said.

"Yes, that's Bobby. Our pride and joy." She gave the kind of laugh that only lives in the mouths of new mothers. "He'll be eleven months old on the 21st. Almost a Christmas baby."

"Can I see him?"

The request was so flat and unexpected, she felt the tiniest thrum of alarm, but quickly reasoned he was simply being polite.

"He's napping right now, and if you know babies, you'll know that any time they sleep, it's a mercy. If I wake him now, he'll be up all night and I have so much to do."

He did not acknowledge her demurral. He said nothing at all.

My mother returned to her tea, mildly troubled. "When did you say you lived here?"

"1927."

The man who'd sold them the house claimed it had been built in 1956. It was of course possible that he'd been wrong, but although the house was falling into disrepair, nothing about it suggested it was thirty years older than they'd been told. Not to mention the fact that her visitor looked, at most, to be in his forties. A child in 1927 would be in his sixties now, and that just didn't appear to be the case at all. However, she saw little sense in pointing any of that out. For reasons of which she was only just now becoming aware, she didn't think he would react all that well to being called a liar. More likely, he simply had the wrong house. No memory is more deceptive than nostalgia.

She glanced up at the clock above the kitchen window. It was just after 11 a.m. My father wouldn't be home for lunch until 1, but at least she could use the excuse of having to cook to motivate her guest to leave. Assuming he didn't interpret that as an invitation to join them.

When she looked back down from the clock, the stranger was sitting across from her at the table, staring with those queer whitish blue eyes. Her heart leapt and she put a hand to her chest. "You startled me."

"What are your plans for the child?" he asked, thereby ringing within her the second peal of alarm in as many minutes.

Her benevolent smile faded a notch. "What do you mean?"

He clasped his hands, interlacing his long, tapered fingers with their dirty brown nails. This close, she could see that his skull was oddly shaped, as if it had sustained some severe injury, possibly more than one. There were dents and hollows and bare patches where his close-cropped reddish-brown hair hadn't grown back quite as densely. It made her think of the wild woodland behind her grandparents' house back in Wisconsin, a veritable fairytale world of scrub and brush and oak and fern only now darkened by the comparison. Above those unsettling eyes, his eyebrows were thin, as if they were just growing back after being shaved. Like everything else about him, his nose was narrow and long, the thin-lipped mouth set in a perpetual moue of dissatisfaction.

"What kind of future do you see for him?" he asked.

My mother shrugged. "Well, I don't know. We haven't thought that far ahead. Does anyone?"

"Some of us do."

"Well, there's plenty of time. Obviously, we want the best for him, and I suppose at some point, he'll decide what he wants to be, and we'll support that. Why do you ask?"

He turned his head to look out the window and she saw there were pale growths on the sides of his neck, like marbles beneath the skin. They moved when he spoke.

"My parents' plans for me were questionable, immoral. They weren't nice people."

"Oh, I'm sorry to hear that," my mother said, and meant it. She wasn't given to bromides.

He didn't hear her. His eyes were out there in the snow now. "I am very old, and very tired."

Seeing an opportunity to wrap a question in an innocuous remark, my mother said, "You don't look that old to me at all."

"It looks different now, this place." He withdrew his gaze from the window and looked at her instead. She wished he hadn't. His attention caused something cold to uncoil within her.

"Well, all things do change over time, don't they?"

"Not the light. The light is supposed to stay the same, just like the dark. The dark doesn't change either. But none of this looks right now. It's like a reproduction."

"I wonder if you might be mistaken about this being the house where you grew up."

"I'm not."

"After all, all of these neighborhoods look pretty much the same."

"1823 Grable Avenue. My father was a carpenter. He made the address plate you still have tacked on the wall beneath your mailbox."

My mother sipped her tea, the only sound in the room the faint ticking from the clock. She regretted admitting the stranger into the house, but as much as she wanted him to leave, she knew better than to try to evict him too quickly and without cause. After all, it was she who'd extended the invitation. He'd merely been looking at the house. A few minutes more and he might well have moved along. Revoking that invite might at best cause offence. At worst? Well, who knew what a man who spoke so strangely might be capable of? She would need to be considerate and most of all, careful. Any man could be dangerous in the wrong light.

"I suppose I should start lunch soon," she said. "Before I do, would you care to see the rest of the house?"

"I doubt it'll live up to my memories of it. It hasn't so far."

Mildly annoyed by his casual dismissal of her home, my mother said, "I got the impression those memories weren't very fond. Perhaps seeing the house in a new light might put them to rest for you. Time moves on, after all, and so do we."

She didn't wait for him to follow her into the hall. If he stayed at the kitchen table, so be it. She would simply wait in the bedroom with me until he got bored of his games and let himself out, or until my father got home, whichever happened first.

She was halfway down the hall to the bedroom when an alarming sound reached her ears, draining her momentum. She stopped, listening, face half-turned back toward the kitchen, where the stranger still sat at the table. She saw he had covered his face with his hands. Behind those long dirty fingers, he was crying. Stricken, she watched him, unsure what to do. In the end, her good heart won out and she returned to the man and placed a gentle hand on his shoulder.

"I want it back," he whimpered.

"Want what back?"

"All of it. I want to start again. To start over. Another chance. It's why I'm here—to demand it from the air in the house, to shake awake the unrealized dreams that live in these walls. I can feel them, don't you understand?"

My mother went to the stove, to the kettle. "Have some tea. I insist. It'll make you feel better."

"I don't want tea."

"It'll warm your bones."

He relented, the desperation giving way to melancholy. "Nothing warms bones born cold. I stopped living here. I don't mean moved out or moved on. I was just a child when I realized I had no life, that my parents had suffocated it, so I became nothing, a ghost haunting this place. That ghost is still here, but it's frozen. It was waiting for me to go out into the world and find myself. But no matter where I looked, I never did."

Back turned to the stranger, my mother popped a tea bag into the cup and filled it with hot water. "It sounds like you've had a rough time of it. I'm very sorry."

He scoffed. "It wasn't *rough*. If you're dead and just refuse to be buried, it isn't *rough*. It's nothing. It's decades of nothing. Paralysis. A waste of time. Years spent sitting quietly in empty rooms staring at the walls waiting for something to happen, waiting to hear a small voice deep down inside me, letting me know there was hope, that I was still alive. But no, nothing but silence. I left myself here and I've come back to get it. I can't leave until I do."

My mother spooned sugar into the tea and turned back to the table. "Do you take cr—?"

There was no one sitting at the table. She looked in time to see the man disappear into the hall, and, possessed of a dread certainty that he was heading to her bedroom, my room, she set the cup down hard enough to empty half the liquid onto the table, and hurried after him. "Excuse me. Hey, wait a minute."

She reached the hall and saw him rush into her room, into the room where I lay sleeping. Panicked now, she rushed to apprehend him, but the door slammed shut in her face. "Hey!" She reached for the doorknob and heard the lock slide home. "Open this door right now!"

He didn't, despite her panicked protestations. He left her out there in the hall, powerless. She only ceased her assault on the door when she heard his voice, low and calm, speaking to her from inside the room.

"How empty we are as children. How pointless. Youth is a waiting room, isn't it? But what is it we're waiting for? Purpose? God? Inspiration? How do we know when to wake up, and when to sleep? It's too easy to say it's the body, or instinct. Why do we fear the dark and embrace the light? How can you create a thing that serves no purpose, for which you have no use except to attend on it and be its slave until it grows wise enough to leave? What a cruel and silly ritual. We'd be better being born dead rather than live long enough to watch our lives taken away by the monsters."

Ear pressed to the door to better hear him, my mother had never been so scared. "Please," she implored him. "Please don't hurt my baby."

"He knows nothing. He's an empty vessel, just like me. He won't feel a thing."

At the threat inherent in those awful words, instinct overruled fear. My mother drew back and kicked once, twice, and again, but the door held. "Don't you touch him. Don't you dare!" she screamed. Inside the room, I began to cry, not an upset cry, not a hungry cry, but of an introduction to a kind of agony I'd not yet lived long enough to know. At the sound, my mother went berserk, kicking and clawing and punching and screaming. Finally, as my cries grew more desperate, more agonized, she launched herself bodily at the bedroom door. There was a crack as the lock splintered, the door swung open, and my mother fell into the room. So intent was she on my well-being, she didn't register that the man wasn't there. There was only me, squalling in my crib.

ALL OF THIS she told to my father when he arrived home for lunch that day. He was so perturbed by her account he took the rest of the day off to be with her, something he never did—not when money was so tight and an unscheduled half day could have gotten him fired. But my mother needed him. He knew it as soon as he walked in the door and saw her sitting on the floor of the bedroom, me sleeping in her arms. She looked like a ghost, colorless but for the red in her eyes from crying. After lunch, he sat with her and they talked long into the night. Neither of them truly understood what had happened in our home. My mother was not superstitious, but there were times when she wondered if the man had been a ghost, or the Devil himself, punishment perhaps, for being lax in her churchgoing. Without experiencing the strangeness firsthand, my father was more inclined to think the stranger a weirdo, some homeless guy looking for a place to bed down, or worse, for a house to rob or a baby to steal for ransom.

My mother was never quite the same after that, never quite as charitable to strangers as she'd been before. The memory of that day in the Christmas of 1981 clung to her, infected her dreams, and made her look differently at her child—at me, who after that day, never cried again.

THE EVENTS DOCUMENTED HERE MIGHT NEVER HAVE been known to me if my father hadn't chosen to share it with me the night before he died. My mother was eight years in the grave by then, expired in the mental institution that had so dramatically failed to save her from her own delusions. My father's doctor had summoned me to see him, assured me if I didn't come, there would not be another opportunity to say goodbye.

That night, I entered a small stuffy room that smelled of sweat, bodily waste, and other callous colors from the palette of indignity. My father was a skeleton wrapped in a sheet, his face a lazy colorless sketch of what it had once been. I might not have recognized him had I passed him in the street. I doubt he'd have recognized me either. The years had not been kind.

"Father," I said, taking the seat beside his bed.

Mouth hanging slack, he looked up at me with morphine eyes, and the notion of a smile flickered across his lips like a stone skipped across a pond. I can't recall when it was we fell out of favor with one another, or why. My teenage years are a blur, each chapter marked by rebellion, violence, and the occasional attempt to end my own life. I know I made him suffer, retribution for some affront that eludes me now. The irony of sundering a relationship when the crime is too trivial to recall is not lost on me, but once the goat has been sacrificed on that particular altar, it's hard to send the devil home.

I reached out my hand for him to take it, and feebly, he brushed it away.

"You're not my son," he whispered, and I waited a beat for the hurt to find my heart. When it didn't, I wondered if I felt nothing because I had already known this to be true.

He told me the story I have just told you, all without once looking me in the face.

"I didn't believe any of that bunk about devils and demons that your mother talked about. Not for the longest time," he said when he was done with the account. "Then there was the night you crashed the car and killed all those kids."

"That was an accident," I said, with no emotion at all. It was the truth. I hadn't meant to kill those kids, my friends at the time, but I also remember being annoyed at them, at Dave for being too loud and never knowing when to shut up, and at Stacey for loving him instead of me. I remember taking my hands off the wheel and the exhilaration of feeling the car rushing through the night unguided. Then it left the road, and I didn't try and stop it. They were drunk and not wearing seatbelts. I'm not to blame for that.

"It was your eyes," my father said, throat choked with tears. Still he wouldn't look at me. "When I came to the hospital, I saw them. Maybe you were in too much pain to hide it like you did all those years. Maybe it was the drugs that tore the curtain down, but I saw. They reminded me of what your mother had said about the eyes of the stranger when you were a baby. Mannequin eyes. Like they were painted on. Pretend eyes. That's what I saw."

"Is this what you called me here to tell me? The same nonsense that drove Mother mad?"

He shook his head. "Mother. Father. You don't even talk right."

"How should I talk?"

"Like you're human."

"And you think I owe you that? A father who leaves his child to the wolves doesn't deserve anything from that child. You're going to die alone after making a stranger of me and that's how it should be. You're the imitation person, not me."

I stood, headed for the door.

His words stopped me. I dared not believe it reconciliation. It was too late for that, and he was too sick and afraid.

"When your mother said she broke down the door and the stranger was gone, I always thought that he'd slipped out the window or the door when she was focused on you. That's not what happened though, is it? He escaped, all right. Into you. Into my child. Just tell me that, at least. Be honest. Tell me the truth so I can die knowing I didn't fail you, that there was never any way to be a good father to a child poisoned by the rotten soul of a vagrant demon."

I looked back at him with my painted eyes and tried to smile.

It didn't fit.

I CHASE THE WINTER, following the snow and the ice to towns large and small, to see if I can find my home, the one my memory tells me is there, but which is never quite the same when I arrive. Perhaps winter itself is the home, but if so, it has never made me feel welcome and I can never find its heart. So I walk on, stopping every now and then when a house emerges from the white like a new drawing, and I stand and take it in, imploring it to reveal its soul to me, imploring it to invite me in.

It's Christmas now.

I want to go home.

BY CHANCE OR PROVIDENCE

JAMES R. TUCK

The road spilled in an undulating, never-ending ribbon, barely discernible from the dust and grit of the desert it cut through. He had walked longer than he had ever walked before, traveling an eternity, each step the same as the one before it a thousand times over.

Forever it seemed.

Eons had passed.

Civilizations had risen and fallen and risen again with new strange ways and customs.

The sky above him had gone cool purple, rich to near-black, starless and empty as an overturned wineglass. Night had crawled over the mountains that made the horizon early, the sunlight of the day had been tepid at best and could not hold up. The sun was a weak and wounded animal, taken down by the long night.

A whisper of wind lifted the hair from the back of his neck, cooling the exposed skin into a prickle of gooseflesh that ran down his back.

He shrugged it away and kept walking.

He was beyond tired; exhaustion had turned from a burden into a companion miles ago. He could not stop here in the dark, inhospitable desert.

He would not look back. To that direction belonged destruction and he had no desire to see the trail of the flotsam or the jetsam of his choices. No, he felt their lagan weight in each scuff of boot heel on asphalt.

The cool wind slid past him again, carrying on it a scent that lodged itself in the rag tied over his face against the dust. Loam-moist and sticky, it crawled inside his mouth, coating his tongue so he tasted it more than smelled it. His head swam, the scent breaking his stoicism, allowing his companion to hold him closer.

He knew that scent; many moonless nights in his youth had been spent surrounded by white smoke and lithe company. It was a scent that, while pungent, did not travel far.

Scanning the expanse in front of him with narrow eyes he saw a glimmer, a shimmer, a flicker of light up ahead.

He fixed his eyes on the light, maintaining his weary stride along the road.

THE EDGE of the low adobe roof hung over the whitewashed walls of the inn, its scalloped edges reminding him of incisors. The timber door hung on wide hinges attached to straps of iron that looked black in the dark but he could smell the tang of rust from where he stood next to the courtyard fountain that may have never held water inside its basin or its fonts.

The door swung outward, revealing a shapely silhouette from the dark inside. He kept his hands by his hips, fingers open and ready. A dull, red dot floated across the shape, flaring to bright orange. A moment later and he was washed over by the heady colitas scent again. The ember moved and flared, the light eating the shadows away as a candle held by a woman caught and burned. The candlelight flickered along her edges, cutting her out of the doorway. She studied him as he studied her, taking in her bare arms prickled from the cold, sinuous body covered in a gown that lay against her, tight as bathwater. Dark hair ate the light, leaving her jaw and cheek to glow in it. Her mouth twitched in a smile that also cast her eyes in shadow to glitter like sapphires in a cave.

He had never seen a woman like her before.

He waited on her to speak; a lesson he'd learned many years ago.

She took a long drag from the cigarillo she had used to light the candle, sticky smoke wafting from the corner of her mouth.

"Hello, Stranger," she said.

He tilted his head, touching his brow.

"You have the look of one who could use a hard drink and a soft bed."

"Truthfully," he said. "I am unsure which of those I would prefer."

Her throat glowed in the candlelight as she laughed deeply. "No need to choose here, both are readily available," her voice deepened, taking a serious tone. "If you have the price for a room."

"I have the means to pay."

Teeth embedded in her bottom lip, she looked him up and down. He felt the rake of her gaze even under his clothes.

"A man like you always will."

She turned on her heel, moving inside the inn.

Across the night came the hollow toll of a bell from some mission in the desert, the sound traveling far on the night air, forlorn as a lost songbird. It hung around him, trying to settle in his chest, to weigh him down more than weariness already did.

He shook it off and followed her inside.

THE INTERIOR SURPRISED HIM; here the outside of the inn was shabby, the lobby was possessed by an unexpected luxury. Benches for guests to wait circled a large hearthstone fireplace, overstuffed cushions sprawled over them as invitation to sit and stay. Thick rugs covered the tile floor, immediately silencing his footfalls. Along the left ran a great counter of polished oak, the woodgrain gleaming rich in the lowered light of the candle in the woman's hand and the low banked fire in the hearth.

Behind it loomed an immense man.

Not obese, but over-proportioned. Large hands at the end of massive arms and a chest like a barrel, he had the ruddy, forge-burned complexion of Hephaestus.

The tooth-crowded smile that parted his dark beard shone more than the candle.

"Captain," the woman tilted her head toward him in greeting.

"Lilah," he returned. His voice matched the rest of him, rolling through the room. "I see you've lured in another straggler."

"No luring necessary, he came to the door and then followed me inside."

"What man wouldn't?"

The Captain turned his attention toward the Stranger.

"You look as if the road has been a long one."

"It always is."

"Well said," the Captain chuckled. "You'll be staying with us on this Yuletide evening?"

The Stranger grunted. "Not everyone recognizes the Solstice."

"Fitting though, isn't it?" the Captain said. "The end of old journeys and the beginning of new ones."

"I find it all the same journey, even when I change direction."

"And if you change yourself? Does the new man walk the same road as the old?"

They stared at each other over the counter, the unanswered question stretching between them, a membrane drawn taut, a skin over a drum, growing thin and thinner and thinner still.

Until the Stranger broke it.

"How much is lodging here?"

The Captain waved away his question, "Never worry the cost on a night of such auspices, first order is to find you a bed."

The woman shifted, drawing their attention to her. "I will lead him to a room."

The Captain pointed a finger at her, "Try to not get distracted along the way."

"Why, Captain," she purred, "I would *never*."

The Captain glared down at her for a long moment before turning back to the Stranger. "Join us tonight, we have a veritable feast planned for the holiday."

"You celebrate the Christ Mass?"

"Nothing so . . . *elaborate* as all that, but we do have our little festivity we share with those under our roof." The Captain bared his teeth. They shone wetly in his beard as he waved them on toward the interior. "If you need anything, Stranger, you just ring and I will have it taken care of."

The Stranger nodded and followed the woman further into the inn.

THE HALLWAYS WERE long and filled with longer shadows that clung to the adobe walls. Wide oak doors lined both sides, all of them shut. They walked a steady pace, but it seemed the doors would remain far away, remaining stationary until they suddenly weren't, lurching forward to be next to him. As they passed by each door, he could hear voices, low and murmuring, snatches of sound that reminded him of nothing more than someone calling home a wayward child. They trailed after him, tugging on his inner ear, distracting him, driving him to interrupt them by speaking to the woman guiding him.

"What is this dinner the Captain spoke of?"

"It will be a lovely affair. I will fetch you in time to attend."

"I am not fit company for dinner," he said. "I have only these shabby traveling clothes I wear."

Lila shook her head. "No one will care how you are dressed; I swear. In fact, your clothes won't be an issue at all."

"Then, to speak plainly but succinctly, I am uncomfortable celebrating the Christ Mass."

Her step faltered, stopping them short. A small line appeared in the center of her brow, drawing his eyes to it before her lip plumped into a frown and distracted him lower.

"I have two questions."

He tilted his head in assent.

"Do you often speak succinctly?" she asked.

"Yes."

She waited for more of an answer. He waited for the next question.

"Are you not a godly man?" Her voice purred, low from the back of her throat.

"I've never been mistaken for one."

She nodded; her face placid but he sensed approval. It may have only been his hope giving that impression, but he trusted himself enough to not lose his head over an attractive woman.

"By chance or Providence, people of every stripe come to this place. Join us for the feast."

"Possibly."

"I will fetch you."

Down the hall came a shimmering light. It danced up on the walls in a kaleidoscope of colors.

The Stranger pointed. "What is that?"

Her hair whipped across his arm as she turned, looking where he pointed. A grin split Lila's face, turning her countenance from a mysterious young lady into that of a feral child seeing the fair for the first time. She grabbed his wrist, nearly burning him with the cigarillo still held between long fingers, it brushed his coat and showered a dribble of red sparks that snuffed out before they struck the floor.

He allowed himself to be pulled forward in her wake, her fingers a manacle, hard as iron around the small bones of his wrist. The light grew brighter as they got closer, heat lightning flashing. Cold moved through the air in drafts, crawling up his sleeve and under his shirt. They rounded the corner to an open door. Before he could plant his feet, Lila pulled him through.

They were in a courtyard.

Torches planted in the ground cast a haze into the roofless open air, turning the starless sky above into a dark smudge, amorphous and shapeless and far away. The flagstone floor of the hallway became flat cobblestones on the other side of a heavy iron threshold. Grass that had grown in their seams had been crushed, staining the edges of the stones in dark patches. Past the cobblestones the grass had been torn to the bare dirt, tufts and divots of soil lay scattered to the edges, along the walls, fresh turned as grave dirt.

The feet that had done the damage belonged to a dozen men who flung themselves across the courtyard square in ecstatic spasms. Some of them held small drums that they hit with knobbed sticks, each player to their own rhythm, laying a blanket of disjointed percussion that combined to form a vascular pulse that bloomed behind the Stranger's ribcage. His head swam as his own heart contracted and held and began to keep time.

Other men in the group clutched thin, curved ivory flutes, each of them playing different tunes. One would lift the flute to their lips and play a long melody that slithered over the backbeat provided by the drummers. The moment he stopped, yanking the flute away as if it were a hot coal, another dancer would begin playing a series of shrill notes that struck the back beat with the same ferocity as a wasp, when plucked from the air, stings the hand that holds it.

The dancers surged forward and swirled past them, skin glistening with sweat. Their hands flailed out, grabbing at Lilah. The

Stranger latched onto her arm and pulled her back, against his side, to prevent her being caught up in their madness.

One of the men, a mop-haired young man with a left eye that drifted to the outside of its socket, lunged close enough that the Stranger got a good look at the flute he held between clenched teeth. The light was low and the man swooped in then was gone but the Stranger recognized the material of the flute from just a glimpse.

It was bone.

Unpolished, raw bone.

He had seen bone of that nature, long, thin, and curved.

He took his hand off Lilah's forearm.

"Who are these men?"

"They are my friends," she said. "They've come to celebrate with us this eve."

"Where have they come from?"

"The highways and the hedges, they have been compelled."

"They appear compelled."

"Don't you find them to be just so *pretty*?"

The Stranger grunted, jealousy smoldering as he watched them dance, eyes narrowed in study. All of the men were what most would consider handsome, each of them knit together, well-formed, and without blemish or handicap. They danced unabashedly, not only flinging themselves around the courtyard but into each other's arms to be lifted and twirled. If they were bothered by his presence as an onlooker, they gave no indication.

It was cool, the night air falling into the courtyard from the open roof, but the dancers all gleamed with sweat, despite most of them being undressed. They trampled their clothing underfoot, all of it covered in the bare dirt, flinging up small dust dervishes when a foot would snag an article of clothing and sling it, fling it a few feet away. None of them tripped, not stumbling at all, even dancing at the fevered pace they were.

Their energy pushed and pulled at him. Their swaying bodies

hypnotized him, a small voice in his brain urging him to join them, to shed his second skin and lose himself to the unsyncopated tune they played. He could sink into it, the primal grunt and thrust of the dance, movement that echoed the contractions of birth, the gyrations of lust, the throes of death. It called to the primate in his brain, to the fish that wriggled its way onto land who still nestled in his DNA. It was inside him, as it is in every man if you scratch him deep enough, to howl at the moon and to chase his food and to destroy anything he could not carry.

Their frenzy made a weight upon him, reminding him of every mile he had walked before arriving here.

"Take me to my room."

THE BED SWELLED AROUND HIM, the mattress soft and loose, filled with some rustling substance. He did not pull the covers down, and, instead, lay atop them. He could smell his own stink, his skin trapped under the same clothes for too many days and too many miles of road.

He was alone. Lilah leaving him at the door with a promise to return soon.

He did not want to attend a dinner.

But he knew that if dark-haired Lilah found him awake, he would follow her wherever she led him.

Hunger was a hard knot behind the buckle of his belt, his stomach folded around itself. He could not remember his last meal, anything that was more than scraps from the road. He had long lost his sense of surprise at what he could do, at what he could survive. Eating something he could not identify that had been crushed flat and baked hard by the unrelenting sun was now an action that did not deserve even a memory to commemorate.

It took him a long moment to roll to the edge of the bed and reach for the phone on the table beside it.

Somehow, he knew when he picked up the receiver that the Captain would be on the other end of the line.

"Yes, Stranger," the bellicose voice rolled into his ear. "What can I have done for you?"

He hadn't known what he would ask before the question was posed, but the moment it was heard he realized part of him wanted something to take him to sleep. If he were not awake when Lilah arrived, she might leave him be.

"I would like some wine, please."

From the other end of the line came a small *tsk*, the barest sound of tongue against teeth.

"I am sorry, we have been out of wine for some time now. There will be spirits at the feast this eventide, but for the moment we are dry."

The Stranger waited for the Captain to suggest an alternative. After a few minutes he gently replaced the receiver on its cradle and closed his eyes, part of him tense at the refusal the other part of him glad for being refused.

THE LAMPLIGHT CRASHED against the edge of his vision, his eyes burning as if he had a fever. Sleep had not come in his room. His mind had traveled too many turns and twists behind closed lids, some things from his near past, others from the distant past.

Too many thoughts of Lilah.

Her dark hair, her dark eyes, her dark scent.

He walked beside her now, glancing at her as he could. She had changed into a diaphanous shift of a dress, the fabric of it clinging to her and flowing around her like a mystery. Her dark hair had been pulled into intricate braids that lifted and swirled, knotted into each other in overlapping strands leaving her neckline exposed. Under her jaw the skin turned silvery in a thin line. It slashed up, curling almost to her earlobe.

He had seen scars before, carried many upon his own flesh, but this did not have the appearance of a scar, it was more a seam, some surgical separation of the skin along her throat although no gap appeared as she turned her head.

"I have a question," he said.

"I will have an answer, even if it not the one you want."

"What is your place here?"

"That is an interesting question, kind Stranger."

"I am not kind," his voice lowered to emphasize his words, "and however do you mean? It is a plain enough inquiry."

"Do I answer you with the location of my residence? Do I give you my status in the hierarchy here? Do we discuss my role in the greater scheme of the universe?"

"How did you come to be here, leading me down this hallway?"

"It is my function as hostess to bring guests to the Master's chamber."

"Who is the master? The Captain?"

She chuckled and it ran across his chest as if she had caressed him there.

"The Captain is the Captain; he is not the Master."

"Who is the Master?"

"This is his inn we all stay at."

"Does he have a name? I will not call another man Master."

"He does not care what you call him, you are his guest."

"Does he have another name?"

"He has many."

"What do you call him?"

"The Master."

"Not *your* master?"

Her arm linked into his as her hip bumped him to turn down a different corridor.

"You are close to becoming boorish and rude."

"One last question, and I will relent," he said.

Lilah nodded her assent.

"When I leave will you go with me?"

She chuckled, soft and low, "Stranger, if you leave, I will be right behind you."

His lip curled against the soft mockery of her tone. "You think I would choose to stay?"

Diaphanous fabric slipped, revealing the dimples of one small shoulder, as Lilah shrugged.

"A free man and a free woman can go as they will."

"Good sir, we are all prisoners here by our own choice."

She stopped short before he could respond. She turned him toward an entrance. The doors had been flung open to reveal a long room. The murmur of voices and the jumbled noises of people moving about matched the scene he saw inside. The room held dozens of people, all standing around a long table that filled the center of the long room. From the door, he could see the table had been set along its length, but he could make out no details in the soft gloom of the low lanterns and candles that provided a dusk of ambiance.

"We have arrived."

A HUSH BLOSSOMED as they stepped over the threshold. It only lasted the moment before voices rushed to fill in the gap and the room was once more blanketed in hushed conversations. His eyes adjusted quickly coming the dark corridor into the room. The people in the room were a varied group, a cross section of age, race, gender, and economic status. Some were dressed in finery, there were several dresses and suits that would be at home at any High Society function. He also found several people to be dressed in what looked to be work clothes, rough sturdy fabrics worn by rough and sturdy people. All of them or clean and in good repair, none of them has shabby as his traveling clothes.

In the far corner he found Lilah's friends. They lay against one another on a set of couches, still diffidently dressed and as unconcerned about that in the crowd of dinner guests as they had been in the courtyard.

For some reason he found their presents to be comforting.

Lilah leaned away from him her arm still hooked in his. She snatched a long-stemmed glass from the tray of a passing waiter. The waiter did not acknowledge the taking of the glass in any way.

She brought the glass around and held it to his face.

"Oh, you must absolutely try this!"

The pink liquid in the glass fizzed and bubbled, releasing gas that filled the inside of his nose. It made a tickling, scratchy sensation like something with too many legs crawling along the lining of his nose.

He did not want it, did not want anything to do with it. Some instinct inside him rose up, a lizard part of his brain twitching something carried over from a Time when what would become man used every sense that he had to avoid being eaten by things larger and faster and more toothed than he.

Lilah's eyes shimmered in the candlelight and his refusal drowned in that gaze.

When she pushed the rim of the glass between his lips, he opened them and allowed her to pour the liquid down his throat in a long continuous swallow that drained the glass dry.

His throat clenched, trying to shut around the vapor but he forced his body to obey. Still, he coughed has Lilah giggled beside him.

His eyes watered, blurring his vision for a moment. When he blinked them clear he found that the other guests were taking their chairs. Lilah gave a tug to his arm and he followed her towards the table.

His head swam, the sounds of the room around him felt as if they had been pushed to the wall and he sat in a cone of only his own sounds. Only the rasp of his breathing, only the rustle of his clothing, only the circadian thrush of his own blood as it fulfilled its blind circuit.

The light in the room took on a different cast, circling the other guests with a nimbus the color of rotten honeycomb. The shadows that coated the ceiling dropped, hanging down the way Spanish moss hangs from a tree.

His chair bumped forward, clacking his teeth together, and he realized Lilah had tucked him into the table and was turning away from him.

His fingers caught the edge of her dress. He clutched it, pulling towards him. Her hand slid along his jaw, the fingers thin and cool against his pulse. He tried to form the words, to ask her why she was not sitting next to him, but they would not come. She leaned close, her mouth near his. He smelled her warm loam scent, the dark spice and clean night of her and it intensified the effect of the drink he had taken.

"I must go do my duty for the feast," she said, her breath hot upon his cheek. "Stay here, I will be back to the table in a bare moment."

"Let me help you."

Her hand tightened on his throat, not enough to hurt, but enough to sharpen his focus. "You are a guest; it is not your place to help."

"You will return?"

"I will, very shortly, now I must go."

Lilah pulled away, moving behind him. As she did, the hem of her dress tore away in his hand, the material thin and weak. He held the scrap tightly and leaned back in his chair, letting the stupor from his drink wash over him.

His brain turned down corridors of its own, reeling inside his brain the way he felt he would reel if he tried to stand and go find Lilah.

His attraction had intensified. More than want, more than animal desire, he felt as if he needed her, as if she were now intrinsic to his very existence. Was the world, all he had experienced of it, simply a holding area until she brought him forth, fully formed into this existence?

He had touched her, she felt as material as any other human. He was not awed by her, wasn't driven to worship her as a goddess. He was no proselyte to prostrate himself before any god or man. He did not worship the air in his lungs or the food that gave him sustenance. He felt her as necessary to him as that.

Something around the table shifted, some energy that changed, He felt it as surely as if someone had jostled him from his reverie. He opened his eyes and found himself staring back at an odd angle. He still leaned in the chair, his face toward the ceiling. The light in the room had brightened and now he could see that the ceiling was a mirror, reflecting him. He looked the same as he remembered but also different, not a whole new man, but new parts. He looked longer and leaner than he remembered. He felt fit, kept hard from the miles he walked across the earth, but in the mirror, he found a scarecrow with bedraggled hair and limbs that jutted at angles, a gaunt, a haggard.

A haint.

Around him rose a collective moan from his fellow dinner guests, one of anticipation. He allowed it to pull his eyes away from the man above him.

The guests along the table all leaned forward, a long knife clutched in every left hand.

A knife like theirs lay in front of him, wrapped in a silk ribbon.

The polished bone handle enough for two hands to grip it lay neath the blade that ran straight, long as a child's forearm. Both sides tapered to a long, wicked point. The edges showed their sharpness as a gleam even in the low light of the room. The center of the blade dipped into a blood groove below the guard.

His left hand moved to it without his guidance, his mind too occupied sorting the purpose of its design to issue a command to his musculature.

This was not cutlery.

Not a santoku.

Never meant for a chef's hand.

This knife had one purpose.

It fit in his grip as an extension of his own hand, of his own body.

Tooth and claw for a creature that had allowed convenience and safety to shrink both to vestiges.

The same moment his hand closed around the hilt a bell sounded, clear and cold, behind him, causing all the guest on his side of the table to turn as he did to see what new turn the evening had taken.

Part of the wall-a part he now recognized as a pair of pocket doors-had slid apart and through it came a cadre of six waiters bearing a large tray on their shoulders as if they were pallbearers. Something large that he could not make out from his seated position lay heavy on the tray. The waiters moved in lockstep, gliding the short distance to the table. They moved with practiced grace, each motion in time and with the preponderance of a ritual completed many times. A hush fell over the guests, each face a grimace of anticipation as the bearers maneuvered their burden to the table and lay it in the center with precision.

They stepped back in unison.

On the tray, in the center of the table, within reach of each and every guest, lay a pale goat bound with red cord.

It lay on its side, breathing deeply but evenly, jutting ribs expanding and shrinking. Its fur was short and smooth, thin enough that the pale pink of skin could be seen though the white of it. His eyes traveled its length, taking in the graceful lines of the beast, the crooks of its shanks a perfect curve, its pink belly unmarred and pristine. The only color to be found on her, the goat was absolutely a *her* now that he had looked, was the black in her narrow hooves and the dainty curl of horn that swept off her brow. Even her eyes, eyes that peered at him from inches away as she had been positioned with her head in front of his place, were so light a brown they were a cream. Those unguent eyes fixed on him, locked him in their gaze. She did not blink, did not close her eyes, simply stared at him. *Into* him. He was seen. Recognized in a way he had never been by a human, much less a beast before.

Her eyes did not close even when the first blade sank into her.

Instead, they widened, nearly doubling in size, as a man on the opposite side of the table, four chairs down, held the hilt of his knife, pressing the guard into her side, the blade sunk between her ribs. Seconds stretched with no movement, time locked in a bubble between the blade, her eyes, and his mind.

A tremble ran down her side, under her pale fur, from the blade to her jaw.

A trickle of red ran free from the bottom of the wound, zigging and zagging until it broke free of the fine white hairs. Once it released onto the curve of her stomach it raced in a straight line to the tray she lay on.

The blood dripped, spattered, and the spell was broken.

The guests surged forward, sinking their own blades in her as she thrashed her head, bleating wildly from the pain, her cries mixing with the staccato of wet *thunks* made by hilts driven forcefully into flesh.

The Stranger held his knife in his hand, but he could not move.

As the goat threw her head back, he saw a mark on her.

A thin line of silver that curled from under her jaw and up toward her ear.

His nose filled with the stink of iron as her white fur turned vermillion, the guests stabbing and stabbing and stabbing with their steely knives.

She thrashed and kicked her bound legs, throwing back her head, slip-sliding on the tray that overflowed with dark crimson, soaking into the cloth covering the table. The tray rattled and dinged, moved and jittered from the force of the thrusts to its occupant.

She let out a long howl, a noise not meant to come from one such as her, it sliced into his mind and he fell back. The knife he had held clattered to the floor as he turned his eyes up and away.

In the mirror above was his scarecrow self but he did not see it.

His vision was only for the beast that lay before his mirror self.

On the tray, bound hand and foot, wounded but not dying was no goat at all.

Lilah.

The horror of it curled inside his chest, and his legs drove him back, up and out of his chair. Hand to his mouth, he stepped back, but stared down at the table, his eyes opened to the truth of what lay before him.

The guests ignored him, caught in their frenzy, their bloodlust, they continued to stab. One blade passed through the cords around Lilah's arms and chest, splitting them open, freeing her upper body. She twisted, faster than he could watch, moving from lying in her own blood to sitting up. He kept moving back as her hands closed on the cords around her legs and tore them asunder.

Her eyes fixed on him, glowing through the mask of crimson that coated her whole being and now it wasn't her blood but the color of what wasn't skin any longer but he had no better word to call it. Her limbs stretched and curved, arcing back on each other and gleaming like polished steel. She had joints still but they were in the wrong locations, clustered together asymmetrically or spread too far apart. She was not a dark-haired girl any longer. She had become something other, something less than human and more than mortal.

Her eyes fell upon him.

Her words echoed in his mind.

Stranger, if you leave, I will be right behind you.

Most of the guests had stopped, fallen back in their chairs still holding their knives but simply staring at the bloody creature before them. Three of them continued to stab forward, lunging at her.

One of them managed to drive the tip of his blade into what was once her hip.

She snapped her overknuckled fingers.

As one, every guest spun their knives in their grips and drove them deep in their own bellies.

His empty fist drove deep into his stomach.

The room filled with the green stench of disembowlment as every lap but his and what-once-was-Lilah's lap filled with gore.

What-once-was-Lilah's hooves tinned a screeching chime on the silver platter she had been carried in on as she clambered to her feet, pink eyes pinned on him. Her jaw worked side to side and her blood stained throat convulsed around a moan that held the echo of language.

He turned and ran from the room.

HE TURNED A CORNER, chest burning, stumbling, mind racing, and animal desperation to find his way out of the inn. Every corridor had turned into a different one. That many steps should have taken him to the outside.

Any moment he stopped he could hear her behind him, a bleating moan calling his name, the name he had not given to anyone under this roof, not even her.

A flickering light at the end of the hall called him forward.

He found himself in small room with a hearth.

"Hello, Stranger."

He turned, the Captain stepped out of the shadows, into the hearth light.

"What is the trouble on this long and holy night?"

Between heaving breaths, he said, "I have to get out of here." He jerked his head, scanning the room. There were no doors save the one he had entered through.

Down the corridor he had arrived in came the hissing wet

scrape of hooves dragged on tile. The *thunk* of them being set down like a hammer on a stake.

The Captain chuckled.

"Let me go!" The Stranger cried.

"I am not holding you."

From the corridor, the scrape, the *thunk*, louder now.

"This place is a trap."

"No, it is an inn."

Scrape. Thunk!

"I wish to check out!"

His name echoed down the corridor in Lilah's voice, clearer now, almost normal save for the vibrating, caprinae vowels. It wrapped around him, lover close, intimate.

Once-was-Lilah shuffled into the room, still the thing that had lurched off the table, still coated in blood gone tacky, drying to black, shrinking to a crust that spiked the short hair of her, leaving pale clean skin exposed. Her eyes still pinned him, glaring pink and now multiplied into clusters of small, smooth orbs like spider eggs. Her jaw slung low, waving beneath a tongue that waved like a child as her long throat worked. He felt the sound inside it in his very bones, a vibration attuned to the essence of him. His true name poured up her thorax, spilling over her tongue, showering him in Lilah's voice. He drowned in the baptismal of it, so submerged in the unholy sacrament he barely heard the Captain, standing witness still, when he spoke.

"My friend, you can check out any time. But you can never leave."

THE HERON IN WINTER

JOHN LINWOOD GRANT

It had been an excellent dinner, the more so because none of the diners—indifferent cooks themselves—had been involved in its preparation. O'Hanrahan, the Irishman who acted as major domo to the household, had prepared and served the entire meal, and would accept no help with the clearing away of the remains.

"Will you join us for brandy, O'Hanrahan?"

"I've no head for brandy, nor for your sort of tales, Mr. Dodgson." The Irishman considered the half-empty soup tureen in his large hands. "And sure now, isn't that a bottle of porter in the kitchen, calling out to me?"

Dodgson hid his smile. "I do believe so. Well, you know where we are."

He led the others through into the small dimly-lit study. There were only three of them that night—Dodgson, his colleague Miss Jessop, and their occasional guest, Lieutenant Redvers Blake.

"A snort, Redvers?"

The young officer ran gloved hands along a bookshelf, his eyes drawn to titles which made little sense to him. These were books he would not care to touch, not with his bare fingers.

"I will, Henry. Be generous with the soda."

Settled in leather armchairs, the diners entered that awkward comfort of those who have known each other for some time, but who cannot be sure of what any one of them might say. All three took slim cigarettes from the case which Dodgson handed round; matches scraped, and brief flares disturbed the darkened corners of the room.

Dodgson, a broad-shouldered man of almost O'Hanrahan's proportions, was clearly the most relaxed; pale, slim Miss Jessop the least at ease. Her long fingers brushed the cameo at her throat, ignoring the glass of brandy by her side.

"You carry something with you, Blake," she said.

"Only d-d-death, as usual." The lieutenant spoke without any particular emphasis, without emotion. Winter rain beat on the window panes behind him, muffled by heavy drapes.

"Your work with Special Branch?" Dodgson looked interested.

"No. A matter of m-m-mills, and uniforms; of ordinary lives. This new B-B-Balkans affair, however…"

But neither Dodgson nor Miss Jessop would be diverted.

"The story, in return for dinner." Dodgson insisted. "You know that's the arrangement here at Cheyne Walk, an arrangement set in stone. You can be what you must be outside these walls, but here we follow the old ways."

Blake smoothed his slim mustache with one finger; neither of the other two could see if he smiled or frowned beneath the gesture.

"Very well."

And so between brandies and cigarettes, speaking crisply above the hiss of the gas-lights, he paid the toll for his meal…

YOU KNOW that there is a meanness and brutality to much of what I do (began Blake), and some tales I would never tell you. This one, however...you must judge for yourselves.

Early last week I received orders that I was to head up Manchester way, and from there to make directly for an establishment belonging to the Rochdale Canal Company, somewhere out in the wilds. The company had begged Whitehall's assistance, and what Whitehall had chosen to send was, well, me.

I asked why, of course. Were we talking insurrection, agents of foreign powers, Bolsheviks—or perhaps even Fenians? No, came the curt response. Simply...difficulties. I was told to wear full uniform, and that a canal company man, Mr. Charles Edgerton, would explain more when I got there. Orders were orders, so I packed a bag, and did as I was told.

The inclement weather down here at the moment is nothing compared to the winter that the North has been enduring. The train was lashed with sleet as it sped towards Manchester, and once in that city I had the devil of a job to make my way to my destination—an isolated spot near Todmorden. A motor-cab, skidding on two inches of packed snow finally managed to get me there later that same afternoon.

I'm not a literary man like you, Dodgson, but let me see...

Picture a landscape of hillsides, almost bare of trees and bleak with snow; villages of grey native stone huddled in valley bottoms, the occasional rearing chimney of a mill or factory, like dead fingers pointing to the heavens. And a building, a badly-wrought brick building set on its own by the canal-side—a toll station and centre of operations for barge traffic. A friendless place which squatted by a basin crammed with idle, canvas-covered barges.

That was Lydgate Stop House, my temporary assignment, and where I was given into the care of said Mr. Edgerton, a damp, nervous man in his fifties.

"Lieutenant Blake, from London," I said, stamping the snow off my boots in his office, "As requested—but I d-d-don't know why."

At least the fire was built high. The room smelled of mould and scorched toast.

"They...they didn't tell you?" Edgerton took a kettle from the stove, and scalded himself filling a large cracked teapot. "Oh dear me."

The milk was almost off, but the tea was welcome enough. I sipped, and waited.

"We...er, we have a problem with Low Hawnsey Cut," he managed at last.

"N-n-never heard of it."

Ah, how I hate these tales within tales. Still, I'll give you the gist.

The company had an antique ice-breaking barge, *Heron*, for when such icy circumstances gripped the network of navigations. Thus, when the hard frost set in, *Heron* was manned by company men and local workers, and sent to open up the seven mile cut to somewhere called Cochrane's Mill.

The mill lay in a deep fold of the Pennines, and the waterway in question, Low Hawnsey Cut, was the main artery to the mill—but the cut was frozen solid.

"Our problem is the...ice-breaking crew, Lieutenant Blake," he said. "They...what with the...body, you see?"

He was a man of many pauses; I was a man without a clue. I suggested that he be succinct, before I took myself back to my cramped but more congenial office at Whitehall.

"The *Heron* started from the basin, here..." said the company man, "And made good progress, until..."

"Until they found a b-b-body?" I suggested, hoping to speed him up. "A corpse in the canal?"

He paled, which was difficult with a man already so wan.

"The crew...saw a body in the water. This was yesterday. They had covered almost three miles, the horses were tired, and they...the tiller-man shouted that there was something...*someone*...in the water, by the patch they had broken moments before.

"Naturally, men rushed to see, and called to the lengthsmen who were on the banks...they have long rakes, you see, to haul sheets of ice and flotsam to the sides. 'A woman!' was the cry, and rakes dipped from *Heron* and the canal bank..."

"They hauled her out, presumably?"

"There was...nothing to haul. The rakes went through the...body, whatever it was. It drifted past the boat, they say, and then...was gone. Vanished. The men would go no further." Edgerton swirled the dregs of tea in his cup. "*Heron* lay near a winding hole on the cut, where she could be turned, when the incident occurred, so they brought her back here to the Stop House, against their instructions. Since then, they talk of spectres, and hauntings, and all manner of unhealthy things...yet the mill..."

"What's so important about this mill?" I pressed him.

Edgerton explained that Cochrane's Mill was a leading supplier of serge, under contract to the War Office. The barges in the canal basin outside were jammed with raw materials for the mill, and given the thick ice, neither those materials nor the finished serge could go anywhere. Bargees were angry; tolls were being lost, and the factories which made up the uniforms in Manchester had their own complaints.

"I can't...can't seem to get them to take *Heron* out again, lieutenant."

My presence now made sense. I was there to bluster, to order, to put steel into these people, to get things moving—and to deal with any talk of 'sightings'. Send that Blake fellow, some idle official must have muttered. 'He has a taste for oddities and nonsense.'

I nodded. "So—water-weed, old rags that the rakes could not catch; too many early b-b-beers, delusions brought on by this bitter cold. I suppose that I should speak to your men."

"You don't believe in...ghosts, lieutenant?"

"I d-d-don't believe in anything, Mr. Edgerton."

Looking slightly puzzled, the man led me out and round to the rear of the building, where eight or nine men sheltered by some stables, oiling various implements, mending ropes, and drinking mugs of tea from a battered urn.

"Blackwood, this is Lieutenant Redvers Blake, of the—"

"North Surreys." Which was all they needed to know.

"Ah, yes. He is here to consider our little…problem."

A thin man with one shoulder higher than the other stood up. Whether his posture was from accident or from birth, I couldn't tell, but it tilted his long head perpetually to one side. His eyes were sharp enough, though.

"Ay up. They goin' to shoot us, if we don't work *Heron*, then?"

I walked closer. "W-w-would that help? I do have my revolver with me." I spoke affably enough, and patted the side of greatcoat.

Several of the men gave out uncertain laughs; others scowled.

"Mr. B-B-Blackwood, I'm here to get the cut working again. If there's a way to do so which involves neither guns nor p-p-priests, I'm open to it."

Blackwood squinted at me. "We saw what we saw. Ned, Harry, Joseph and all the rest, even them as leads the hosses. There were a woman in the watter, and then there weren't."

"A woman? Did you recognise her?"

The fact that I didn't immediately dismiss his words seemed to throw him.

"Recognise, sir? There were no…face, like, nobbut a blur. She had mebbe a dress, shawl, it were hard to tell. And summat white, like a flower, pinned to her." He touched the lapel of his grubby jacket. "'Bout here."

It was an odd detail. The others agreed, though not everyone had seen the flower or broach, whatever it was. These men had had time to confer, but there were none of those typical 'rehearsed' lines to be heard. Most said it had been a woman; almost all thought that the body had been drifting along in the same direction as the weak current, which was some product, beyond me, of lock gates, sluices and the reservoirs above Cochrane's Mill.

"When would you take *Heron* out again, n-n-normally?"

Blackwood considered the grim, snow-speckled afternoon which gripped the toll house, the basin, and the low hills around it.

"Should mebbe be out now," he admitted. "But the light's goin', and the hosses aren't ready."

I had no wish to remain up North any longer than needed. "Mr. Edgerton, Mr. Blackwood. We'll sail—or whatever you canal p-p-people call it—first thing tomorrow. I'll be on the boat."

"But—"

That earned them what might be called an 'army stare'. "And I hope you have a cot ready for me somewhere in this Stop House of yours."

I was given a room cluttered with dusty ledgers and unidentifiable tools; Edgerton was sleeping in the toll-keeper's bedroom, and the toll-keeper in the office downstairs.

Supper was a fatty chop and a slurry of heavily-boiled peas, peppered with attempts by Edgerton to tell me things I didn't really need to know.

"We rely, you see, lieutenant, on the steady flow, yes, the steady flow of industry...each broken link costs everyone. Our investors, the bargees and the families, who have to eat; the mill-workers who must be on short hours until goods move in and out...you understand?"

Low Hawnsey Cut did have to be opened, it seemed.

I SLEPT BADLY; there were missing tiles on the Stop House roof, with the resultant whistle of icy blasts across my room throughout the night. At first light I abandoned my cot and shaved in a bowl of cold water. There was a hot brew waiting down below, accompanied by cheese and stale bread buns. 'Baps', the company man called them.

"They have *Heron* ready," said an unshaven Edgerton. "Come, I'll take you. I don't...participate myself, of course."

Of course.

We made our way over frozen ground, away from the basin and the double lock which led into the Rochdale Canal, heading northwest for the first stretch of Low Hawnsey Cut itself. It was an unromantic stretch of grey water, stone-lipped and bordered by no more than the occasional stunted hawthorn, their leafless forms bent over the tow-path as if they sought to reclaim it. I was surprised to see a team of six horses stamped and blew clouds of steam by the water, already harnessed to…an odd boat indeed.

Heron was a wooden barge of forty foot or more, maybe eight wide, with a great iron rail running down the length of it, fixed with metal stanchions to stand about three foot above the planked deck.

"She has, you see…" panted Edgerton, clearly not a fit man, "Protective plates bolted to her sides. As the horses pull, the men grip the rail…and roll the barge, first one way then the other. This and the forward motion shatter the ice."

Blackwood and four others had turned up to man the icebreaker, six less than her normal crew, I was told—and those few stalwarts hardly looked cheerful. Their faces fell further when a large heavily-wrapped woman came striding down towards us.

"Alma." Blackwood reddened. "Get 'ome."

The woman glanced at Edgerton and myself, sniffed and turned to Blackwood.

"To hell wi' thee, Layton Blackwood." She strode across the gangplank, onto the barge, and took up a position at the rail. "If tha cannot get t'men to do it, someone must."

"His wife." Edgerton dabbed at his nose with a handkerchief. "A…lively woman. Well, Blackwood will be on the tiller, and if you stand there with him, you'll see the way we work."

A mutter or two, and the rest of the crew was in place. Alma Blackwood was a head taller than the men, and as she rolled up her sleeves, I saw muscle enough to drop a donkey in those arms. Her husband clearly didn't wish to discuss her presence, but called out for the 'hosses' to begin their steady plod up the tow-path.

The wind had dropped, leaving a chill mist clinging to everything, but we were mercifully free of yesterday's snow or sleet. I braced myself at the stern, careful not to be in the way of the tillerman, and *Heron* shuddered as the ropes went taut and she began to move.

"Old, solid oak, and iron plates," said Blackwood. "She'll break an inch, mebbe more."

I could see fragments of ice still clinging to the banks of the cut, glinting whenever the weak morning sun broke through, but the way ahead showed only fragile skins reaching out from those fragments. Occasionally a jumble of dead leaves and detritus had frozen into a block by the tow-path. Stone markers on the bank showed each half mile; the horses hauled, silent in the mist except for the thump of their hooves. We were an island of quiet, no talk between those on the rail; most of them had pipes out, and were staring down at the water as they smoked.

"How much farther?" I found myself speaking in a hushed tone.

"Less'n a mile," said Blackwood, hunched over the tiller. "*Heron's* a heavy bugger, with all that iron, and the best hosses are on the Rochdale. We'll get...there."

There.

Where they had seen the apparition, if such it was; where they had stopped the barge, and baulked at going on.

Heron surged, slowed, surged, as the lads at the horses showed their jitters, not regulating the pull as well as they should.

"Steady, there!" I call over. "Nice and steady."

Blackwood accepted a cigarette from me.

"The army must want them uniforms bad."

"D-d-doubt the army cares that much. What it doesn't want is canal companies and m-m-mill owners bothering it."

Which earned me a thin smile.

"You a regular, then, lieutenant? Seen action."

They always want to know, and what they want to know was: Have I killed anyone? The Fenians ask it, when cornered in dank cellars; the pacifists ask it at polite dinners. Children ask it, and old men always wonder...

"I've seen enough." I said, and turned away.

We hit thin ice ten minutes later, but that meant nothing to *Heron*'s bows. Some twenty yards ahead I could now see the untouched sheet which blocked the cut. The men looked nervous. I slipped off one glove, and gripped the rail at the stern, reaching into the barge with my damnable, unwanted gift, listening...

Nothing. Scarred timbers, iron, years of duty, but *Heron* was what she seemed. I could sense no malice, no unnatural influence within her.

Blackwood's eyes were fixed on the others.

"Ready, lads. You'll want to hang on there, lieutenant."

Edgerton's explanation hadn't prepared me for the moment of action. As the barge came close to unbroken ice, the tiller-man set up a call—a canal shanty, I suppose you'd call it.

"Hold, and..."

Those at the long rail tensed themselves, boots scraping on the deck.

"Onside! Offside! Let her run, and...Onside! Offside!"

With the first word of command, the crew—without letting go of the main rail—threw their weight in the direction of the towpath, and with the second, lurched towards the other side.

"Onside! Offside!"

Heron shifted with them, rolling in the water, and hit the thick ice like a slow, twisting bullet. A great grinding and cracking sound arose about us as the ice-sheet splintered; the timbers of the barge moaned, but held.

Fascinated, I watched as the frozen surface of the canal shattered, throwing up inch-thick plates of ice and a spray of ugly water. Men who had followed the tow-horses, willing to work as long as they didn't have to be on the barge, unshouldered rakes with clawed tines and dragged the broken ice to the banks, hauling some slabs out of the water altogether.

It was practised, organised.

"Onside! Offside! And let her run, me bullies!"

I threw off my greatcoat, and went to the rail, next to Alma Blackwood.

"You object, madam?"

Dark eyes narrowed. "Hold t'rail tight, lad. I'm not fishing thee out."

This was work. All had to time their movements perfectly, and to do so gripping a freezing iron rail, with wet planks beneath us. I thanked my heavy army boots for joining me, and I cursed my arms, which were aching after only ten minutes of lurching and wrenching.

"Onside! Offside! And...Lord, look!"

It wasn't difficult to spot what should not have been there—a shadow, emerging from under the ice ahead. Not a woman this time, but possibly a child.

The body was floating a few inches below the surface to our larboard. Offside, as Blackwood would have put it. I let go the rail, and went forward, picking up one of the long rakes on the deck.

This child—a boy, I thought, maybe eleven or twelve years old— drifted face-up in the cut, but the face was wrong. The eyes, the mouth, were smudges, the whole head indistinct; likewise, the drab clothes were vague, as if seen through muslin.

I dipped the rake, but already knew what would happen—the curved tines passed through the apparition without resistance.

Worse for the mood of *Heron*'s crew, I was not the only one who could see that there were more such dark blurs, slipping out from under the ice before us...

"Steady!" I snapped, hearing alarmed mutterings and curses behind me. "There's n-n-no harm in them."

The horses had been stopped; *Heron* was barely moving. The mist had thinned, but I could see dark, heavy clouds gathering. More snow. For a brief moment every living eye was on me—the army man, stiff, expressionless in his wet uniform. These are the times I hate, the times I use. Depressing, how men will follow a uniform into peril, however stupid or venal the wearer.

"Double wages." I stared round at the worried faces. "We b-b-break another hundred yards or so, to see whatever has been laid out for us to see. D-d-double wages for today."

I had no authority for this, but could not see the pale, worried Edgerton denying me.

"I'll be on the rail with you," I reminded them. "B-b-but they'll not give me a brass farthing more for it. Pity the poor bloody soldier."

Alma Blackwood responded with a snort of amusement, which broke the mood. "Hunnert yards, aye. I'm game."

"Alma—" Her husband fingered the tiller, hesitant. She was shaming them, as she had done when she boarded the barge.

I clapped my gloved hands together. "Settled, then. Whatever these are—lost souls or echoes—they can't hurt us."

Which may have been wishful thinking, but suited the moment.

"Echoes?" said the big woman. "Echoes of what?"

"People who've d-d-drowned here over the years?" I had no idea, in truth. "Memories?"

The next man along shivered, and I decided it was best not to explore the matter further at that time.

"Mr. Blackwood?"

"Aye—I s'ppose."

He called out to those who were leading the horses, cursed the lengthsmen for slacking in their task of dragging broken ice to the sides, and the barge began to move forward again. Onside, offside, and into the next slab with a crunch, and a crack like a rifle being fired. Fault-lines shot across the surface, and Heron made another few yards, sheet-ice breaking into manageable chunks for the rakes.

"Cut's nobbut two year old," said Mrs. Blackwood as we lurched to starboard with the rest. "Meks no sense there'd be s'many drowned, like."

"We'll see."

It was not a sight that inspired enthusiasm in me, I admit. As the ice shattered, those dim forms floated towards us with a painful slowness, and no one could be immune to their presence. They did at first seem like rags and water-weeds from a distance, but as we closed, they could only be visions of people. Boys, perhaps also girls, women in long skirts and shawls, a man in working clothes—but the hands and faces indistinct, blurred. I knew there was no point in using the rake again, or seeking any physical contact-and what sensitivity has been forced on me is useless without touch.

"D-d-do any of you," I said, in a loud clear voice, "Know these people? Can you tell me anything about who they might be?"

The crew peered into the water with reluctance.

"Them's the dead." A thin, red-haired man on the other side of the rail crossed himself with his free hand. "The dead, come t'warn us of oor sins."

"Bloody funny way o' doin' it," said Mrs. Blackwood. I was warming to her. She had a broad face, a broad accent and a bluntness which I could appreciate.

My gaze was on the water; as the apparitions passed *Heron*, I saw that they grew more tenuous, as if dissolving, until nothing could be seen of them.

Snow had begun to fall, and given the mood of those around me, I could see little point in continuing. I understood that Cochrane's Mill was only three miles off, where the cut curved around a spur of scree-marred hill.

Might as well have been fifty miles.

"Have the team unhitched, Blackwood, there's a g-g-good chap. I think we're done for today."

There was no way to turn *Heron* around at this spot, so she was tied up. Men and horses made their way back, the men moody and quiet, the horses content enough that they would soon be stabled, and at their feed.

When we reached Lydgate Stop House, Edgerton came out, and

saw plain enough how people were going into huddles, making occasional gestures towards me.

"It happened...again?" He brushed snow from his cheek.

"Worse this t-t-time." I followed him into the office and set myself to steam by the fire. It was easy enough to give him a summary of the day's progress.

"Will they go out tomorrow?"

"With me, p-p-possibly. But I've something to do, first. I need a riding horse, and a local guide. Where does Alma B-b-blackwood work, normally?"

"She oversees some of the looms at Cochrane's Mill. Her husband knows the area, though..."

"Better that it's her."

He huffed and sighed, but made arrangements.

By four in the afternoon, with constant light snow, I was back on the tow-path, a skittish mare under me and Alma Blackwood striding alongside. She didn't ride, laughed at the idea.

"Ah walk God's earth, like it were meant. They call this God's Own Country, did tha know, Lieutenant Blake? Meant for hard women, frit of nowt."

"My name's Redvers. You m-m-might as well use it."

"Alma."

"So what are the men saying?" I edged the mare around an icicle-tipped hawthorn.

"Nowt and summat. 'Bad fortune for all', and 'Needs t'vicar and his book-larnin',' that sort o' talk. They're not sure, but seein' tha work t'boat fair took them. None o' the bosses would ha' done that."

We came to the section where *Heron* was moored, lonely by the bank. Faint ripples on the open water; a cold gleam to the ice. None of the earlier phantoms remained, but there was yet another dark figure in the water, drifting slowly as before. I dismounted.

"Are you game to look, Alma?"

She spat out chewing tobacco, and followed me to the edge,

which put us no more than five feet from the 'apparition'. It was clearly female—and the face was more distinct this time. A high forehead, thick eyebrows...I fancied the eyes were closed, but that was harder to discern. Alma sucked in a breath.

"Hettie Cowton, ah'd swear. See, she's gotten that red shawl on."

"When d-d-did she die?"

"She nivver did. Ah saw her this morn, fit as anything, afore I came down. On her way to t'mill. Works t'looms, she does. Sithee, cut's froze over solid to Cochrane's, so how'd she get down 'ere? Meks no sense."

It did not.

"A red shawl, a white flower. Your husband saw the f-f-first..."

"A white rose, he were thinking, as he said to me. Tha knows, like t'flower o'Yorkshire." She turned from the water. "Lieutenant...Redvers, then. Queer sort o' name. It dunt seem like tha's ower fussed by this. Tha's seen ghosts and t'like afore?"

We regarded each other, whilst soft flakes gathered on our shoulders. Two different worlds, tight-wrapped in the cold—the mill woman, and the man who fed the hangman.

"I've seen worse. It's what they p-p-pay me for."

She nodded.

"Our Uncle Alf 'ad a stammer, when 'e went down the mines."

"Did he get over it?"

"Not before t'shaft collapsed and took 'is 'ead off. Us didn't notice it s'much after that." She laughed, and trudge on towards the mill.

I wondered if she'd ever considered joining the army. We could have used men like her.

WATER MADE INDUSTRY. Alma explained it as we rounded the scree and came in sight of Cochrane's Mill. Two small reservoirs fed the mill, which thrived on steam from its own boilers, and the flow, polluted with washings from the textile sheds, went into a basin directly by the mill. The basin, now iced-up, then fed the cut which ran to the Rochdale Canal.

There isn't much to tell you about the mill. A massive four story building, facing the water as I said, and an engine house to the back and centre, like the servants' wing of a mansion, with a two hundred and fifty foot chimney rearing above all. Pale brick, with the occasional terracotta moulding, set against gloomy hillsides which harboured rows of small cottages. It was a dour land, making dour folk.

"Come wi' me."

Alma took me through broad, open gates to one side, and into the behemoth. I followed her her up flights of steep stone steps to the second floor, where mechanical looms clacked across the length of the floor, making the most abominable noise. Ropes, pulleys, and beams; the smell of sweat and chemicals.

"There!" she said, pointing to a loom-worker with a distinctive crimson shawl around her shoulders. "That's Hettie Cowton."

The woman at the loom turned her head for a moment, and yes, the likeness was unmistakable, the clothes identical. We had seen the semblance of a living woman drifting as if dead in the icy waters of the cut, where she could not be.

"How do, Alma." A man in a worn, over-tight suit sauntered over. "Thought you were down at Lydgate Stop House."

"Ah'm to help this gentleman, the maisters say."

"Lieutenant Blake, N-n-north Surreys," I said. "Whitehall send me about the hold-ups with the serge."

He shook my hand. "Bert Gault, foreman for Cochrane's. Aye, it's a rum do. Hear some lass or summat drowned in the cut, spooked the canal men."

"Something like that." I imagined that this afternoon's news would spread like wildfire once the men around the Stop House went back to their homes.

"How's it going with the cut, sir?" asked Gault.

"Can't say, as yet. Three miles still frozen. It'll be p-p-pack mules between here and clear water, at this rate."

He took this idea more seriously than I'd expected.

"Might be done, with carts and suchlike. I'll tell the bosses, if needs must. But you're here, so must want summat."

"I n-n-need the feel of the place."

He frowned. "Alma can show you round, as good as any, I suppose."

"Much appreciated."

In truth, I didn't want a tour as such. I wanted to find a girl with a white rose, or a white silk flower, that sort of thing, pinned to her blouse or jacket. Was it possible that all the drowned were from this mill?

Alma knew everyone, be it for the time of day, for a word about 'snap' as they called the food they took at breaks, or for news of Low Hawnsey Cut. She said little about the latter. We walked the weaving and finishing floors, watched carders at their work on the raw wool; we edged away as boys ran past, carrying huge bobbins. The place was an ants' nest built of Northern brick.

"Hang on." We were back by the looms, and through the dusty air I saw a flash of white. I almost ran, skidding up to a young woman at a loom, much to her dismay. I would have put her at seventeen or eighteen years of age, and she wore a grubby white silk rose pinned to her lapel.

"Mister, I've dun nowt—"

"And there's nowt to worry on," said Alma, huffing up behind me. "Meggy, this 'ere's a gentleman wi' t'canals."

"I don't mean what I says," the girl whimpered. "I'm not reet, Alma. You know that."

My guide caught Gault's attention, mimed taking this girl from her place; the foreman looked to me, and nodded.

We walked to the stairwell, the three of us, and I knew there was something wrong. Meggy Whoever-she-was was frightened. Alma leaned close to me.

"She's allus been slow, mebbe a bit touched. There's no 'arm in 'er, though." In a louder voice, she said: "Tha must tell Mr. Blake 'ere whatever is botherin' thee."

Soft brown eyes shifted in my direction, then to the older woman.

"I been hearing it, Alma, these last couple of days. It's so loud, like God's shouting at me. Like thunder, it is, in me head. I tells them 'Summat bad's coming,' but they laughs at me. 'Meggy Gaines, daft as our dog.' They won't listen..."

She was weeping; I hauled out a handkerchief and gave it to her.

"Like thunder?"

Meggy nodded, pulling on a length of thin blonde hair. I took her gently by one hand.

"This feeling you have—when d-d-did it start?"

"Three, four days ago, sir. But it's me—I'm touched, like they say. Allus getting 'feelings', I am. Me mam hits me for it."

I tried to smile in what I hoped was a considerate manner. "Maybe I'll have a word with your mother about that, Meggy."

"Go on, lass, back to tha place," said Alma. "Not so long 'til knockin' off time."

Thunder.

What was thunder? A storm coming? I am not, thank some pitiless God, a psychic, but I felt uncomfortable, ill at ease.

"Is it n-n-nonsense, what the girl says? About 'feelings'?"

The tall woman paused, frowned. "Meggy were reet about Young Alf losin' a leg in t'ropes, last summer, like. She said as he'd not be walkin' again, and that were t'day afore it 'appened. But she says all sorts..."

I was painfully aware that most so-called 'sensitives' relied on keen observation, co-incidence, and clever half-truths. And yet...

"Has anything changed in the last few days, Alma? Here at the mill, I mean. Or did anything happen, three or four days ago, before *Heron* first went out?"

She thought hard, then called Bert Gault over and asked him

the same question. He had to work it over as well, chewing on an unlit pipe.

"Nowt much, sir. We've had a bit of trouble, like, with the looms and the carding machines—first they run too fast, then too slow. I telled the bosses as we should have engineers out, in case the boiler, or the piston fittings—"

"Take me there. Now."

Too surprised at my tone to argue, they led me down again, and into the engine house attached to the main mill. The noise was worse than elsewhere, the hiss and clatter of great pistons; sharp bursts of steam and men yelling at each other.

"It's a triple-expansion engine, you see—" Gault began, but I pushed him aside. Pulling the leather glove from my left hand. I pressed my bare palm to the nearest wall, and listened.

The inanimate can be sullen, unwilling to share its slow existence, but I waited, seeking some connection. My fingertips stroked the coarse surface of the bricks; Gault and Alma Blackwood watched me, perhaps just as they watched Meggy Gaines when she had 'feelings', and then I found it. Cochrane's Mill spoke to me.

You understand that objects, places, have no voice, not as such. What I hear is what they have heard, felt, seen—and this building spoke of rushed construction and poor foundations, which it might have withstood. Worse, it spoke of a flaw in its beating heart, deep in the engine house. A flaw that was worsening, a fatal wound.

The building itself expected thunder, and destruction, soon...

"Clear the mill!" I yelled at Gault and Alma.

The foreman stared at me as if I were mad. "I can't—"

My revolver slid easily from its holster, used to the work. I didn't aim at anyone, but I showed it plainly for any who were watching the scene.

"For God's sake, clear the mill! Get them all out!" I locked my gaze on Alma Blackwood, and she did not disappoint me.

"The whistles, Bert," she said, urgent. "The fire whistles."

He gaped, but then ran to the wall, where a heavy iron handle protruded from a cabinet. He pulled down hard, and somewhere outside a steam whistle shrieked, loud enough to be heard over the engine noise. Others sounded off within seconds, and I caught the thin shrill of something akin to policemen's whistles on the floors above.

A system—at least they had a system.

My left hand was still pressed against the wall, and I could hear it coming, pain which lanced through brick and mortar, pain which would twist an iron beam like a child's liquorice stick.

I made for the nearest way out, shouting at anyone I met to get as far away as possible.

A panicked, puzzled crowd of workers jostled down the stairwells, out into the main yard, and I urged them further away, helped by Alma.

"What is it?" she grunted, pushing confused boys aside and out of the gates. "What's 'appenin'?"

"You'll know soon enough." I saw stragglers still coming out the mill, and wondered if I could be wrong—but then I heard the thunder.

The first roll of it was apparently the sound of the boiler exploding; it felt as if the hills shook, but that was probably an echo of the blast. We ran, all of us—I grabbed a dazed girl by her waist and carried her bodily away from the mill yard; children shrieked and had to be made to hurry…

The ground definitely moved only a moment after that, for whatever carnage there had been in the engine room, it must have torn at the roots of the great chimney.

Two hundred and fifty foot of brick, cast iron and terracotta, the chimney trembled, swayed—and fell. Not lengthways but down, the entire mass collapsing in stages into the mill's main body, shearing through the upper floors. A cloud of dust and debris filled the air for a moment, obscuring our view…

"Dear Jesus!" gasped a man behind me.

Slowly, ever so slowly, the entire south face of the mill broke away, sliding into the frozen basin. I saw a boy scrabble at a wooden beam, screaming—and saw him fall, still screaming, into waters which churned with masonry and ice...

IN THE QUIET STUDY, Blake lit a cigarette.

"There were two hundred and n-n-ninety three survivors," he said, "And seventeen people crushed, killed instantly—or missing, presumed d-d-dead. Two men, eleven women, and four children."

"Dear God," said Dodgson.

"Meggy Gaines was amongst the dead; I found her b-b-body myself, under a shattered loom frame."

"A damned bad business. So...the figures in the water..."

"Matched the seventeen who died, as far as I could establish afterwards. We searched the rubble as best we could, but the main building was at that time too dangerous to venture in far. Most of those killed had fallen into the basin with the collapse of the mill's upper floors—they're still hauling d-d-debris from the water.

"I stayed at Lydgate Stop House two more days, and took *Heron* out again; we opened the cut all the way, so that emergency supplies could be run directly to the communities around what was left of Cochrane's."

The study fell silent, apart from the rattle of rain against the window; Dodgson rose and went to lean on a bookcase, his half-empty glass in his hand.

"You're an odd fellow, Blake."

"Am I?"

"For heaven's sake, had you not been there, it would have been a tragedy of terrible proportions. Your actions probably saved over two hundred people."

Blake shrugged. "M-m-makes up for some of those I've killed, I suppose. You might as well give the credit to Mrs. B-B-Blackwood, who took it all in her stride, and made sure the alarm was sounded."

Miss Jessop shifted in her chair. "You mentioned a red shawl on one of the figures in the water. I presume Hettie Cowton was among those who were lost."

"She was."

"A procession of the dead to come. Ghosts of the living, headed by your poor Meggy Gaines with her white rose, the first apparition they met. I wonder, did she herself form those images, without understanding what they meant? Or was some other force at play?"

"D-d-did her no good, either way" said Blake with a sour look. "P-p-perhaps it was simply what had to be."

Thunder sounded outside, and Redvers Blake stared at the curtains, without seeing them.

"Henry, I'll t-take a dash more of that b-b-brandy, I think," he said. "But forget the soda, this time, old chap."

THE WRECK OF THE CHARLIE SOL

JIM BEARD

"Well, let's get on with it, then."

Commander Lawrence looked at his lit cigar and placed it back to his lips drawing another drag. Savoring its flavor he glanced up at his subordinate standing at the window gazing out at London's twinkling lights.

"Clouds coming in there, sir," announced Lieutenant Lynns with a jut of his narrow chin. "Rain looks like."

Lawrence stood up from his comfortable chair and ground his cigar out in the tray. "When *doesn't* it look like rain, eh?" He picked his uniform coat off the hook by the door and slid one arm and then the other into it. "Lynns, chop-chop. Let's get to it."

"Aye, sir."

As the two men marched down the corridor after exiting the room, Lawrence heaved a sigh. "Should have been done long ago, back when we first started. Why the devil did we wait?"

The lieutenant seemed to consider it, then shrugged. "Can't rightly say, Commander. Funny how it just got, well, *put off*, I guess."

"Well," said Lawrence, standing up a bit straighter and squaring his shoulders, "it's the last one and we can put this file to bed." He frowned as he recorked the brandy decanter next to him. "And then you and I are off on a new assignment."

They neared the end of the corridor and their destination. Lawrence let the lieutenant go ahead to open the door set in the wall there, and as he did he considered the younger officer. He was a good sort, a trustworthy, honor-bound man, but lacking in something...gumption? Perhaps. The commander wanted Lynns to speak up more, show a little more *initiative*, something to distinguish him from the last assistant he'd been assigned. There were some days he even wished the lieutenant would, oh, *argue* a bit with him about a detail or an entry for the file; anything, really.

A moot point now, the commander reflected as they went through and stepped out onto the skiff dock. *One last ship and we're done.*

Their pilot, a bored-looking midshipman, saluted as the approached and the two officers boarded the skiff quickly. It bobbed a bit as they stepped in and Lawrence took stock of the pilot and noted some hesitation in his demeanor when he'd indicated their destination. Normally, he'd have let it go, knowing the tiny skeleton staff of the drydock installation to be generally aimless in their duties, but something about the young man's attitude piqued his interest.

"We're not inconveniencing you today, are we, Midshipman?"

The pilot stiffened slightly and kept his eyes on the wheel as he swung the skiff around and pointed it toward the outer arms of the drydock facility. "No, sir, Commander. It's just that, well, the ship we're going to..."

"Belay that, Midshipman," Lynns cut in. "There's no call for that. This is the last one and we'll take as we have all of them." He glanced at Lawrence with a raised eyebrow. "This one has a bit of a *reputation* among the staff, sir."

The commander watched as great hulks of ships appeared out of the darkness and then disappeared again as the skiff passed, its lights lingering on each only for a moment. The darkness all around them possessed a kind of oppressive weight, he mused; not even the twinkling stars held their usual charm for him. In fact, every aspect of the day felt full of portent and seemed to be conspiring to cast a shadow over the last inspection.

War, he thought. War had darkened everything over the past year as he and the lieutenant worked through their orders, making an otherwise important task for their superiors a thankless miasma of rote and regulations. The commander tried to keep feelings of duty and dedication to the cause intact within him each and every day, telling himself the work was not only necessary but could help tip the balance in his navy's favor. Alas, instead he and Lynns struggled with completing the mission—and neither one of them could put a finger on exactly why. And now this, a simple midshipman pilot with superstition over a blasted old wreck...

"Ridiculous," he murmured. Then louder: "One more and it's done. In and out, *reputation* be damned."

They skirted around a pair of corvettes they'd inspected a month or so before, and a small landing duck that was marked for scuttling. When the pilot sketched an overly wide swing-around across the bow of an aging destroyer, Lawrence frowned and made a mental note have a talk with the young man about dramatizing what was only to be a regulation ride to their destination.

Ahead, in the darkness, he could just make out the lines of the ship. The last ship.

"Pull up some more lights, Midshipman," he ordered. "I want to get as good a look at her as possible as we make the outer inspection."

The pilot moved about as he switched on large lights that shone out from the skiff and illuminated the hull of the ancient, massive heavy frigate. Lawrence felt like the ship absorbed the light somehow, and he actually brought his hand up to his eyes to rub at them, but realized how foolish the gesture was. Instead he focused his gaze on the great vessel and wondered again why they'd left it to the end of their mandated mission.

"All right, Lynns," he said, turning his head slightly to look at the lieutenant. "By the numbers. Nothing different than we've done a hundred times already. Give me the details."

The skiff slid along past the frigate, its lights sweeping across its side, highlighting features, but not defining the ship all together. The passengers saw how dark its hull was and recalled that in its prime the navy held to different standards than those of the modern fleet.

Lynns voice took up a drone of statistics. "The *Charles L. Solway*, decommissioned fifty-one years ago, six-hundred meters stem to stern, thirty-eight gun emplacements, total of twelve decks not counting the bridge half-deck, maximum crew allotment of two-hundred twenty."

"How old?" the commander asked.

The lieutenant pursed his lips when he looked up and found the answer. "One-hundred eight."

"Good Lord," Lawrence sighed. "Two—no, *three* wars ago."

Lynns nodded as he looked over his information. "She was decommissioned after the Battle of Four Oaks. Took some heavy fire and was deemed too damaged to be recommissioned or salvaged."

The commander's eyes ran over the section of hull facing them. That didn't seem right to him; overall the frigate appeared intact, just very, very old. It reminded him somewhat of an ancient mansion, its lines speaking to another era of shipbuilding, one that—

Movement. In one of the frigate's lower ports—a figure.

"There," said Lawrence, pointing. "Someone's in there!"

The lieutenant was at his side in an instant, his eyes darting back and forth between the ship and his data. He shook his head. "W—with respect, sir, there shouldn't be anybody on her. She's been locked up tight for, hold it...fifty years or more."

"Welcome to the *Charlie Sol*," the midshipman muttered to himself. The commander whipped his head around to skewer the man with a sharp look.

"What's *that* supposed to mean, mister?" He glanced back over his shoulder; the port in question was empty. No figure was evident. He frowned even deeper and swung his attention back to the pilot. "Take us 'round her to the other side—Lynns, structural integrity?"

The lieutenant nodded, his eyes still raking over the ship's hull, missing nothing. If he questioned his superior's sighting of a person on the frigate, he showed no signs of it. "I'd say all good, sir. For being decommissioned due to battle fatigue or damage, even, she looks intact."

The skiff came around the stern and began to make its way down the length of the ship, its lights still playing along the metal, creating odd shadows that danced in and out of the onlookers' vision. It dwarfed the drydock around it, a beached whale lying alongside an old wooden ladder.

"There's the lock," Lawrence indicated with a jab of his index finger. He looked at Lynns. "All right, then. Suit up and let's go over."

Both men glanced only casually at the planet London spinning below them as they tethered across the infinite chasm between the skiff and the *Charlie Sol*. At the airlock, the commander was slightly bemused when Lynns was forced to cycle the portal manually, something he hadn't witnessed in many years. Once open, a great, yawning mouth of utter darkness faced them, and not terribly inviting.

Inside the massive vessel, Lynns shut the airlock door behind them. As the last bit of starlight winked out, Lawrence looked around at the absolute darkness of the inner chamber, the only illumination from the lieutenant's small datapod and that seemingly struggling to not be absorbed by the inky black surroundings.

"Power?" asked Lawrence. Something about the darkness was

unnerving him. For a moment all he heard in his helmet comm was his companion's breathing, but the man finally spoke up.

"None, and I've put the code in three times."

"All right, then," Lawrence replied with a sigh. "Helmet lamps, but mind the usage. Let's run down the checklist and expedite this thing. Interior structural integrity, AI assessment, the works." He pressed a stud on his glove and lights on either side of his faceplate sprang into being, sending out two cones of illumination onto the wall across from him. As it happened, a door appeared in the light.

They exited the airlock into a broad corridor running to their right and left. Even with both men's' lamps on, the shadows persisted. Lawrence directed the lieutenant to take the right while he took the left and to report any anomalies as he went along. They departed with nods to each other and made their way down the corridor, their magnetic boots making for the usual slow progress in the zero gravity.

The commander noted very little debris floating around him as he walked the length of the corridor, simply little bits of this and that, most likely from the rooms that flanked him. Some doors stood open while others were still shut with no rhyme or reason. He was also pleased to see there were no signs of stress on the bulkheads or ceiling; perhaps the ship *would* be a good candidate for refurbishing and reentry into active service.

"Lynns, did you say something?" He automatically raised a gloved hand to tap at his helmet near his left ear, a compulsion from his early navy days he'd never been able to conquer. His helmet, while not exactly new, was for the most part state-of-the-art and its comm shouldn't need to be jostled to work properly.

The lieutenant's voice issued from Lawrence's comm almost immediately. "No, sir. But...funny you should ask, because I'm hearing something."

The commander controlled his breathing and adjusted his speaker to include extra-suit sounds. Listening intently, he heard nothing at first, then...tapping. Metal on metal.

"Something's just loose somewhere," he said, though he realized he didn't say it very confidently. "Surprised at you, Lieutenant. How many times have we—"

"Sir, listen," Lynns cut in. "It's not sporadic. It's a steady rhythm."

Lawrence frowned. "All right, yes it is. Go ahead and figure out where it's coming from, then."

He waited for a reply. Ahead of him, the darkness appeared to be weakening the beams from his lights, absorbing their illumination and moving toward him. "Lynns?" he asked, impatience lacing his voice.

"Engine room, sir. I *believe* it is, at least. Should be a turn in the corridor directly ahead of you at twenty feet or so. I'll meet you there shortly."

Lawrence wasted no time moving on. The assessment was already becoming tedious and lengthy; he could just see it growing problems at every turn. Up ahead a larger door than what he'd passed behind him loomed out of the dark. Stopping before it, he informed the lieutenant he'd reached the engine room and was heading in. The door had to be opened manually.

Darkness beyond, but that didn't surprise him. He trained his lights on banks of control panels that looked like a row of grey tombstones of old, and above them the towering engine cylinders themselves, silent sentinels dominating the room with their size and presence, albeit powerless. Lawrence could see they were intact, though, and nodded to himself with a grim smile. *At least that's something,* he thought. At the very least the ship could most likely—

He felt it in his stomach first, then in his head. It was always that way with him with the abrupt entrance of an atmosphere and gravity. The engine room remained cloaked in deep, dark shadows, but somehow something had changed without any evidence of power to the ship that he could see.

Something behind him. He hadn't heard or felt the door

open...*turn around you idiot*, he willed himself, but found the action impossible. Why? He felt his face flush as anger surged into his veins. Just turn around!

A figure stood before him, suited, but with no helmet, its face obscured by the dark though the commander's helmet beams were nearly right on it.

"Lynns? What did you do? How the hell did you get power back on?"

The lieutenant glanced nervously at his datapod. "Not me, sir," he protested. "I felt it same as you—I can't explain it."

Lawrence took a step toward him. "And why in God's name do you have your helmet off?"

The younger man offered a shy smile. "Air, sir. There's *air*. Stale, but it's there."

The commander wanted to remonstrate him on many, many points of flagrant disregard for rules, protocol, a whole host of things, but Lynns face suddenly came over all confused and the abrupt change stopped him in his tracks. "What is it, Lieutenant?"

Lynns raised one hand in a feeble gesture resembling pointing. "Commander," he sputtered, "behind you..."

Wheeling around, Lawrence spied a light blinking on a control panel across the room, one small rhythmic burst in the inky darkness, drawing his eye like a beacon.

"How—how," he sputtered, looking back and forth between it and Lynns. "You said there's no power..."

Amazingly, the lieutenant stepped past him and over to the panel. His hand reached out to hover over the light, but did not touch it. If the commander was closer, he might have seen the man's hand shake a bit as it hung there over the blinking.

"It's a *comm*, sir."

Lawrence was on him in a flash, pushing him aside and studying the panel himself. He did not reach out to cover the light with his hand, but inwardly he struggled with an urge to open the channel. "Someone's playing a game," he said finally, his voice resolute. "The midshipman—our pilot. Must be." He looked back at Lynns. "Get him on your own comm, ask him what the hell he thinks he's doing."

Within seconds the lieutenant looked up at his superior and admitted defeat. He couldn't raise the skiff at all.

The commander twisted around and stabbed at the blinking comm light. At first, when the channel was opened, the line was dead-silent. Then, quietly, as if issuing up from some unfathomable pit, a voice came forth. The two men both bent over the panel, listening. Lawrence even removed his helmet when he thought it would help. He shook his head with confusion; it made no sense whatsoever. The voice grew in intensity, but was undecipherable, a scratchy warbling that sounded human, yet also like nothing the officers had heard before.

And then another voice joined it. And another, and another.

Lawrence jabbed at the comm control angrily. The light stayed on, as well as the voices, a low cacophony of overlapping sounds from some strange nether world. They grew plaintive in tone, then desperate, as if crying out in great distress, yet perhaps from many different places.

"It must be a playback of some kind," Lynns suggested. "I wonder if—"

The commander cut him off by slamming his fist down hard on the panel. "You're not looking at the bigger picture,' he seethed. "Forget that it might be a—a playback—where is the power coming from?"

Lynns' brow furrowed. He listened intently to the voices and his eyes grew wider as his face blanched.

"Sir, I—I think they're—they're saying your name."

The dismissal came easily enough to the commander's lips. "You're imagining things, Lieutenant. Let's move on. Too much to do."

He straightened up again and turned to march toward the door. Back in the corridor, he waited for Lynns to catch up before speaking. "We need to find the AI. Find it and we'll find the source of these anomalies. What deck is it on?"

The lieutenant scrolled through files on his datapod until nodding at the answer. "Three decks up, sir—oh. And, sir? This is very interesting. I just came across a file I hadn't seen before. It says that we..." He looked up with disbelief in his eyes. "...we are not the first assessment team on the *Charles L. Solway*, as I thought. There was one twenty-five years ago. They listed the ship as 'not able to be refurbished.'"

Lawrence chewed on that for a moment, then stalked down the corridor looking for a ladderwell, his mind working furiously.

It had said his name. His. Name.

AS THE COMMANDER opened the hatch to a ladder, he thought he heard something in the shaft. Quickly sticking his head in, he trained his lights up the ladder into the darkness. Just as the illumination fell upon the hatchway up one level, it caught the edge of what looked like the bottom of a boot just stepping off a rung and disappearing through the opening.

"Blast it!" he swore. "There's somebody up there! There *is* someone on this ship!"

Not waiting for his subordinate he shoved himself through the hatchway and grabbed hold of the ladder to begin to pull himself up it. It had been years since he'd used a ladder to go from one deck to another on a ship, but he wasn't about to let a trespasser get the best of him. Hand over hand, foot over foot, he ascended, his head tilted up and lights on the opening he saw the figure go through. Below him the lieutenant was shouting to him about the ship's crew lists, about a name...

Have to catch him, he thought to himself. *What would make anyone think they have the right to be on this ship?*

Someone had said his name.

"Stop!" he bellowed as he neared the next deck up. "That's an order! Stop right now!"

When Lawrence stepped through the hatchway himself, he found only an empty corridor and still more inky, deep shadows. Behind him, he heard Lynns ask if he could see the person as the lieutenant emerged from the ladderwell out of breath and clutching his datapod.

The commander ignored him and stalked off down the corridor, looking left and right for signs of the intruder. Almost immediately a heady feeling of claustrophobia assailed him, just as if the walls of the ship suddenly lurched forth to close in around him through the prevailing darkness. He gagged, his stomach heaving to the point of him nearly vomiting, but he held it down and reached out to steady himself against the corridor's wall. All around him the shadows congealed, a living mass attempting to infiltrate his suit, his skin, his brain. Something touched the side of his head and he flinched violently; to his surprise it seemed to be his own hand, perhaps verifying his skull was still intact and not invested with ropy tendrils of darkness.

"Are you all right, Commander? I—I want to show you something strange I found here on my—"

Lawrence waved Lynns off and found his footing again to tromp back down the hallway, determined to catch the fleeting figure and beat a few answers out of him. In this way, the commander's anger fueled his renewed forward motion.

Up ahead—or was it somewhere off to one side?—the sound of footfalls reached the men's ears, a definitive noise that produced visions of their quarry. Lawrence increased his pace, now with both arms out in front of him as he progressed and the weak beams of his suit lamps only barely defining his hands in the dark.

Within minutes they'd traced the footfalls to an open doorway. Peering inside, squinting to make out any details of what lay beyond the portal, they saw it was crew's quarters.

"What's that hanging there?" Lawrence asked. He pointed to

something dangling apparently from the room's ceiling and stretched out in uneven loops from one wall to its opposite number. Parts of it sparkled when his light touched upon it.

It was a *decoration* of some sort, he thought. A whiff of a scent came to his nostrils. Perfume? A hand, soft and gentle, caressed his cheek, his neck...

"Look here, sir," said Lynns, standing in front of a small mirror that hung on the wall over a sink. Written in a cheerful hand across the glass were the words "Merry Christmas!"

"Christmas?" The commander's voice came out a combination of strained and surprised. "When did you say she was decommissioned, Lynns?"

The lieutenant seemed mesmerized by the decorations as he turned his head to look them over, his own lights playing across their aged glitz and sparkle. He stopped on the ruin of what was most likely a small, artificial tree drooping over itself in a corner by the bed. "Fifty-one, sir. Battle of Four Oaks..."

"Which," continued Lawrence, "if I remember my navy history, was just before the celebration of Christmas was no longer allowed in the fleet. Something about it interfering in the carrying out of sailors' duties."

He turned in place, taking in the symbols of the ancient holiday, feeling nothing for it himself. The decorations sat and hung there lifelessly, hollow reminders of a time when command was lax, his opinion, in discipline among the crew.

"Well, Lieutenant, we've wasted enough time here gazing at the past. Back to it. I'm certain that somehow the AI is still active and is..."

Lawrence realized then he was quite alone in the room and talking to himself.

A queer sort of panic clutched at him, drying his throat and allowing him only a raspy rattle from deep in his throat. Lynns' name would simply not come out. To make matters worse, it was abruptly very, very cold in the room, unlike the moderate temperature that had existed throughout the areas of the ship the two men had traveled through to that point.

His name. They said his name.

The commander summoned his courage—a strange situation for him after a not-brief navy career—and walked toward the open door of the quarters, despite it barely being discernable from the rest of the Stygian gloom all around him. With each step his suit lights stuttered and his heart took up the same unnatural rhythm.

Stop it, stop it, he commanded himself. *Find Lynns, complete the work, leave. That's all you have to do.*

Another voice in his head, one he couldn't recognize, followed that with *If only it were that easy.*

He moved out into the corridor and stood there for several minutes calling out the lieutenant's name and then trying different channels on his suit comm. Disgusted, he took a few steps into the shadows though he had little idea of where he was headed.

Why did he rely so much on Lynns? The thought confronted him as he attempted to sort through and organize his brain for the task ahead. The man was competent enough and as a team they'd searched through and assessed a few hundred ships, hadn't they? But, as he mused earlier, Lynns lacked vision and initiative—but here he had disappeared, literally into thin air. Why hadn't he himself been more involved in the data? Why did he leave it to his subordinate? He was in the middle of an unknown ship from an era he wasn't familiar with and...

Someone walked alongside of him; he could feel the distinct presence of—a man? A fellow crewmember? Then were more all about him, walking and running past him, unseen yet there, all on their way to destinations that were important to them, part of their own tasks, their own missions. The commander considered turning his head to look at them, but decided there was no point to it since they weren't actually there.

Thoughts assailed him, ones strange to him, a veteran of so many years in the service. What was he doing? Where was he? He was in the middle of an immense, dark, artificial construct, a metal and plastic ship floating tethered to an even larger metal and plastic framework floating in orbit around a planet moving through an airless vacuum across a galaxy. Somewhere in another part of that galaxy conflict raged, battles between other ships that tore them apart and wasted lives, lives of those that piloted the ships and had no real cause to clash save for what their superiors told them was there cause.

Stop it.

The clanking sound returned, off in the distance, both up and down and side to side. His collar lights flickered again, seemed to grow dimmer. The dark was a living thing, pressing at him and lowering the celling while raising the floor. Something touched him on the shoulder—how could he feel such a light touch through his suit?—and he turned to see what was indicated: another ladderwell.

No, that wasn't correct. It was a lift.

The commander entered the lift, though a part of his brain told him it was ridiculous since there was no power on the ship. In fact, he made up his mind there and then to put his helmet back on before the air evaporated and he was caught in the deadly vacuum. Centering himself in the lift he turned to look back at the motionless doors, finding them to be quite motion-ful and closing in front of his eyes. The lift activated and began to rise. Somehow he knew where he was going: To the bridge.

A light blinked on a console to one side, demanding his attention. It reminded him of Christmas lights. Had he ever celebrated Christmas? Perhaps as a boy; it was already forbidden when he joined the navy. The telltale kept calling to him, so he reached out to press it.

Voices came to him, even through his helmet, though not thru his comm. It was a few at first and then more, chaotic and urgent. Then, in the middle of the din a stronger voice broke through, this one with a commanding tone, demanding something. What? Lawrence could almost make out the words, but they flitted about on the edges of his comprehension. The superior voice called out again and again and the other voices answered it, in a way, faltering and unsure and desperate. Then, and the commander's heart sagged when he heard it, that voice began to falter itself as it also grew unsure and broken in its demands.

The last thing he heard—had he heard it, actually?—was his name. Someone was calling his name.

The strange performance continued to play out in his mind as the lift lurched to a halt and its doors slowly ground open with painful jerking motions.

He closed his eyes, not wanting to see the bridge. Why? He couldn't say, but someone nameless terror had taken root in his chest and risen to his brain while listening to the voices. Where was Lynns? Why did he care? He has the datapod; he would be able to sort this out. No, he left his post, ran off in fear, had primed himself for a court-martial. The commander was alone. He alone had to complete the inspection, and that duty demanded he view and assess the *Charles L. Solway*'s bridge.

The sound of the opening doors stopped and slowly, hesitatingly, he opened his eyes. All he saw before him was darkness. A tiny respite flowed over him, a small pad of comfort. He trained his lights ahead of him, wishing they could pierce the darkness. Thank God, he thought, the bridge was just one more dead area of the frigate. He'd look around and be on his way.

His lights weakly illuminated a bulkhead and with a spike of panic he saw he was only looking into a corner of the corridor outside the lift. It didn't open up directly onto the command deck of the *Solway* such as it did on modern ships of the line. Crewmembers exited the lift into an alcove and then stepped around to enter the—

Lawrence looked out at the planet London spinning slowly before him in all its blue-green glory.

HALF THE BRIDGE was simply gone, a huge rent in the very bulkhead of the ship taking the place of the opposite side from where he was standing. Through it, the planet could be viewed rotating serenely. All else in front of him was destruction.

And bodies. Crewmembers floated before his eyes, mainly dark silhouettes against the illuminated London. There was wreckage from the ship, too, pieces of decking, ceiling, consoles, and more floating amid the corpses, brushing up against each other in their directionless meanderings. Dim telltales blinked on and off here and there, fireflies among the tombstones.

The commander stared, his mouth open, unmoving. His eyes would not blink, as if they were frozen and unable to *not* see the tableau spread out across his vision. He felt something drip off his bottom lip and realized it was his own spittle. A body drifted close to him, its face just about in view as it moved languorously into the cone of light from his suit. Somebody somewhere was saying something.

Saying his name.

"No-no-no-no-no-no..."

It was his own voice. His hands flailed about trying to connect with something solid nearby, something he could push back from to propel him away from the scene. He willed his legs to move, to begin to take him back to where he started. It was like walking backward in quicksand. The floating corpse appeared to be reaching out to him, to anchor itself to something real and alive...its mouth moved, shaping words, or a name...

The back of his head bumped up against a wall—no, it was the doors to the lift. He jabbed his fingers at the activator panel, but it wouldn't open. Thankfully, he couldn't see the ruined bridge anymore, watch the bodies floating past as they rotated through the destruction. This enabled him to turn his head and look for—there! A ladderwell. He reached out to push aside the covering over the opening to it and somehow scrambled inside the shaft. His heart started again, or at least that's what it felt like.

Down, down. He ordered his body to go down the ladder and the ever-prevailing darkness closed around him as if his entire body was being fitted with a glove.

INCREDIBLY, the shadows pressing in on him helped him to think.

It has to be the A.I., he told himself as he lowered his body down the ladder. *Has to be. The hull is intact. We saw it ourselves. Lynns confirmed it.* That thought made him pause. What if...what if the lieutenant was behind it somehow? Some kind of a joke? That could be it. That most certainly could be it.

He clung to that idea and it comforted him to some small extent. What else made sense? As if in answer, the staccato clanking suddenly sounded again, and all around him. It grew in intensity until the metallic miasma nearly deafened him in the confines of the ladderwell—and the darkness.

A tap at his shoulder brought him to a halt in mid-step, mid-clutch. *What do you want from me?* he called out in his mind. *Why do you keep showing me things?* Then, *Stupid fool! You just told yourself it was the A.I.! Who are you talking to?*

But they had called out his name. His own name.

No almost completely distrusting his feeble lights, he reached out a hand to grope around at the wall of the ladderwell on the side he's been tapped. His gloved fingers connected with a doorway and then the edge of a door. Gradually, he slid it aside to make room for his egress, having absolutely no idea how many decks he descended into the bowels of the *Charlie Sol*.

Stepping out from the ladderwell, the commander tabbed his comm and called out to Lynns. No reply, of course. Looking left and right down the corridor he'd entered, he hesitated. *What are you doing?* he asked himself. *Waiting for a sign? Which way to go? You're a Navy commander with decades of experience on ships—make up your own mind!*

The metallic clanking was lessened in the corridor, but he determined it seemed to be stronger from the left, so he put one foot in front of the other and began to stride in its direction. With every step he felt more confident, more sure of his idea of it being a prank, something his fellow officers had put together and enlisted Lynns to carry it out. Yes, that's what was going on.

Has to be.

He repeated that to himself like a kind of mantra until he saw a light up ahead of him that wasn't his own. It drew him to it, creating a cooling effect on his fevered brow and he moved toward it, but not quickly. The commander felt he had time; weren't all the problems they'd been having because they'd rush into the task?

The ship—he understood it better now. Once again he thought of it as an old house, a huge "pile" as his great-grandfather used to say of big mansions on Old Earth. The *Charlie Sol* was just like that, a fine old relic of a different time that had a quality that was hard to define, something that spoke another language. That was it; the frigate had a language all its own. The commander felt it all around him. The immense size, the bulkheads, the hull, each deck...and the crew. They were part of it, too, like any good ship of the line. The crew was an integral part of the ship. One would be lost without the other.

A small smile came to his face as he walked down the corridor toward the light ahead. It wasn't a bright light, more like a soft summer glow in the sky as the sun set and the night took over—or was it like a sunrise?

A door up ahead stood open and he saw the light was coming from somewhere past it, in a room just beyond. He approached the door not with trepidation, but with the sure sense of understanding he enjoyed when an inspection was wrapping up and he knew just how to classify the ship in question.

The room was a mess. Literally just that: a crew's mess. Lawrence stepped inside it and looked around, good memories of similar rooms on ships he'd served on in his past coming to mind, comfortable areas where the crew could relax, have a meal, unwind.

The room was filled with crewmembers. Not one of them looked at the commander as he entered. The light came from the crew.

Some of them were running in slow motion, screaming. Some were on the floor, bleeding, and with limbs or parts of limbs missing. One of them had no head. A few of them looked to be trying to help the wounded, some of them crying. Still others cowered in corners or under tables, their faces wracked with fear or confusion or both. One crewmember stood on top of a table yelling, attempting to get everyone's attention while just below him two more did unspeakable things to each other. No one was looking at them or paying them any mind.

In-between all the chaos, sometimes ever overlapping it, crewmembers could be seen to be celebrating Christmas by handing gifts to others, unwrapping gifts, or perhaps simply eating a meal and chatting amiably with the person next to them at the table.

Was someone calling his name? Yes, yes—there it was!

Parts of the ceiling were caved in here and there. Some tables were crushed beneath debris, along with crewmembers. A huge Christmas tree was standing solitary and still in one far corner, a mute sentinel to the confusion and celebration. Small colored lights strung around it blinked on and off cheerfully.

Oh, God, why do they keep calling my name?

Commander Lawrence himself stood and stared silently, his mouth twisting on his face, his teeth on and off his bottom lip, chewing at it. His eyes were wide and wet. Down at his sides, his hands convulsed into fists and then opened again, his fingers working themselves into odd angles over and over.

Off to one side, not too far into the room, sat Lieutenant Lynns on the floor. He had his helmet off still, his legs sprawled out before him and his arms wrapped around his torso. He was bobbing back and forth at the waist, his eyes dead and staring ahead. The commander watched as a crewmember came into view right in front of him, just appeared there from nowhere with its face screaming in horror and pain merely an inch or two from the lieutenant's. Lynns' dead eyes looked right into those of the phantom's and together they screamed and screamed.

Lawrence walked over to him to see if he could help somehow.

ONE WEEK later the commander stood on the command deck of the Navy destroyer *Redolent* as it broke orbit from London and began to pick up speed to exit the system. Out its side bridge windows he could see the drydock facility quite clearly.

The destroyer's captain stepped up to Lawrence and noted his fixed gaze. "Not regretting it, Commander?"

Lawrence broke his stare and looked at the captain. "No, no; not at all. Task over, onto the next. You know how it is. A bit of this and a bit of that swirling around, that's all."

The officer nodded and smiled. He himself turned to look out at the drydock, now nearly empty of ships. The navy had been busy pulling one out after another to either be towed to a repair station or, in some cases, be destroyed.

"You see that one there?"

The captain glanced at Lawrence to see what he was on about. He followed the man's indication to a big, bulky shape tethered to a portion of the drydock; an old, old frigate. "Yes, I see it. Lord, quite an ancient one, hey?"

The commander nodded. "Do me a favor, will you? Blow it up."

"You're serious?" asked the officer, not knowing whether to smile or frown. "I mean, we're not exactly a demolition scow, but I suppose we could…"

The great ship sat there, proud-looking in a way, but if it had anything to say before its execution it was lost on Lawrence. A thought occurred to him just then and he stepped over to a nearby console and with a few pushes of keys on the computer began to cycle through data screens.

No. Nothing in the crew lists for the old ship. His name wasn't there. He hadn't even been born yet.

"Never mind," he said finally. "Don't bother." Turning away from the window he clapped a hand on the captain's shoulder and gave it a friendly pat before walking off.

"The *Charlie Sol*'s had quite enough war and destruction to suit it, I figure," he said over his shoulder. "For a long, long while."

THE DOLLMAKER

JAMES A. MOORE AND CHARLES R. RUTLEDGE

I

"Trust me, Henry," Charles Dickens said as he alighted from his cab at Dorset Square, "I've seen every trick these spiritualists use and this performance won't be any different."

"I'm sure you're right, Charles," Henry North said. He had been saying similar things for most of the cab ride from Dickens' house in Tavistock Square. Dickens seemed to have a inexhaustible supply of anecdotes about fraudulent mediums. Still, since the great man was the owner and editor at Household Words, the magazine for which Henry was a sub editor, Henry thought it best to agree with his employer.

"Why the stories I could tell you of fishing rods and sheets sculpted with flour," Dickens went on. "Of spirit cabinets and spinning tables."

Henry said, "From what I understand, this medium doesn't use any props of that sort."

"We shall see," said Dickens. "We shall see."

They had reached their destination, a tall house among a row of tall houses facing the square. Henry stepped up and knocked on the front door. The panel swung inward, revealing a young woman in a dark lavender dress. She was fine boned, with dark hair and wide eyes of an unusual shade of green. Henry was suddenly aware that he was staring.

"Good evening," Henry said at last. "I'm Henry North and this is Mr. Charles Dickens."

The woman smiled. "Of course, Mr. North. So very pleased to meet you. And Mr. Dickens needs no introduction. Please come in, gentlemen. Now that you're here, we may begin. I am Charlotte Kenworth."

Henry nodded, and stepped into the foyer with Dickens close behind. He was surprised that a lady of such obvious means would answer her own door.

As if reading Henry's thoughts, Charlotte said, "I hope you will forgive me the rather unconventional greeting, gentlemen. I send my servants away when I am giving a sitting. It's the only way I can keep a staff."

"Completely understandable," said Dickens. "I suppose they find the rapping on tables to be unsettling."

Charlotte laughed and Henry felt a tug at his heart. She said, "Oh, I don't do any table rapping, Mr. Dickens. No trumpets nor displays of ectoplasm either."

"So my colleague here tells me," Dickens said.

"You are familiar with my techniques, Mr. North?"

"Somewhat. I've read a few of your monographs and spoken to some who have made use of your abilities."

"I'm quite flattered, sir," Charlotte said. She led the two men into a small parlor where they found two other people, a man and a woman, seated at a round table in the center of the room.

"Ah, the circular table," said Dickens.

"We must adhere to some conventions, I fear," said Charlotte.

"This is Mr. and Mrs. Hargrave. It is Mrs. Hargrave's late sister Amelia whom we shall be attempting to contact this evening."

Henry though the Hargraves looked more like brother and sister than husband and wife. Both were thin and angular. He put their ages at around forty. Greetings were exchanged and Henry could tell that Mrs. Hargrave was considerably impressed at meeting Dickens.

"Oh, Mr. Dickens," she simpered. "I have read all of your works and I assure you that they have given me many hours of pleasure."

Dickens, ever susceptible to praise, inclined his head. "Thank you, dear lady. You may soon be reading about yourself in Household Words."

Mrs. Hargrave laughed. Given how Dickens would likely portray her, Henry doubted that she would be so pleased later. The great man had already written two scathing articles about believers in the spirit world for the magazine. Perhaps Mrs. Hargrave hadn't read all of his works after all.

Charlotte Kenworth moved around the room lighting candles that were placed on various surfaces. Henry recalled reading that candles were very important to attracting spirits. When she had finished, she turned down the gas flames and took her seat at the round table. She indicated chairs on either side of her and said, "If you gentlemen will be seated we will begin."

"I see that you do believe in a darkened room for you séance," Dickens said.

"As I indicated, certain conventions are unavoidable. If you would like, sir, you may examine the room for wires or other carefully hidden devices before we begin." She smiled to lessen the sting of her words, but her eyes were frank. Henry decided that it would be all too easy to become fond of Miss Charlotte Kenworth.

Dickens gave a short, but genuine laugh. "That won't be at all necessary, my dear. We are in your hands."

Charlotte smiled again. "Then begin by taking one of those hands,

Mr. Dickens, and everyone join hands with the person on either side of you. One last convention that I shall request is that you do not relinquish your grasp on your neighbors. The circle must remain unbroken."

Henry gladly took Charlotte's offered hand and grasped that of Mrs. Hargrave on his other side. Charlotte looked around at the others in the circle and then focused her gaze on the middle distance.

"And now a trance?" Dickens suggested.

"You may enter one if you like, sir, but I shall remain lucid."

Dickens frowned and Henry had to struggle to keep from smiling.

Charlotte said, "We are here this evening, seeking the shade of Amelia Porter. If you are listening, Amelia, please speak with us. You sister Mary wishes assurance that you are well."

Henry found that he was waiting with a startling sense of expectancy, as if he fully expected the spirit of Mrs. Hargrave's sister to speak. The room remained quiet and empty save for those seated at the table. Henry could almost feel the smugness radiating from Dickens. He was doubtless composing his new article in his mind at that very moment.

"Amelia Porter," Charlotte repeated, "I know that you are happy and fulfilled in the land beyond, but your sister has need of comfort. Won't you come to us for just a moment and speak with her?"

Henry felt something cold brush across the back his neck. There was no discernible draft in the room and yet the candles flickered and guttered. Henry saw something out of his peripheral vision; turning his head slightly to his left, he realized that a figure was now standing behind Charlotte's chair. It was a woman, tall and thin, with an unarguable resemblance to Mary Hargrave. The figure was hazy and indistinct, but it was there.

Thanks to Dickens, Henry knew of ways that this effect could be faked. Hidden panels, magic lanterns and the like. But he knew, somehow, that this was no trick. This was something real from another realm. He glanced over at Dickens to find the great man wide-eyed and staring. He too, sensed that he was seeing something outside his experience.

The figure's lips parted and in a breathless whisper, she spoke a single word, "Beware..."

Charlotte Kenworth sat up very straight in her chair. Henry felt her fingers tighten spasmodically on his own. She said, "There is another presence here."

Charlotte jerked backward, her spine tight against her chair. She threw her head back and her eyes went wide as she gazed upward at the ceiling. The figure of Amelia Porter vanished and was replaced by another. This one hung in the air, arms and legs flailing weakly. It was a young girl with long golden hair and large brown eyes. Her mouth opened wide, oh so impossibly wide, and she began to scream. Henry had never heard a cry of such terror and undeniable anguish.

Charlotte was jerking around in her chair as if suffering a seizure, making inarticulate grunts deep in her throat. Her grip on Henry's hand had become so tight as to be painful but he couldn't pull free.

The girls' wailing reached a higher pitch and Henry became aware that there was yet another form in the room, long, tall, and dark, like a shadow freed from its caster. Long, thin arms reached out toward the girl.

"No!" Charlotte screamed. "You can't take her!"

The shadow turned from the girl and reached toward Charlotte. An instant later, the woman was lifted up from her chair, her hands torn free from Henry and Dickens. She hung there in the air, a macabre parody of the levitation tricks of other mediums.

As Henry gaped in helpless horror, Charlotte's head began to tilt backward and her back began to arch. There was a series of loud popping sounds as her neck broke and her spine splintered, and then she went flying across the room to land in a heap against one wall.

Henry heard himself screaming and as he watched, the shadow turned back to the child and flowed across her, obscuring her from view. A moment later, the shadow vanished.

Henry slumped forward in his chair. Looking around he saw that Mrs. Hargrave had fainted and fallen from her chair. Mr. Hargrave was staring straight ahead, a thin stream of saliva drooling from one corner of his mouth. Charles Dickens was looking at the spot where the shadow and the girl's spirit had been.

Henry took a long shuddering breath, and then said, "My God, Charles. What have we stumbled across? That...thing, whatever it was, it's killed Miss Kenworth."

Dickens shook his head, still staring at the spot the spirits had vacated. "I don't know, Henry. I simply don't know. But that girl. I recognized her."

"She's the ghost of someone you knew?"

"No! That's just it. I know that child. She isn't dead!"

2

Henry awoke from a nightmare and sat up, unsure for a moment of where he was. It came back with a jolt. He had been sleeping, almost fully dressed, on a sofa in the main sitting room of Tavistock House. Dickens had offered him a bedroom, but Henry had preferred to sleep in front of the large fire in the sitting room. He hadn't relished the idea of stretching out in unfamiliar darkness, and after the events following the horrible occurrences at Dorset Square, he had been grateful not to return to his bachelor flat.

Not that Tavistock House was much better occupied. All of Dickens' family were at Gad's Hill Place, Dickens country home where he spent most of his time now. Henry wondered that Dickens hadn't already sold Tavistock House, but he supposed sometimes it was convenient to have a home in the city. In any case, there were only two servants and a cook currently in residence at the London house.

Henry stood up and stretched. The fire had burned low and he stirred it with a poker and added some wood. Then he fished his pocket watch from his coat and checked the time. Almost six in the morning. He wondered if Dickens was awake yet. Inspector Field from Scotland Yard had certainly kept the two of them long enough, but then Henry knew that had he been with anyone except Charles Dickens the previous night, he would have been sleeping behind bars.

Once Dickens had recovered his wits, the two men had gone out and found a police constable, sending him to the yard for Dickens' good friend, Inspector Field. Field had arrived in a hurry, and Dickens had given him a very edited version of what had happened, leaving out all references to the ghost-child and the shadow. He had told the inspector that Charlotte Kenworth had produced the ghost of the sister of Mrs. Hargraves and then gone into a seizure of some sort.

Henry had been able to tell that Field didn't believe the story, but neither of the Hargraves had been in any condition to contradict it, and Henry had no intention of doing so. Dickens could work all that out later with Field. For himself, Henry was both saddened at the death of Charlotte and frightened and confused by the things he had seen and couldn't explain.

The door to the sitting room opened slightly and a footman stuck his head in. "Mr. Dickens requests that you join him for breakfast in half an hour sir. You may use the washroom down the hall if you wish."

Henry thanked the footman. So Dickens was already up. Perhaps he hadn't slept. He was known to suffer from insomnia under normal circumstances. Henry made his way to the washroom and, after performing his morning ablutions, he went to the dining room.

Dickens was at a sideboard, loading a plate from several covered dishes. He nodded a greeting at Henry and then seated himself at the large dining room table. Henry had little appetite, but he took some eggs and toast and went to join Dickens.

"How are you this morning, Henry?" Dickens said.

"Truthfully Charles, I don't know. It all seems like some terrible dream."

"And yet it isn't."

"No. What was that thing we saw? That killed Miss Kenworth?"

"I find that I am forced to rethink much of what I believe about the physical world," Dickens said. "There truly is more between heaven and Earth than I have dreamt of."

"And what are we to do?"

"The first thing will be to visit the home of Simon Current."

"Who is he?"

"I told you last night that I recognized the little girl who appeared in the room. She is Simon's daughter, Violet. We must go and see that she is well."

Henry nodded. That seemed a reasonable thing to do. And at that moment, he needed all the reasonableness he could find.

Two hours later, Henry and Dickens took a cab to Current's home, which was located on Montague Street, not far from the British Museum. Dickens led the way to the front door and when a butler answered his ring, Dickens inquired if Current was home.

"He is, sir," the butler said. "But I do not believe he is receiving visitors."

"Please tell him that it is Charles Dickens."

The butler raised his eyebrows. "I will sir. If you gentlemen would care to wait in the library I shall go and tell him you are here."

The butler led them to the library and hurried off. A very short time later, a thin and haggard looking man came into the library and grasped Dickens by the hand. "Charles. Thank you so much for coming, my friend. I wish it were under better circumstances."

"Is something wrong, Simon?" Dickens said.

Current looked surprised. "Oh, I thought you had heard and

that is why you called so early. My daughter Violet has been taken seriously ill."

Dickens shot Henry a warning glance. Then he said, "I am terribly sorry to hear that. What has happened?"

"The doctor doesn't know. He's in with her now. When her mother went to wake violet this morning the child didn't respond. We haven't been able to wake her yet."

"But she's still..."

"Alive? Yes, thank God. But the doctor tells me that her heartbeat is weak and her breathing shallow. I am something of a wreck, I fear."

"I shouldn't wonder," said Dickens. "And of course, I hope fervently that she will be well. Henry and I shall go. We were just in the area and I thought you might like to join us in visiting the Museum."

"Thank you for thinking of me, Charles, and for your well wishes. I must get back to Violet now."

"Of course, Simon. We will see ourselves out."

Dickens turned and hurried out and Henry rushed to catch up. When they were in the street, Dickens said, "Damnation, Henry! I had hoped that we would find the child well."

"Do you think then that it really was her spirit we saw last night?"

"Spirit. Soul. I don't know. We need to speak to someone knowledgeable in such matters."

"Do you know of such a person?"

"Perhaps."

3

Montague Street was quiet enough. One would hardly know that a child was ill and sliding toward a slow death.

Doctor Gareth Quincy was not optimistic about young Violet Current. The girl lay motionless on her bed, barely breathing, and he scribbled notes to himself. She did not appear to have any injuries, but her pallor was nearly bleached to the color of fresh cream and even the spray of freckles on the bridge of her nose seemed to have faded. Her hair, normally alive with curls, was currently wetted to her scalp by the remains of a fit of sweating and moaning that had come on suddenly and then faded away.

Worst of all, even while she was silent, there was a look to her face that spoke of tremendous fear. Her eyes flickered nervously under closed lids. Her lips parted and she let out small, terrified panting sounds before she fell once again into a restless slumber.

Simon was beside himself, of course, and poor, dear Corinne was very nearly incapacitated. At the moment they had both left the room at Gareth's insistence. They wanted to stay. They wanted to help, but he needed to concentrate and assess what the possible source of the young girl's sudden collapse might be.

He had checked her arms, her legs, her neck, behind her ears, and even examined her privates, looking for any sign of disturbance. It was rare in London for an insect or spider to kill with a bite, but it could happen, especially with all of the vermin coming into the ports from other countries. Most of the beasts didn't survive long in the colder climate, especially the insects from India and Africa, but better to be safe than to overlook a simple possibility.

Gareth looked away from the girl for a moment and studied instead the doll that rested on her nightstand. It was positioned so as to look down on Violet in her sleep; a guardian against nightmares and ill fortune. It was a marvelous likeness. The mouth smiled lovingly, the eyes glowed with vigor. The hair, the same as dear Violet's, as it should be seeing that had come from her very head. As a family friend he had been there to see the look on her face when she received the prize only a few weeks earlier. Her face lit with joy and she held the beautifully rendered doll in her hands and danced from one foot to the other with excitement.

He remembered then that the doll had made a musical note when she swung it about, and he'd wondered about that. Corinne had explained that the noise came from a bell hidden away inside the doll, a trademark of the man who created the prized figures.

He couldn't remember the name of the dollmaker and frowned at that thought. His own Sally would be of an age where she might well want a doll of her own and if she was going to have one, it needed to be of the finest quality.

Violet moaned again and shifted slightly on the bed. Her legs fidgeted, sliding back and forth, scissoring lightly as if she might be swimming or running in her sleep.

"Running from what, I wonder?" He paused at that, not certain what had made him have such a notion.

He lifted his stethoscope into place and moved to check Violet's pulse again.

As he slid his hand over her chest a rustle of fabric whispered to his left.

There should have been no sounds, but he ignored the unexpected noise for a moment, concentrating on Violet's heartbeat. It was there, but weak, so weak. Even softer than before.

Her flesh was cool to the touch and Gareth shook his head, unconsciously chewing on the coarse hairs at the edge of his heavy mustache.

As he reached to check her eyes again for any sign of jaundice, the ringing sounds struck him. It was faint, almost a faded as poor Violet's pulse.

He looked toward the elaborately crafted doll where it perched and blinked his eyes in surprise.

In a perfect world he could have claimed that the doll had been shifted by his own motion, but he had not moved enough to even disturb the curtains in the still room and most assuredly would have known if he'd collided with the heavy wooden furniture enough to move anything.

The doll was facing him. A moment before it had looked down upon Violet like a guardian angel but now the sweet, innocent face stared in his direction, the glass eyes seeming to look directly into his own with an unspoken challenge.

The smile on that face, still lovely, did not seem quite the same as before. There was a twist to the mouth, he was sure of it, that had not been there before.

"Madness. I've been up too many hours." This was the second house he had been to in the last week where a young girl had taken ill. He was being kept busy enough for three doctors simply because of the inclement weather. Adding in children falling into comatose states was merely tasking him to be more vigilant. He hoped he was up to the challenge.

Gareth closed his eyes for a moment and rubbed at his temples, feeling the hard muscles that knotted beneath his flesh.

The bell rang again, far more clearly than it had before, and Gareth looked up.

The doll had fallen forward and now was only inches from him, the eyes staring into his from so short a distance that his image of the face was distorted.

"Gads!" He pushed back from Violet's bed and nearly overturned the chair he was sitting in.

The doll had not fallen. It was standing as surely as if he had placed it carefully on its small, flat feet in their meticulous boots.

Unsettled, Gareth rose from the chair and pinched at the flesh between his thumb and forefinger, checking for pain response, needing to know that he wasn't dreaming. Exhaustion caused the oddest dreams in him.

The pain was real and he was looking right at the doll this time as it moved. The hellish thing took another step forward, looking into his face as it reached for him with delicately sculpted fingers.

Gareth stepped back and promptly stumbled into the chair he had just vacated. Despite his best efforts he could not maintain his balance. Both he and the chair fell over with a loud clatter.

Immediately he heard the sound of footsteps coming his way. "Doctor Quincy! Gareth? Are you injured? Is Violet well?" Simon pushed open the door and rushed to him, helping him to his feet and upending the chair in almost the same motion. The man was bristling with nervous energy.

On the bed Violet remained in the same state, her mouth opened in a silent gasp, her skin so pale it was nearly translucent. Her small hands fluttered nervously, trapped birds trying to fly away.

Gareth responded while shaking his head. "I'm sorry, Simon. I must have drifted into a slumber. I gave myself a start looking at Violet's doll." He shook his head, embarrassed by his own actions.

"Violet's doll? The Harringdale?" Simon frowned in his direction. "Do you know, I haven't seen that thing in days."

Simon was looking toward the end table where the doll had been standing. There was no sign of the doll.

4

The wind coming off the Thames was as cold as the grave and when it caught the buildings the right way, it howled a low, mournful note.

Jonathan Crowley walked down the alleyway without hesitation. Somewhere up ahead there was a killer and he intended to find and destroy that killer, exactly as he'd been asked to.

The fog was heavy along Butcher's Row and moved in wavering phantasms. Over half the figures he saw with his eyes were mere parodies sent forth by the winds or by something else. It was sometimes hard to say.

Kung Li had written to him and asked him to help with whatever was stalking the Limehouse area. No one was quite certain; they only knew that when the bodies were found, they were desiccated. Dried, bloodless husks.

The freshest body was only a hundred yards behind him. She'd been such a lovely little girl the last time he'd seen her in Shanghai and now, twenty-seven years later, she was a withered shell, dead before she knew what happened.

One deep puncture mark along the base of her spine was all that he saw of the killer and all that he needed to see.

The problem with commerce is sometimes the demons from one place found their way to another.

He didn't know the name of that particular beast, but he had seen them before and he knew how to destroy them. A simple mixture of salt, silver and grave mold, properly employed and mixed with the right incantations would settle the matter.

First, however, he had to catch the damned thing.

"Where are we going, Mister Crowley?" The voice was nervous and winded. Not surprising when he considered the source.

"We're following a demon, Simms."

"I-there's a church right across the way. Will we need to find holy water?"

"It's not that sort of demon, Simms." He could feel the headache wanting to start even as he spoke.

"Begging your pardon, Mister Crowley, but what other sorts are there?"

"Not every monster is afraid of your God, Simms."

Simms was a good man, but not very open-minded when it came to the rest of the world. For him the only parts that mattered belonged to the British Empire and only spoke English. Crowley was rather surprised that the fellow had decided to join him in the fledgling China Town, which was nearly a foreign land to Simms's way of thinking.

Simms took in a deep breath and Crowley winced. The man was a decent enough sort but he was about to go on a tirade regarding the foreign population and how it was not a blessing for the Crown.

He had been asked to take the man along as a guide. He had been asked nicely. Simms had been born in London, true enough, but the city hadn't changed that much in the last seventy-five years and Crowley knew his way around. Still, he had been asked nicely by people he respected.

Simms did not speak. Crowley frowned at that and slowed his walking pace, listening for the man. Perhaps his heart had given out. Simms was not in the best of shape.

He turned to face the round little man, seeing him through a caul of fog, and found the demon he was looking for perched on Simms's shoulders and back. It was a parody of a human shape. It wore a cloak, and there was a top hat falling from the bald, greasy pate of the nightmare. Once it might have even been human, but now it was more like a tick than anything else. The face was distorted, pulled into segments not unlike an insect's, that tapered into a long proboscis, which was currently thrust into the back of Simms's neck. Great, greasy red orbs stared from where eyes should have been. The flesh of the thing was a white as a fish's belly and almost as wet in appearance.

The rotund man was screaming, but no sound came from his mouth. Trails of spittle drooled down from his teeth and dribbled across his chin. The limbs of the thing on him were short and thick and bent in the wrong way. Heavy fingers sank deep into Simms's greatcoat and tore the fabric.

Simms was already dead. His eyes rolled back in his skull and his round face thinned, the skin sagging and then pulling tight as the life essence was drawn from his body.

Crowley cursed. He'd been wrong. This was not at all what he thought he might see. In fact, he'd never seen anything like it before. Part of him thrilled at the idea of encountering a new form of evil. Most of him recoiled. Unprepared. He was unprepared for what might be coming his way.

Crowley took two steps forward and reached for the pouch he'd already set aside. Silver, salt, grave mold. They often worked on more than an occasional Chinese nightmare. He spoke seven words not heard ever before on British soil, and threw the dust into the air.

The demon tried to escape. It leaped back, powerful hind legs kicking Simms's body forward. The shape rocketed backward, pushing off of the alley's narrow wall and dropping down again, jumping a second time, then a third.

Crowley ran after it and heard a sound come from it like laughter. The noise rebounded off the narrow walls of the alleyway and as Crowley watched the damned thing hopped again, leaping across the distance of the arrow alleyway and striking the wall on the other side. It hit and leaped again and a moment later it was gone, leaving behind only the corpse of a decent, if xenophobic, man and a tattered top hat.

"Bloody hell." Crowley heard the sinister laughter growing more distant. He'd let himself be caught off guard and unprepared. He was getting careless and he could ill afford that luxury. That sort of behavior led to unfortunate deaths.

The ruined remains of William Simms fell to the ground and broke like fragile china. The form within his tweed suit collapsed into dust, bones and a few wisps of dried, malnourished hair.

"Damned foolish of you, Crowley," he said to himself. "You've cost that poor wretch his life."

He stared after the source of the wicked laughter that bounced still between the walls of the local buildings.

"I am going to have to kill that damned thing." If Simms agreed or disagreed, he offered no argument in either direction.

5

Despite the fact that he was a great reader and collector of books, as well as a prolific if amateur poet, Henry had somehow never found the bookshop called Thackeray's in Charing Cross Road. Following Dickens into the store, Henry was amazed at the size of the place. Shelves stretched out in all directions and a dizzying array of staircases promised many more shelves on upper levels.

The place belonged to George Thackeray, who Dickens had assured him, was no relation to the more famous owner of that particular surname.

"But he does have a large selection of books about the occult," Dickens had said, "As well as a great deal of personal knowledge about the subject. One would almost think the man a sorcerer."

They found Thackeray behind the store's front counter, going through a stack of small leather-bound volumes that had apparently arrived with the morning post. A large pile of brown paper and twine was still strewn about the counter.

"Ah, Charles!" Thackeray exclaimed upon seeing his friend. Thackeray was somewhat portly with a ruddy complexion and white hair that stuck out in all directions. "What are you doing about at this time of day? Well, never mind. I've made some fascinating acquisitions since your last visit."

Dickens said, "I am certain that you have, my friend, but I fear that I haven't come merely to browse today, George. I have a matter I wish to discuss with you."

"Of course. I am all attention."

Dickens gave a very brief account of what had occurred at the séance, leaving out the names of the people involved. Throughout, Thackeray stood with his thumbs jammed into his waistcoat, nodding occasionally.

"A bad business," Thackeray said at last. "A very bad business indeed."

"I had hoped you might have some advice or be able to recommend some books on the subject."

"As it happens," Thackeray said. "There is someone here right now who might be of more help than either myself or any of my books. A veritable expert on the occult in all its forms."

Dickens said, "And he is in the shop?"

"Yes, in the back looking through my most recently acquired grimoires. He has the most extensive knowledge of blasphemous books of any man I know."

"Well I would certainly welcome his opinions," said Dickens.

"Give me but a moment and I shall fetch him."

Thackeray waddled toward the far end of the store and paused looking down a long row of books. "Mr. Kharrn? Might I trouble you for a moment? I have a good friend here who has a matter that may interest you."

A moment later, Henry heard the old floorboards creak as someone approached. Whatever he had expected of an expert in occult matters, it wasn't the man who came striding from among the shelves.

The man was a giant, surely almost seven feet in height, and with shoulders so broad that he was obliged to turn sideways to move among the shelves. His black suit had obviously been tailor made, for no common clothing would fit him. He had black hair, worn rather long, and an old white scar ran down one side of his deeply tanned face.

Thackeray said, "Mr. Kharrn, this is Mr. Charles Dickens and his associate, Henry North."

Kharrn nodded. "I've enjoyed you books, Mr. Dickens." His voice was deep and rumbling. "How may I help you?"

Kharrn wasn't British, and Henry couldn't place his accent. He didn't appear to be American and he certainly wasn't French.

Dickens said, "I am attempting to help a child who seems to be in some terrible danger. It is something of a delicate matter. There's a coffee house across the street. Perhaps we could go there and talk, sir."

Kharrn said, "That would be fine. I've looked through all of Thackeray's books already."

"And found them wanting?" said Thackeray.

Kharrn smiled at the book dealer. "And found them safe for the public. You know the kind of books I seek."

"I do, and should one appear I shall contact you with all haste."

The three men adjourned across the street and Henry found them a table in a back corner. Kharrn leaned a wide, flat leather case against a wall. Henry had noticed that the giant kept a close eye on that case. Once they were seated, Dickens gave yet another account of the events at the séance. This time, Henry noted, he added more details.

When Dickens stopped talking, Kharrn said, "It sounds like a soul stealer of some sort."

"Are there many sorts?" said Henry.

"Far too many," said Kharrn. "The child's soul may have escaped briefly and she was drawn to the séance by the receptive conditions. The creature came after her and retrieved her soul."

"Is she dead do you think, Mr. Kharrn?"

"Just Kharrn. No mister. Her soul may still be alive. It depends on why the creature wants it. Some entities of that sort feed on souls. Others merely collect them. And there are doubtless others with different purposes which I've never encountered."

"You make it sound like there are hundreds of malevolent specters lurking out there."

Kharrn leaned forward. "If you knew what hovered just beyond the circle of light you call reality, you would run screaming into the comfort of madness."

The giant's blue eyes seemed to glitter with an almost feral light, and Henry had to fight the urge to shrink back from the man. "What will become of the child?"

Kharrn took a swig of his coffee, then said, "If her soul isn't reunited with her body soon, she will cease to be."

Dickens said, "A few days ago I would have laughed at such a notion but now I've been forced to admit the world holds many mysteries I cannot fathom. We must help the girl Kharrn. We must."

"Take me to her," Kharrn said, rising from the table.

6

Mrs. Catherine Stewart smiled at her daughter Eve's antics as the child capered and danced along beside her as they made their way through the crowds of shoppers on Regent Street. And why shouldn't the child be happy? Her fondest wish was about to come true because this was the day she was to receive her doll from Harringdale's.

The process had been a long one. First Eve had to go for a sitting while the dollmaker, Harringdale sketched her, for he made each doll in the likeness of the child, and then she had had to grow her hair out long so that the doll's hair could be made from it. Each Harringdale was an exquisite work of art. And for what the man charged, they had better be.

Catherine and Eve reached the shop, with its brightly painted storefront and its display windows full of dolls of all sorts. In addition to examples of his special dolls for girls, there were also clowns and soldiers and circus animals. There were even examples of more fantastic creatures, like gryphons and unicorns and dragons. It seemed that the man could make anything.

They stepped inside, grateful to be out of the cold and the press of the crowd. Shopping at Harringdale's was by invitation only. A chime rang as the door swung shut and Mr. Harringdale came out of a doorway in the back of the shop. His mode of dress, as always, was that of an earlier day. He wore the clothes of the previous century and a white powdered wig was perched upon his head. He had small, narrow eyes, a somewhat pinched face and a smile that was almost too wide and which never seemed to leave his face.

"Good morning, my dears," Harringdale said. "So good to see you."

"Is my doll ready?" Eve piped.

"Eve!" Catherine said,

"Quite all right, Madame," Harringdale said. "Of course she's excited. It's a big day. A big day indeed!" Harringdale walked across the gleaming white and black tiled floor to the front counter and lifted a white box from under the counter. "And here she is."

Eve hurried over to the counter. Harringdale opened the box

and slid several layers of tissue aside. A small, smiling face peeked out from behind the paper. Eve said, "Oh! She's beautiful!"

"So she is, my dear. And now she's yours." Harringdale's grin grew wider, if that were possible. "And do you know what?"

"What?" cried Eve.

"And now you are hers as well."

7

As Henry watched, Kharrn rested one huge hand on Violet Current's head. He sat very still at her bedside, the whole of his attention focused on the child. Violet's physician, a man named Quincy, hadn't been pleased about being bundled out of the room, but Dickens had convinced Simon that Kharrn was a specialist and needed his privacy. Simon, desperate for anything that might help his daughter, had complied.

Finally, after several minutes had passed, Kharrn looked up and said, "Her soul is somewhere far from here, but it lives. However, the link between Violet's soul and her body grows more tenuous. She won't survive the night if something isn't done."

"Is there anything you can do?" said Dickens.

"Perhaps. My friend Decamp would be better suited to this, but there isn't time to try and reach him, so I'll have to make the effort. It would help if I knew how her soul had been taken. Dickens, has your friend mentioned any new acquaintances or has he recently purchased any art objects or collectibles?"

"Nothing that he has mentioned to me." Dickens paused for a moment. "Though he did say that Violet's new doll has disappeared."

Kharrn's eyes narrowed. "What sort of doll?"

"A very expensive one. Made by a man called Harringdale. They're all the rage in society circles now. Every gentleman's daughter must have one, and quite a few ladies of greater years own them as well."

"And Violet had one and now it is gone?"

"That's what Simon said. Apparently Dr. Quincy thought he saw it earlier this evening here in this room, but obviously it isn't here now."

"We'll discuss it further once Violet is out of danger." Kharrn stood and walked to his leather case, which he had left near the room's door. He picked up the case and returned to the bed. He unsnapped the latches on the case and removed a big, gleaming axe with two blades, like the kind Henry had seen in illustrations of Vikings.

"Good God," Dickens said. "What is that?"

"My axe," said Kharrn.

"I can see it's an axe, man. What are you going to do with it?"

"Probably make a demon very angry. Now stand away. It would probably be best if you left the room, but at the very least move over to the far wall."

Kharrn stood by Violet's bed and held the axe in front of him. Henry knew the big metal weapon had to be very heavy, but Kharrn held it without apparent effort. Slowly, the big man began to turn. Henry felt his heart lurch as something appeared in the air, a wavering band of pale light that seemed to flow from the axe to somewhere else. Kharrn stepped away from the bed, keeping the axe in contact with the nebulous ribbon, as if he were following it toward its source.

Without warning three things occurred. Kharrn whipped the axe back and then cut through the ribbon, Violet sat up in bed and started screaming, and the same shadow Henry and Dickens had seen at the séance appeared in the room.

The door burst open and Simon and Dr. Quincy froze in the doorway, staring at the spectacle of a tall, shadowy figure looming over a giant man with a gleaming axe. Henry glanced over at Dickens and saw the great man staring with wide eyes.

The shadow slid forward, extending talon like fingers toward Kharrn. The big man lunged in, swinging the axe. Where the blade struck the shadow, the specter shattered like a pane of dark glass. The greater mass of the creature began to back away but Kharrn went after it, striking again and again.

The shadow thing reared up, spreading out like the hood of some great cobra, and then flowed forward, surrounding the giant man. For a moment Henry could see nothing of Kharrn, as if the thing had swallowed him whole. Then he saw a gleaming blade break through the darkness, and Kharrn cut his way to freedom. The shadow being seemed to be getting smaller as the big man continued his attack.

Kharrn pressed forward, striking again and again. The shadow screeched and wailed and finally broke into dozens of fragments. Those fragments dissolved into a black mist that swiftly faded away.

"There," Kharrn said. "Now it can't re-form and come after the girl again."

"What was it?" Henry said.

Kharrn shook his head. "A servant. A thing used to collect souls for its master, whoever that is."

"Father!" Violet cried and Simon hurried across the room to embrace his daughter. "The big shadow had me, father. It was keeping me somewhere cold and dark."

Simon looked over at Dickens. "Charles, you must tell me what I just saw. Good Lord, man. What was it?"

"Whatever it was, Kharrn here defeated it. Violet is safe now. Isn't she Kharrn?"

"As safe as she can be. As I told you, that thing was merely a servant. A puppet. We need to find who or what is pulling the strings." Kharrn looked at Simon Current. "Tell me about this Harringdale doll."

8

Gareth Quincy looked at the man walking beside him and shuddered. He was a fine enough fellow, until he smiled. It was those teeth, and the expression of his face, as if he were both enjoying a private joke and possibly considering taking a bite from the doctor's face.

"I know we haven't had an opportunity to speak in quite some time, Mr. Crowley, but I remembered your penchant for the unusual, and, well, I've encountered something very unusual, indeed."

They had met under the worst possible circumstances, and Gareth hadn't even remembered that they'd met until the business with the doll started up. There had been a dead woman, and there had been blood and screaming and even now he didn't want to remember the hellish night.

He pushed the thoughts aside.

They walked along the darkened road heading for Regent Street, and though they had never been to the dollmaker's shop, Quincy felt a nervous flutter in his stomach.

"Well, I appreciate you showing me the way, my good man." Crowley was dressed in finery for an evening out, his greatcoat moving in the evening chill, his gloved hands immaculate. Still, despite the perfect attire, there was something disturbing about him.

Pools of light ran from the gas lamps, but it was still dark, and foggy, and every time they moved away from those illuminated areas the doctor suppressed a desire to run. It had to be his imagination but it also seemed to him that every time he grew more nervous, Crowley's smile grew brighter.

The man was speaking to him, but he barely heard the words. "This dollmaker, is he someone famous?"

"Oh, Harringdale dolls are apparently in very high demand." He pointed to the front of the shop, which was small, but immaculate.

Crowley looked at the building and walked slowly, the smile fading from his face.

"Do you see something?"

Crowley's hand waved as if to swat an annoying bug, and Quincy took the hint. The man was now on the job as it were, and that meant the rules had changed.

"Well..." Crowley squinted at the building and turned his head slightly to the side as he examined the door, the windows, and the building itself.

"Well, this is different, I dare say." Crowley was speaking to himself.

In order not to feel lost in the situation, Gareth spoke up. "I have heard nothing but praise for the craftsmanship and artistry of the dolls. The one I saw earlier was spectacular, very nearly a perfect example of the young girl who owned it."

"The same young girl you were caring for?"

"Indeed."

"You said she'd been helped out by another man. Tell me about him."

"Well, none other than Charles Dickens himself came to visit, and he brought with him very possibly the largest man I have seen in my entire life. The man was as solid as a wall, easily a foot taller than me, with dark hair and a long scar on his face."

Crowley frowned. A foot taller and dark hair. Was he carrying an axe, or a long flat case?"

"An axe! Yes he was. How did you know?"

Crowley's smile was as unsettling as ever. "Because I know the man in question. Unless I've missed my guess you're talking about Kharrn."

"I do believe that was the man." Gareth shook his head. What was the likelihood of two men that specialized in matters best not considered arriving in London at the same time?

"Small wonder the girl is alive. Kharrn has ways of handling the night terrors of the world that are direct and often useful."

Crowley moved forward and touched the air in front of the dollmaker's shop. His fingers pressed against that air as if pushing against glass. He could see the fingertips of Crowley's hand press and flatten.

"Warded." Crowley hissed the word and pulled his fingers back. Gareth saw the blood from those fingers drizzled down the air and turn to ash. Crowley's fingers were bleeding openly for a moment and then the wounds faded away.

"Good Lord, Mister Crowley! Are you injured?" He walked closer and looked at the fingertips that he knew had been bleeding as surely as he knew his own name. There were no wounds now. The skin was unmarred.

"I'm fine, as you can see. But whomever this Harringdale is, he has prepared for unexpected company. There are powerful wards here, the sort meant to kill anyone with mystic abilities who is foolhardy enough to venture in this direction."

Gareth reached out and slid his hand through the air where Crowley had touched it. There was no resistance. "It seems fine to me."

"That is because you are not touched by the mystic. You're a fool, and you may well be touched, but not by the mystic."

"Whatever do you mean?"

"I just said the area is warded. It is warded against people like me, priests and shamans and sorcerers. It is not warded against doctors of medicine." Crowley looked his way and the anger there was enough to make Gareth step back. "Had you been adept in the wrong specialties, you'd have burned your damned hand off, Quincy."

"Do you mean to say I could have been harmed?"

"I mean to say you're luckier than you know. Often times when someone activates a ward like this they stay active. Whether or not you are what the wards defend against crossing or touching the barrier could well have destroyed you. You are fortunate indeed that this dollmaker wishes to be subtle about his defenses."

Crowley stepped closer and smiled. It was not a kind expression. "You've asked for my help and so you have it, but don't be foolish about these things. If you see me being cautious remember that I am likely better at healing myself than you will ever be, physician."

"Very good, Mister Crowley." The man's brown eyes regarded him for several more heartbeats and then he backed away and nodded.

"Now, where did you see Kharrn?"

"He was with Charles Dickens, as I said."

"Yes. So you did. But where did you see him?"

"He was at the house of a dear friend of mine. I mentioned that, didn't I?"

Crowley stared at him again, much harder this time. "Yes. Now, where were they? What location? Is it in this city? Is it nearby? Will I have to go to bloody Scotland to find them?"

"Oh." Gareth shook his head, embarrassed by his responses. "No. They're just down the road a bit, unless they've gone somewhere else. I felt the need to get in contact with you because, well, to be completely honest I'm not sure why."

Crowley waved a dismissive hand. "That's because I implanted the desire to contact me if you ever again ran across something supernatural when you were just a child."

"Beg pardon?"

"Never mind. The important thing here is that I want to get in contact with Kharrn, because whatever this is, it's powerful and I'd like to survive an occasional encounter."

"Beg pardon?"

"Never mind."

Sometimes being patient with foolish people was harder than he liked to think about. That was definitely the case here. The good doctor meant well, but he was not emotionally prepared for dealing with things of an otherworldly nature.

Crowley shook his head and stepped back as something with a terrifying power moved closer to him on the other side of the wards.

Whatever it was, the presence of it was enough to blot out the moon. He could not see it, but he could feel it, towering high above him, dwarfing the city of London. Whatever it might present itself as, dollmaker or puppeteer, or something else, it hid a great deal of power behind a mask of humanity.

How he wished that were the exception. Something about the world was changing, and Crowley was not pleased by that notion. Whatever it was, it seemed to awaken darker threats, and that at a time when he desperately wanted to leave hunting monsters behind.

Crowley looked at the building and saw the power that had gone into warding it. Whatever was behind that barrier had a powerful desire to be left alone.

He had no intention if succumbing to that desire.

"I believe we're going to have to look for Kharrn before we do anything else, Quincy."

"No reason. I'm already here."

Crowley heard the familiar rumbling voice and smiled. Sometimes it was nice to run across a figure from his past.

9

"Crowley," Kharrn said. "I'd been wondering when I'd run into you again."

"How long has it been?" The rather sardonic looking man Kharrn referred to as Crowley said. "At least fifty years."

The man had to be joking. Some private jest between the two men. Neither of them could be much older than thirty. And what was this man doing here? And why was Dr. Quincy with him? Henry had too many questions.

When Kharrn had asked to see Harringdale's Doll Shop, both Henry and Dickens had been only too happy to leave the Current home. It was while they were preparing to go they realized Dr. Quincy had disappeared at some point. Henry had assumed Quincy had been unnerved by their encounter with the shadow creature, and had simply gone home. Yet here he was on Regent Street, in the middle of the night, with this smiling dandy.

Kharrn turned from Crowley and stared at the dark front windows of the shop. His brow furrowed and he frowned. "There's something in there."

Crowley said, "Noticed that, eh? The place is guarded by some of the most powerful wards I've ever sensed. I was about to come and find you so you could help me learn what exactly resides within."

Dickens, who had been listening to the conversation without saying anything, stepped forward. "Just what is going on here? Kharrn, who is this man?"

Kharrn said, "Someone you want on your side. You were looking for experts on the occult. Crowley here is one of the most knowledgeable men in the world."

Dickens said, "Oh, I see. Very well then. I am Charles Dickens. Your servant, sir."

"I know who you are," Crowley said. "Kharrn, what brought you here tonight?"

"I ran into a soul stealer. I suspected it had something to do with the man who runs this shop. Now I'm sure of it."

Kharrn gave a brief account of what had happened to Violet Current. Crowley seemed to take the outlandish tale in stride.

Crowley said, "It's no simple soul thief, my friend. The power emanating from inside the building is almost painful."

"Yes, I can feel it now," Kharrn said. "We have to get inside."

"I can get us inside, I think. I just wish we knew a little more about what might be waiting in there."

Kharrn grinned and hefted the case that held his axe. "Just get me in there. I've killed men, demons, and gods."

"You see, Quincy?' Crowley said. "I told you he was just the man for the job."

Kharrn said, "Henry, you and Charles need to move away from here. Go down the street and be ready to run."

Dickens said, "Now see here, Kharrn. I really don't..."

"No, you really don't." Crowley said. "You need to do as Kharrn says. When I open those doors all hell may break loose, and I assure you I am speaking neither figuratively nor rhetorically."

Dickens stood for a moment, trying to meet Crowley's gaze and finding he could not. He turned away. "Come along, Henry. You as well, Quincy. These madmen may be right."

10

Once the other men had moved away from the front of the shop, Kharrn opened his case and removed the axe. He watched as Crowley took a stance in front of the shop doors and raised his hands. He was reminded of another time, long past, when he and Crowley had stood with a group of Templar Knights at the gates of Ascalon, where Jackal-headed, Egyptian demons had made the crusaders fear the night.

Crowley muttered some sort of invocation, and a diffused light began to play around his fingers. He moved his hand forward, feeling for the outer limits of the protective wards. There was a bright flash of light, and Crowley staggered back.

"Damnation. I've never felt that kind of power."

Kharrn said, "Let me try."

The big man swung the axe back over one shoulder and then lunged forward, aiming the heavy weapon at the shop doors. This time the light flared even brighter and Kharrn was actually lifted off his feet and thrown backwards, to land rolling on the hard cobblestones. Crowley stepped forward immediately and renewed his assault on the barrier. His hands glowed bright.

He grinned as he pushed his way through to the door. "Hurry, Kharrn. I can feel whatever it is already marshalling its power against us."

Kharrn rolled to his feet, shaking his head like a bull. He charged forward and slammed his axe against the doors. He felt something pushing against him, as if he were swimming against some strong current. Then wood and glass shattered and he and Crowley were inside the Dollmaker's shop.

Gas lamps from outside did little to illuminate the interior of the large front room. The inconstant light threw back reflections from the glass eyes of the small figurines which sat on every surface and on the shelve that lined the shop's walls.

Kharrn said, "Evar's bones. I wonder if every one of these dolls is the simulacrum of a child here in the city."

"Still swearing by your old gods, I see," Crowley said. "But to answer your question, yes, I think each of these small horrors represents a stolen soul."

It was unnaturally quiet in the shop, as if the wards designed to protect the building also kept out the sounds from the street. Thus, the sudden squeaking of the polished wooden floorboards seemed far louder than it would have under normal circumstances.

Kharrn turned toward the sound and saw two hulking figures emerging from a wide door in the back of the shop. They were taller and wider than Kharrn, and as they moved into the feeble light coming through the windows, he could see that they were misshapen, with mismatched limbs and lumpy, featureless faces. They moved forward with halting, jerky motions.

"They appear to be some sort of automatons," Crowley said.

"Dolls," said Kharrn. "Giant dolls."

"And unfriendly from the look of them."

The things picked up speed as they came. Kharrn rushed to meet one of them and swung the great axe. He sheared through a questing arm, sending a shower of brass gears and springs spattering to the floor. The other arm, the longer of the two, swung out and struck Kharrn across the shoulders, slamming the big man into one of the walls. Dolls fell all around him as the robotic horror stalked closer.

The second creature reached out to grab Crowley, who evaded its grasp. Crowley caught the arm, and with a huge pull, wrenched it free of the creature's shoulder. Fowl, brackish oil spurted from the stump. Using the arm as a club, Crowley struck the automaton again and again.

Kharrn got to his feet just as the creature reached him. Using his almost 300 pounds, the giant man rammed the thing with his shoulder, shoving it backward. It teetered for a moment, off balance, and Kharrn took that opportunity to raise his axe high and bring it down on the monster's skull. He heard a loud screech and then one of the shadow creatures he had seen earlier rose from the mechanical man and vanished into the darkness of the shop's high ceiling.

Seconds later, a second shadow fled the wreckage of the automaton that had been attacking, Crowley. Crowley looked down at his fine suit, now bespattered with oil and grimaced.

"Oh dear," a voice said from the shadows. "You've ruined my toys."

Both men turned toward the sound. A small, wiry man, dressed in the style of the 18th century stood there frowning at them.

11

The man was dressed in woolen pants, a white cotton shirt and a heavy vest, all of which hid partially under an apron with several small tools locked in place. He had a white, powdered wig on his head.

He looked at them with wide eyes and a small scowl of confusion on his long face. "I don't believe either of you are supposed to be here."

"I don't believe you're supposed to be stealing the souls of children, either, and yet, here you are with an array of dolls designed to capture and feed on the lives of young girls."

"To be fair, I could certainly have done far worse to them. They don't truly suffer as a result of my actions. They simply drift off to sleep and never awaken."

Crowley smiled. "'I'm sure that's supposed to be a comfort to their loved ones. What are you?"

"I'm a dollmaker. I make dolls."

"Whereas Kharrn is a corpsemaker. He makes corpses of the sort of things that steal the souls of children."

Kharrn nodded. "It's true. I'm very good at my chosen occupation."

The small man smiled and his eyes blinked. "I'm certain of that. You made very short work of my guards."

"Well, they didn't seem very welcoming."

Crowley nodded his agreement. "Enough of this, Let the children go."

"It's far too late for that. They're serving a greater need now than they could have ever imagined."

"Oh, what sort of need?"

"They feed me and I in turn feed my masters, and in time we will all wander together through the Outer Darkness."

Kharrn scowled and shook his head, "None of the children asked to serve you. They wanted dolls."

"And they got them," The small man stood taller, his chest puffed with pride. "I make the very finest dolls around, lifelike and very nearly perfect."

Crowley walked over to the closest shelf. "I've whittled better in my sleep." One hand reached out and plucked one of the dolls from a shelf.

"Be careful with that."

Crowley smiled. "Are they particularly delicate?"

"No, but—"

"They look rather sturdy." He tossed the doll toward Kharrn. "Does this seem well made and solid to you, Kharrn?"

Kharrn held the doll in his massive hand. "Seems well crafted. Certainly worth a few coppers for the craftsmanship."

"They do, don't they? Still, that one looks lifeless. Empty. What a shame."

The dollmaker looked toward Kharrn. "Coppers? That shows what little you understand about craftsmanship." His thin lips peeled away from teeth that seemed too large for his face. "I am handsomely compensated for my work."

"I'd have to agree. All it costs the young girls are their very souls." Crowley stepped closer to the small man, fully aware that what he was dealing with was hardly human, despite appearances. The power of the thing was obvious enough to him and he suspected to Kharrn as well. "I'd say the cost was too high by far for a pale imitation of the true treasure."

"A pale imitation?" The dollmaker's voice broke as he repeated the words. "My skills are second to none, sir!"

"Your skills? You call murder a skill?"

Kharrn said, "To be fair, murder is a skill. But these dolls?" His hand closed on the head of the doll and an audible crunch could be heard through the small shop. "These are hardly treasures." Kharrn's eyes stared at the small man, the challenge very obvious. "I've seen your carvings, Crowley. They're far superior."

The shopkeeper stepped past Crowley, barely even seeing him as he returned Kharrn's glare. "I'll tear your body apart for that." The words were a trembling hiss, the expression on the dollmaker's face one of pure hatred.

Kharrn released the ruined effigy and flakes of paint and strands of dark hair fell from his hand like a flurry of snow.

The Dollmaker screeched then, a thunderous sound that shook the windows in his shop. Crowley looked at the back of the man's head and studied the Dollmaker, looking for any signs that he was more than human; it was not hard to see the spots where the human facade were failing.

"Those who walk behind the angles, the gods of the Outer Darkness, have always been arrogant, but when did they start getting sloppy, I wonder?" Crowley's words were measured and deliberately insulting,

The Dollmaker's head snapped around at a nearly impossible speed, and the eyes that looked at him were lined with red, a color that slowly moved to cover the whole of the orbs until no sign of pupil or iris showed behind the crimson smears.

"What do you mean?"

"Your seams are showing. You fail to look as human as you might." Crowley stared hard at the man. He was lying but he had no intention of giving that fact away. Had he dealt with the followers of the creatures? Yes, but this thing, this Dollmaker, was a different creature entirely. "If you make your dolls this poorly I'm amazed that you sell any of them." To make his point Crowley kicked out at the closest shelf and sent every doll on it, a full dozen of the magnificent works, falling to the wooden floor.

The Dollmaker let out another screech and this time, it began to change, shifting away from the human facade it wore and becoming something else entirely.

The change was impossible to miss. Like the creatures the Dollmaker had sold itself to, the man was no longer human, and the rules he had been limited by had changed significantly.

He *unfolded* himself. The wig flew off, and the heavy wrinkles at the back of the man's head and neck—the sure sign to Crowley that he had been hiding something—opened up. The man simply stopped being a man as the extra limbs he'd been hiding came into view.

There are creatures that can camouflage themselves. Chameleons change their color and other things, stranger things, hide their true nature behind pretty packaging. The same was true here. The skin at the back of the Harringdale's head blossomed open, and the pressure in the shop changed to reflect the fact that he was opening a doorway into a different realm. The air that came from behind him was cold and whirled into the room amidst a sudden fog caused by the temperature difference. The very air seemed to steam, the cold so far beyond what was already present that there was simply no way around the changes. Those impossibly long limbs struck the parquet floor and scurried for purchase even as the body continued to spill outward from the opening at the top of Harringdale's skull.

The limbs came out as what looked more like the legs of a crab than anything else. They were long and pale and barbed and, as Crowley watched, they telescoped, unfolding at joints that were not immediately visible. The body of the man stretched like a cloth sack held open. His face crumbled in on itself and more of that obscene form pushed itself into the world.

There were perhaps ten legs, all of them joined to an obscene, bloated body that shone wetly, as if freshly born into the world. The body also sported seven arms, all too human in shape even if the skin was a pasty gray. Three separate faces came out of that body, each worse in appearance than the previous. Each vaguely resembled that of the Dollmaker, but all of them sported the same sickly flesh. The eyes were bloodied, the mouths drooled still more blood, and sported teeth that belonged in a boar's head, tusks and all. Two of those faces bore all the intelligence of an idiot, nearly expressionless, with muscles that twitched and shuddered, but the third had cunning. The third was vividly alive and furious.

"I am not a failure, you fool! I am not weak, and I am not merely an afterthought! I am a god!"

Even as the gloating face spoke, the body continued changing. The back of the round body split and from that fresh wound came a spiny shape, something between the tail of a scorpion and a tentacle. It moved easily, a seemingly endless array or orbs attached to each other like links of a chain, but with more deliberate and malicious intent. At the end of this last limb there was an opening that could have been a mouth, but instead of teeth there were barbs thrusting outward in each direction.

Kharrn gripped his axe with both hands and went into a fighting crouch.

Crowley felt himself smile. His eyes looked at the nightmare before him and tried to study every detail of the thing.

Puddled at the ground under the shape was the body of Harrington. Clothes and flesh alike were discarded, dropped into a jumbled mess. The long legs bent at four different spots each an impossible jumble of limbs that should not have worked, but did.

One hand pointed at Kharrn and another at Crowley. "You have offended me, gentlemen. You are not welcome here."

Kharrn shook his head and stepped forward, sweeping the twin-bladed axe as easily as a man might swing a walking stick. One of the axe heads cut into the closest leg, slicing through the heavy exterior and into the meat, wedging there.

The Dollmaker screamed and tried to pull its leg back with limited success. Kharrn ripped the weapon away from the wound and swept in a hard half circle before slamming the blade into the other side of the same limb, cutting through like a woodsman attacking a sapling.

The Dollmaker reared back on the rest of its legs and then dropped down with the force of a guillotine. The stinger on the top of the round body slammed into the ground, narrowly missing the giant man as he slipped to the side.

"Do you have any idea how many gods Kharrn has killed?" Crowley's grin was pure venom.

All three of the faces at the front of the bloated body turned toward Crowley, each and every one wearing an expression of hatred. "I'll kill you last!"

Crowley reached into his jacket pocket and found his collection of ingredients. What he sought, and happily found, was a long crystal that was jagged on one end and nearly smooth on the other. The dark stone held no special properties, save that when he'd had the spare time, nearly a decade earlier, he'd carved a particular set of markings into the sides.

He spoke seventeen syllables last heard on the planet some time before the fall of Babylon, and then tossed the stone at the Dollmaker.

The creature flinched back, eyes wide, perhaps expecting an actual physical attack. In the meanwhile, Crowley slid around to the left, making certain that the thing kept its attention on him instead of on Kharrn.

The crystal hung in the air for exactly five seconds before it shimmered, vibrated, and then vanished.

The Dollmaker stumbled back toward Kharrn, squeaking in surprise.

"What did you do?" All three heads swiveled and the faces twitched, two mirroring the surprise of the last.

Crowley smiled. "I shut a door."

"No! Nonononononononooooo..." Harrington backed up again and then let out a shriek as Kharrn brought his axe down on a second leg and split the limb away from the body; the stench of the thing's insides was repugnant and both men nearly retched.

"I'll kill you both, but not just now!"

One of the creature's segmented legs lashed out, striking Kharrn in his chest and sending him staggering backward. The big man grunted at the impact. The Dollmaker ran at the front of the shop and crashed through the door, taking part of the wall with it. Crowley started after the scuttling horror. He knew Kharrn would be right behind him.

12

"I don't know why we should stand here freezing in the street," Charles Dickens said.

"Kharrn and Crowley may need our help, Charles," Henry said.

"I think Mr. Crowley made it perfectly clear that..."

Dickens' words trailed off and his mouth hung agape as he stared over Henry's shoulder. Henry turned to see something from the nightmares of a madman come smashing through the front of

Harringdale's shop. It was like a cross between a crab and a scorpion, but of monstrous size, and it had not one, but three human faces. It came scrabbling their way and Henry, Dickens, and Dr. Quincy hurried to get out of its path.

A few seconds later, Kharrn and Jonathan Crowley ran out of the hole made by the creature, dodging falling rubble as they leaped into the street. The crab monster was rushing away with surprising speed, heading toward Piccadilly Circus.

"Kharrn!" Henry called. "What is that abomination?"

"It's Harringdale. He's a servant of the Outer Ones," Kharrn said as he rushed past.

"Oh, of course." said Henry. *What was the man talking about?*

Henry started off after Crowley and Kharrn. He had never considered himself a brave man, but he felt he needed to see this adventure through, if only for the sake of the unfortunate medium, Charlotte Kenworth. Her horrific death had been all but forgotten in the maelstrom of subsequent events.

The three men rushed toward Piccadilly Circus. Dickens and Quincy, both well out of training, soon fell behind. Though it was late at night, there were still many people milling about at Piccadilly. Screams rang out as the monster crashed through the crowds, knocking them aside with its claw like appendages.

"It's getting away, Kharrn," Crowley said, "The damn thing is too fast on all those legs."

Kharrn looked around and then pointed toward a two-horse open carriage. "We'll use that."

The giant ran over to the carriage. A driver in fine livery goggled at Kharrn and he climbed into the seat beside him. The man said, "Here now, what are you doing?"

"We need this carriage," Kharrn said.

"Get down right now. This Carriage belongs to the honorable Geoffrey Brown. You can't just…"

Henry winced as Kharrn struck the man with one massive fist, knocking him from his perch. Kharrn gathered the reins is his huge hands.

"Get in if you're coming," Crowley said, climbing into the back.

"Terribly sorry," Henry said to the driver, who was sitting on the ground, rubbing his jaw.

Henry barely had time to scramble in beside Crowley. Kharrn snapped the reins and wheeled the carriage around, causing it to wobble on two wheels for a moment before careening off in pursuit of the monster. Henry was thrown back in the seat. The crowds in Piccadilly Circus hurled themselves aside as the carriage rattled on the cobblestones and veered onto Haymarket Street.

"I think it's heading for the river," Crowley said.

Kharrn grunted in agreement, concentrating on driving the carriage. The horses were difficult to control, doubtless because of the unfamiliar driver and the scent of the thing they pursued. Henry had always found horses to be sensitive creatures.

The benighted streets of London rushed past at a dizzying pace and Henry was sure that, at any moment, Kharrn would take a turn too quickly and the carriage would overturn, killing or maiming them all.

Still, they managed to keep the creature in sight, and when it turned onto Northumberland Avenue, Henry knew that Crowley's surmise was correct. The monster was heading for the Thames. And why not, since it resembled some great crustacean more than anything else.

Just before the monster reached the river, it turned toward the massive construction site of Joseph Bazalgette's ambitious Embankment project and disappeared among the scaffolding and rubble.

Kharrn reined in the horses, vaulted from the cab, and charged after the monster. Crowley leaped over the cab's side and ran after him. Henry tried to keep up. The construction site was a bewildering maze of equipment and materials. Henry had written an article about the project. It was designed to incorporate the main interceptor sewer from West London and the new underground railroad, as well as a retaining wall along the North side of the Thames.

Henry turned a corner around a huge stack of metal pipes and found Kharrn and Crowley standing at the edge of a gaping hole. Deep furrows etched in the damp ground showed that the creature had come this way.

"Do you think this is that horror's lair?" Henry said.

"It went down there for sure," said Crowley.

"And so will we," said Kharrn.

"I don't recommend you accompany us, Henry," Crowley said.

"I've gone this far. I'll see it through to the end."

"You very well may. But suit yourself."

"Enough talk," said Kharrn. He dropped into the dark pit.

Crowley grinned. "One thing you can say for Kharrn. He's single-minded."

Crowley rummaged through his coat pockets and produced a small, translucent crystal. Henry heard him mumble something he couldn't understand and then the crystal gave off a pale, blue light. Henry tried not to dwell on how he had produced the light. He had seen too many strange things already.

Crowley followed Kharrn into the pit. Henry steeled himself and went in a bit more cautiously than the other two men. That turned out to be fortunate, because he almost stumbled down a steep incline. He saw Crowley's light bobbing ahead and hurried to catch up.

They were in a wide tunnel with surprisingly smooth sides. Henry wasn't certain if it was part of the construction or something the creature had made. It sloped gradually downward, and as they descended, Henry became aware of a sound of rushing water. That struck him as strange, because unless his sense of direction had become hopelessly confused, the tunnel angled away from the river.

The tunnel widened without warning, and Henry found himself in a great chamber. Crowley tossed his crystal to the floor and its baleful glow illuminated the entire chamber. It looked to be a natural cavern, with stalactites hanging from the roof. A fast moving torrent of water rushed along the far end of the cave, some unknown tributary of the Thames. That explained the sound of water.

The room was filled with effigies, strange statues molded from clay and stone. Some bore vague resemblance to human beings, while others were creatures almost too terrible to gaze upon. Apparently the Dollmaker made more than dolls.

The creature itself was standing before some sort of altar. It contained the most abominable sculpture of all. A great mass of writhing flesh with many eyes and many screaming mouths. The Dollmaker turned as the three men entered. One of its three faces was twisted with rage, while the other two drooled and howled in mindless fury.

"You may have sundered my link to my masters," the Dollmaker shrieked at Crowley. "But this is my place of power. Here I shall contact them anew."

"Not if we don't give you a chance," Crowley said, starting forward.

The Dollmaker said, "You'll be dead long before you can reach me. I told you I'd kill you."

The stone and clay figures began to move, lumbering toward the three men. Something that looked like a satyr with the head of an octopus reached out for Henry, who screamed in spite of himself.

Kharrn said, "Finish him, Crowley. I'll hold these things off."

The giant man rushed into the throng of simulacra whirling the twin-bladed axe. Chunks of stone and gouts of clay flew as he cut his way through them. Henry found that the things were ignoring him now, concentrating their attacks on Kharrn.

Kharrn smashed one figure and beheaded another. As Henry watched, the man's facial expression became more and more savage, as if he were unleashing some beast he kept chained within himself. Anything that came within the reach of that great axe was destroyed. The automatons swarmed around him and he hewed through them like some ancient god of war.

As Crowley ran toward the altar, the creature scuttled forward to meet him. Henry felt the air in the room change, like the feeling of an approaching thunderstorm. He understood somehow that Eldritch energies were dancing around both the Dollmaker and Jonathan Crowley.

The Dollmaker roared and charged toward Crowley, the massive tail of the thing lashing out, striking again and again as the man dodged around it. Each impact sent shockwaves through the ground, breaking earth and sending stones dancing across the uneven surface. Henry fought to keep his feet.

Crowley failed to dodge, and the massive stinger on that hellish limb punched through his chest and exploded through the back of the dandy's clothes. His bleeding, broken form was hurled through the air and fell to the round only a yard from where Henry stood.

"There! Dead! You are dead! You will never win against me or my masters!" The bloated body of the Dollmaker danced a multi-legged jig and the faces all bore similar furious grins.

The smiles on all three faces faded when Jonathan Crowley stood up. One idiot expression, one angry scowl, and a gape mouthed howl of blind rage replaced the victorious joy.

Crowley looked toward the Dollmaker and coughed a wad of bloody phlegm. His smile was gone, replaced by a look of cold anger. Henry could not decide which bothered him the most. The fact that the man who should have been dead was standing again or the fact that his unsettling smile had faded away.

The crystal that Crowley had enchanted still did its work, and the chamber was lit well enough that henry could see Kharrn methodically chopping his way through the stone effigies, shattering them with his axe, grunting and growling as the things attacked. The big man was battered and bloody. He could see Crowley himself standing slowly as the hole in his chest pulled itself closed, leaving his clothes in shreds and his flesh impossibly intact.

He could see the horror that was the Dollmaker as it screamed its fury into the air and shivered with barely suppressed fury. "I killed you! Kindly stay dead!"

That elicited a very small smile from Crowley. Moment later his hands were moving in a series of gestures and his lips whispered words that Henry could barely hear, sounds of some sort that made his eyes ache and his ears ring.

The Dollmaker stepped toward Crowley, shaking all three of his heads. The eyes wandered madly, as if trying to find a place to focus but not seeing Crowley at all.

The man's voice grew louder, and as it did Henry shook his head and looked away himself. He could not see the man without feeling acute pain run through his skull. So he looked instead at the monstrosity that was the Dollmaker and saw the body shudder in revulsion, saw the way the little flesh that still looked human began to smoke and bubble like pork fat thrown on a hot skillet.

"What are you doing to me?" All three mouths made sounds, but only one of them spoke the Queen's English. The other mouths gibbered and the only thing all three streams of noise had in common was an underlying note of panic.

The Dollmaker backed into the wall of the cavern and tried to get away, tried to push further than the curved stone would allow in an effort to escape the rising sound of Crowley's unholy words.

Around Kharrn the statues grew still as the Dollmaker's concentration was broken.

The great tail of the self-proclaimed god split then. The flesh ruptured and what spilled out burned the stone behind the Dollmaker and the ground at the beast's numerous feet. The scream of pain that came from the Dollmaker was enough to deafen Henry for a moment and he took two steps back just as the creature thrust backward again, this time with enough force to split stone.

The stone broke and as it did, water erupted from the broken wall with enough force to propel the Dollmaker into Jonathan Crowley. The ceiling above them all fractured and more water, and dust alike, came spilling down. The bodies locked together in a tangle of limbs, and Henry saw one of Crowley's hands grab the idiot face of the Dollmaker and watched fingers clamp down hard enough to split skin and pulp muscle. The Dollmaker screamed and Crowley let out a roar of laughter even as the wall crumbled and a fountain of water smashed the both of them backward, driving them to the edge of the underwater river and then into the darkened waters.

"Crowley!" Henry yelled as man and monster disappeared into the swirling water. Rocks and dust continued to fall from the roof. Henry felt a vise-like grip clamp on his shoulder and then Kharrn was pushing him toward the tunnel mouth.

"The whole cavern is coming down," Kharrn said. "Hurry back up the tunnel."

"But Crowley," Henry said.

"I'll go after him. Now go!"

Kharrn shoved Henry into the tunnel and even as he did so, the entire roof came down with a roar. Henry's last sight of Kharrn was in the pale glow of Crowley's crystal, and then he was gone. Henry turned and scrambled up the slope as debris fell all around him. The tunnel itself was collapsing inward and Henry barely managed to crawl from the mouth and get clear of the tumbling rubble.

He stood for a moment, staring at the shallow depression where the tunnel had been. The Dollmaker was destroyed. But at the cost of two more lives. Kharrn and Crowley were buried beneath tons of rock and dirt. No one could have survived that.

13

Two days later.

Kharrn pushed his shoulder against the final layer of debris that covered him. He had been steadily digging upward for the better part of two days, sometimes passing out from lack of air, but always waking again and going back to work. Most of the bones that been broken when the cavern roof had collapsed were healed, though the tips of his fingers had to keep regrowing, since they were all he had to dig with.

With a great heave he burst out of the ground, gulping lungfuls of air. It was night time and the construction site was empty of workers. Just as well. Kharrn crawled out of the ground and staggered to his feet. A hundred or so yards from where he stood, the dark waters of the Thames flowed away into the night. Was Crowley out there somewhere? He had trouble believing that his fellow immortal had drowned in the underground river.

Oh well, he'd turn up again or he wouldn't. Kharrn turned back towards the gaslit streets of London and began to walk.

CONTRIBUTORS

JIM BEARD

Jim Beard became a published writer when he sold a story to DC Comics in 2002. Since that time he's written official Star Wars and Ghostbusters comic book stories and contributed articles and essays to several volumes of comic book history. His prose work includes the novella *Kolkchak: The Last Temptation*; co-editing and contributing to *Planet of the Apes: Tales from the Forbidden Zone*; a story for *X-Files: Secret Agendas*; *Gotham City 14 Miles*, a book of essays on the 1966 Batman TV series; *Sgt. Janus, Spirit-Breaker*, a collection of pulp ghost stories featuring his Edwardian occult detective; *Monster Earth*, a shared-world giant monster anthology; and *Captain Action: Riddle of the Glowing Men*, the first pulp prose novel based on the classic 1960s action figure. Jim also currently provides regular content for Marvel.com, the official Marvel Comics website. Look for Jim on Amazon at Amazon.com/author/JimBeard, on Facebook at Facebook.com/TheBeardJimBeard, and on Twitter at @WriterJimBeard.

CLIFF BIGGERS

Cliff Biggers began working for Jim Steranko's Mediascene in the 1970s; since then, he has written literally millions of words for numerous magazines, including more than 1,750 issues of Comic Shop News. He has also written comics and short stories, including tales in *Skelos*, *A Lonely & Curious Country*, *Mighty Warriors*, *Pickman's Gallery*, *Occult Detective Magazine*, and elsewhere. His first short story collection is tentatively slated for 2021 release. What does he do when he's not writing? He'll let us know when and if that ever happens.

KEALAN PATRICK BURKE

Hailed by *Booklist* as "one of the most clever and original talents in contemporary horror," Kealan Patrick Burke was born and raised in Ireland and emigrated to the United States a few weeks before 9/11. Since then, he has written five novels, among them the popular southern gothic slasher *Kin*, and over two hundred short stories and novellas, including *The House on Abigail Lane*, which is currently in development as a TV series.

A five-time Bram Stoker Award-nominee, Burke won the award in 2005 for his coming-of-age novella *The Turtle Boy*, the first book in the acclaimed Timmy Quinn series.

As editor, he helmed the anthologies *Night Visions 12*, *Taverns of the Dead*, and *Quietly Now*, a tribute anthology to one of Burke's influences, the late Charles L. Grant.

Most recently, he adapted his work to comic book format for three volumes of John Carpenter's *Tales for a Halloween Night* series of anthologies and contributed a short story to Mike Mignola and Christopher Golden's *Hellboy: An Assortment of Horrors*. He recently completed a new novel, *Mr. Stitch*.

Kealan is represented by Merrilee Heifetz at Writers House and Kassie Evashevski at Anonymous Content. He lives in an unhaunted house in Ohio with a Scooby Doo lookalike rescue named Red.

AMANDA DEWEES

Although Amanda DeWees grew up in Atlanta, her inner life has always taken place in crumbling mansions on misty English moors. Her books include *With This Curse,* winner of the Daphne du Maurier Award in historical mystery/suspense, and the Sybil Ingram Victorian Mysteries series. Visit her at AmandaDeWees.com to learn more.

JOHN LINWOOD GRANT

John Linwood Grant is a writer/editor from Yorkshire, UK, with over fifty short stories and novelettes published in magazines/anthologies during the last few years, including *Lackington's Magazine, Vastarien, Weirdbook,* and *Space & Time.* He writes disquieting dark fiction, particularly period supernatural tales. "His Heart Shall Speak No More" was picked for *Best New Horror #29,* and his novel *13 Miller's Court* (with Alan M. Clark) won the 2019 Ripperology Books award. He is the editor of *Occult Detective Magazine* and various anthologies, including two volumes so far of *Sherlock Holmes & The Occult Detectives.* His first collection, *A Persistence of Geraniums,* was set in the Edwardian era, and a further collection of his weird fiction, *Where All is Night, and Starless,* will be out from Trepidatio next year.

LEANNA RENEE HIEBER

Leanna Renee Hieber is an actress, playwright, tour guide and the award-winning, bestselling author of Gothic, Gaslamp Fantasy novels for Tor and Kensington Books such as the *Strangely Beautiful, Magic Most Foul, Eterna Files* and *The Spectral City* series as well as the *Dark Nest* saga of Space Opera novellas for Scrib'd. *A Haunted History of Invisible Women,* Leanna's first foray into non-fiction, focusing on narratives where women are centered in haunted houses and ghost stories, will release in 2021 from Kensington. Her work has won 4 Prism awards and has been included in numerous notable anthologies such as *Queen Victoria's Book of Spells* (Tor) and her books have been translated into many languages. She crafts fun Gothic and Steampunk accessories for Torch and Arrow at Etsy.com/TorchAndArrow and works as a ghost tour guide for Manhattan's Boroughs of the Dead. Hieber has been featured in film and television on shows like *Mysteries at the Museum*. For writers' resources, free reads and more visit: LeannaReneeHieber.com.

WILLIAM MEIKLE

William Meikle is a Scottish writer, now living in Canada, with more than thirty novels published in the genre press and over 300 short story credits in thirteen countries.

He has books available from a variety of publishers including Dark Regions Press, Crossroad Press and Severed Press and his work has appeared in a large number of professional anthologies and magazines.

He lives in Newfoundland with whales, bald eagles and icebergs for company and when he's not writing he drinks beer, plays guitar, and dreams of fortune and glory.

JAMES A. MOORE

James A. Moore is the award-winning, bestselling author of over forty horror and fantasy novels, including the Seven Forges and the Serenity Falls and Blood Red series. He has edited anthologies, written comic books, co-authored books with Christopher Golden, Charles R. Rutledge, Mark Morrison and Jeff Strand. He is currently at work on new collaborations with Charles R. Rutledge and Christopher Golden and is preparing to work on book six in the Seven Forges series. He resides in New England with his wife, Tessa, and their dog Murry.

JOSH REYNOLDS

A professional author since 2007, Josh has over thirty novels to his name, as well as numerous short stories, novellas and audio scripts. Born and raised in South Carolina, he now resides in Sheffield with his wife and daughter, as well as a highly excitable dog and something he hopes is a cat. A complete list of his work can be found at JoshuaMReynolds.co.uk.

CHARLES R. RUTLEDGE

Charles R. Rutledge is the author of *Dracula's Revenge* and *Dracula's Ghost*, and the co-author of three books in the Griffin & Price series, written with James A. Moore. His short stories have appeared in more than two dozen anthologies. He owns entirely too many editions of the novel Dracula, keeps soil from Transylvania on his desk, and is seldom seen in daylight.

JEFF STRAND

Jeff Strand is the Bram Stoker Award-nominated author of almost fifty books, including *Pressure, Dweller, My Pretties, Clowns VS. Spiders*, and *Autumn Bleeds Into Winter*. Several of his books are in development as motion pictures. He hates cold weather, but conquered his fear to write this story. You can visit his Gleefully Macabre website at JeffStrand.com.

JAMES R. TUCK

James R. Tuck has written 11 novels, over a dozen novellas, and has lost count of the short stories. He has been a tattoo artist for 25 years and he used to throw people out of bars for money.

Printed in Great Britain
by Amazon